ACCOUNTING
FOR EVIL

ACCOUNTING FOR EVIL

Parker & Parker

To order additional copies of this book, contact:
Xlibris Corporation
1-888-795-4274
www.Xlibris.com
Orders@Xlibris.com
22864

CONTENTS

PREFACE

Excerpt from "Five Minute History Lessons"
Edition: 511 A.R.
Topic: The Green Realm

Thousands of years ago, the humans of Planet Earth foresaw an end to life on their world. A fortunate few of their people fled the doomed planet in generation ships, each headed toward a promising star and the hope of a habitable planet. This time is known as the Great Dispersal.

After centuries of travel, a few lucky ships found worlds they could settle. Each new world tested its settlers, who struggled to survive and struggled to hold onto any shreds of their knowledge and their sense of civilization. As millennia passed, the people adapted to their home worlds. Unique races of humans emerged.

Technologies, too, emerged and developed. When the Thalians discovered space tuck and hyperspeed, they had the means to travel astronomical distances in days instead of centuries. They set out to find their lost cousins.

First, the Thalians discovered Planet Lavar and its descendant race of humans. Thus began Reunification and the discovery of 20 habitable worlds, some previously unknown to humans. Today, in 511 A.R. (After Reunification), we humans are joyful citizens of the Green Realm, a union of eleven Great Dispersal worlds, five second dispersal worlds, two colony worlds, and two outpost planets.

We will not rest until we have accounted for all the generation ships and all descendant humans, no matter what their state or condition might be.

Each re-unified race is precious, and each reunified human is: "Well found!"

CHAPTER 1

Alarm

"Look out! It's . . . mmf!"

Even as she heard Lute's warning, Ardra Wythian caught her first smell of the attack force and heard the whisper of foot on sand. In one motion she spun, crouched, and drew her blaster.

In the arid gully before her, she saw Lute Cullen, team botanist, on his knees and gagged by an arm clenched around his mouth, his left arm twisted back at a rude angle. The arm doing the gagging was attached to a short, wiry man with green-tinged hair, squinting eyes, and a button nose—a Wanderite. Another short, wiry man of identical features stood next to him, but this one held a lance in both hands, and the weapon's copper-colored tip rested against Lute's neck. Both attackers wore beige smocks that fell to their knees. Their feet were bare and their skin matched the color of their smocks.

With a brief flare of anger, Ardra realized that she had only herself to blame for this standoff. She had left the safety of the spaceport without her sergeant's approval and come out into the desert with a civilian to meet the reclusive Wanderites. And here they were.

"Why have you attacked us?" Ardra demanded as she straightened slowly, blaster leveled at the man with the lance.

"You stepped on our toes!" he snapped. His hands tightened on the shaft of his weapon.

For a moment Ardra was at a loss for words, wondering—what toes? what is he talking about? Then she remembered Kafka, the strange Wanderite she had met in town, and she borrowed a couple of his phrases. "We only wanted to flap gums and follow the leader to your chief."

"Follow the leader?" asked the lance man turning his head to look at the arm twister. "Flap gums?"

Ardra saw their grips relax, so she took the next step and eased her blaster down until it pointed to the ground by her foot. In response, the lance tip withdrew from Lute's neck and gave a wink of reflected sunlight as it swung up toward the sky and the lance butt slid down to rest on the sand. With a sigh of relief, Ardra put away her sidearm. She stood tall, the better to impress these men with the black uniform she had sweltered in during her hike across the desert.

"I'm PKF Ardra Wythian, Peace Keeping Force Officer First Class," Ardra said formally. "I'm investigating the murders of two people from the spaceport, Retro. And my friend is Botanist Lute Cullen of the Green Realm survey team."

The two Wanderites stood mute and blinking before her, so Ardra tried again, "I'm Ardra. My friend is Lute. What are your names?"

"I am Jex . . . jex," said the arm twister, "and my brother is Jex . . jex. You stepped on our toes to flap gums? Did Lute step on our toes to flap. gums?"

"Yes, Lute too. I don't understand. Do you and your brother have the same name?"

The arm twister released Lute, who pulled his arm forward with a gasped "Thank-you".

"Our names are not peas in a pod. I am Jex . . . jex and my brother is Jex . . jex."

"I can't hear a difference," Ardra said.

"It sounds like there's a difference in the pause between syllables," Lute said as he gingerly rose from his knees and rubbed at his abused shoulder.

The arm twister stepped forward, reached out a wary forefinger and touched the mottled green skin of Ardra's cheek. "Elya?" he asked. "Sister?" The Wanderites knew Elya Udell as the anthropologist among the survey team, the woman who sought to understand their ways.

"No, Elya is my mimi . . . er, cousin, not my sister." By coincidence, Ardra was distantly related to the anthropologist. Both were members of the race of humans from Planet Olid, known throughout the Realm for a keen sense of smell and camouflage skin. Their coloration had developed over the millennia as a means to be invisible in the green jungles of Olid. In the early years, camouflage was their best defense against the fearsome empress lizard.

"Ah. Elya and Ardra are truce-cousins." The two Wanderites looked at each other and nodded solemnly.

Just as the situation seemed destined to relax, Skrif, Ardra's cone-shaped companion robot, sped into view around a corner of the gully. Abruptly, the companionbot reversed its thrust to stop a respectful distance from the gathered humans.

"I beg your pardon. Excuse me," said the robot.

The Wanderites made hissing sounds and waved their arms and lance at the new arrival.

"Park it, Skrif," said Ardra and the companionbot quickly lowered itself to the ground and powered down its antigravity and its minijets. The Jexes approached the robot on tiptoe then prodded and poked at the strange object. Skrif remained inert; it would take much more than a copper lance tip to mar its durmet surface.

"That's Skrif," said Ardra. "It's . . ." But how could she explain a robot to people who had no mechanical technology? She tried a non-threatening smile and finished her sentence, "It's harmless." To herself, she rationalized that Skrif was mostly harmless. Certainly, if anyone or anything threatened Ardra, Skrif would intervene.

"Follow the leader?" she repeated when the Wanderites exhausted their need to push at the robot.

The twins nodded slowly in unison, turned, and glided down the gully. Ardra motioned Lute to follow her and Skrif to take the rear. She wondered how the natives traveled so smoothly and silently; she felt like a lumbering automaton by contrast and she studied their movements for pointers.

In a dozen paces, the Jexes dodged into a narrow cleft and the arm twister dropped to dig at a low ridge of sand piled up against the wall of the gully. After a brief flurry of burrowing, the man pulled away a mat of woven grass to reveal a hole in the shape of an ellipse, the longest axis no more than a meter in length and the vertical axis significantly less than half a meter. A waft of deep earth filled Ardra's nostrils. It was the scent that had led her into the gully and into the ambush.

"Follow the leader." The fellow with the lance flopped onto his belly and squirmed into the opening. As soon as his toes disappeared, his brother wriggled after him. Lute eased down to his knees and peered into the black opening.

"I hate closed spaces. This is crazy," he sighed.

"The opening is too small for me," said Skrif. "We mustn't enter. It's too dangerous, too unpredictable."

"We came out here to talk with a local clan," said Ardra. "This is vital to the investigation."

"But if you signal for help I won't be able to come to your aid."

"Then you might as well head back to town. We'll be back before nightwatch. If I'm not back in time for my shift then you can raise the alarm. It's better this way. You know where we went in."

"What if the invitation is a trap?"

"A possibility, but I'm better armed and I'm ready."

"I protest."

"I understand, Skrif." Ardra looked down at Lute. "How about you? Would you like to go back with Skrif?"

"Not a chance." Lute shook his head at the offer and at his own foolishness. Then he pulled off his pack, dropped flat behind it, and pushed it ahead as he crawled slowly out of sight.

Ardra agreed with both Skrif and Lute. It was unpredictable, dangerous, and crazy; she should be out here conducting a proper investigation with her PKF sergeant instead of being teamed up with a civilian trained only in such matters as the distinction between herbs and grasses. After checking back up and down the gully for sights, sounds, and smells and finding nothing of note, Ardra bent to the opening and called in, "Lute? All clear?"

"It opens . . . it opens . . . right . . . right up, up, up," his answer echoed out. So Ardra flattened against the ground and slid into the hole. "I can't believe I'm doing this. Grime!" she muttered. She could feel sand working into her clothing and sticking to the sweat on her stomach.

Ardra felt ahead with her hands as she crawled. The tunnel went straight for two meters, made a quarter turn left, then a quarter turn right. After the second turn she saw light and four pairs of feet, three sets bare and one set wearing hiking boots. Then she slid out into a round chamber and stood up next to the others.

There was a third Wanderite in the group armed with a lance, a sentinel, Ardra speculated. He looked like the first two except his nose was a bit rounder and a gashing scar snaked down his left arm from shoulder to wrist. He stared at her but said nothing.

As Ardra beat the sand from her uniform, the arm twister slithered back out the passage, made some scratching, rustling sounds, and reappeared feet first. He was closing the door, she decided. She checked their surroundings.

The chamber they stood in was perfectly round in circumference and domed at the ceiling, about three meters high and five meters in diameter. Running a hand over one wall she noticed marks left by scraping tools. The light in the room came from a narrow trough that had been hollowed into the wall and ran around it at eye (for her) level. The trough was filled with oil, and lighted wicks floated in it at intervals. There must have been air vents somewhere, for a draft tugged at the flames.

On the wall away from the entrance, three passages, lit like the chamber, curved out of sight. Ardra reached out and dipped a finger in the trough. She sniffed it and felt a surge of triumph. This oil tied into the first clue she discovered where Surveyor Cara Stine was murdered.

"I am called Ardra," she said to the new man. "And you are . . . Jex . . . jex?"

"No, I am called Jexjex," he replied. It figured she would get the pause all wrong. The sentinel then winced, looked at the empty space over his left shoulder and barked, "Heshaleeniapi! We speak Standard."

Lute stared at the space, turned to Ardra and mouthed, "Do you see anything?" She shook her head and wondered why she had felt a sudden chill of fear that she might.

In the gully outside of the cavern, Skrif watched as two sinewy arms reached out of the opening and pulled mat and sand in to fill the entryway. The arms moved with efficiency born of practice and the hole and the arms quickly vanished. A breeze gusted up the gully, brushed sand over the truncated trail of footprints, and stroked at the re-formed barricade. The robot was alone.

"If I were a coredrill I could cut the rock and widen the entry. Then I'd be inside with the others," Skrif thought. Unfortunately, no one robot was capable of all specialties. As a companionbot, Skrif was gifted with language and communication skills, logic capabilities, and a versatile, maneuverable form. As a coredrill, it would be big and powerful and not much else.

"Coredrills can't play even the simplest game of chess," Skrif reminded itself.

A minute passed after the arms had buried the entry and Skrif carefully monitored its audilink connection with Ardra. It was silent. Impossible. Humans in new situations were incapable of being silent for so long. Skrif sent out a rebound pulse to test the connection. The pulse did not feed back.

"Oh dear," Skrif thought. "Now we have no communication. She can't signal if something goes wrong, if she needs me to raise the alarm early."

A sensible human would discover the loss of audilink function and decide the risks now outweighed the benefits. A sensible human might retrace her steps and return to Skrif in the gully. Skrif scanned the sand barricade unhappily; it did not expect to see any mottled green Olidan hands pushing the sand aside.

"Is it my imagination or are we going in circles?" Lute hissed over his shoulder. The arm twister and the lance man had turned Lute and Ardra over to the sentinel, who now led them at a brisk glide through a curving maze of tunnels. As he flowed along, he carried on a one-sided conversation with the empty space beside him, high and left.

"I'll eat dust? You'll eat dust." Pause. "Never . . . never."

Ardra's ears popped. She whispered forward to Lute, "We're definitely descending but the stone around us must be causing interference because my locator isn't working here underground. I don't know what our bearing has been. Maybe we're spiraling down or maybe not. Which direction do you think we're turning in?"

"Left."

"We'll need a guide to get out of here." She didn't bother to add that her impression was that they were turning to the right. "I think there might be an optical illusion to the curve of the tunnel walls."

In the wash of air at the rear of the procession, Ardra could smell the distinctive scent clusters of each man. There was the odd whiff of Boolean musk. She distracted herself by worrying about Skrif; if the locator wasn't working it was a sure bet the audilink was down as well. Hopefully, Skrif would not be raising frenzied alarms—yet. Manually, she switched on her belt recorder; she didn't want any word of her encounter with this clan to be missed.

"At least it's cooler in here than out under the suns." Lute shrugged.

"Right." Ardra wiped the sweat from her palms onto her tunic and swallowed a prickly lump in her throat. At the PKF Academy she'd tested negative for all phobias, claustrophobia included, so why were her hands sweating?

"Despite her brilliant deductive abilities and excellent policing skills, Officer Wythian has shown an unfortunate tendency for impetuous action." Thus read Ardra's most recent evaluation report. Maybe it was right. Her need to search the desert for the Wanderites could be seen by some as impetuous. Her sergeant definitely considered her first day on Wanderer to have been marred by an impetuous act. She had gone straight to the first murder scene.

But it had paid off. It always did. Every step that brought her to this cavern had made perfect sense. Once more, she reassured herself that she was on the right track and that everything was finally coming together.

She sniffed the oil on her fingers again and the smell carried her back to her first day on Planet Wanderer.

CHAPTER 2

Life and Death

On hands and knees, Ardra approached the boulder. The hair on the back of her neck prickled to attention.

"The scent is close. I'm getting closer," she reported to Skrif, her PKF companionbot and her only companion in this wilderness. To herself, she muttered, "Relax, it's just a rock. It's not going to attack." Still, she ached to draw her sidearm and follow it around the edge of the stone, just in case some weird new creature leapt out at her. Here, on Planet Wanderer, where surveying had only begun, no one knew for certain which life forms were harmless and which innocuous-looking creature carried a deadly secret.

Behind Officer Wythian, Skrif adjusted its antigravity and minijets to hold a position two meters above ground level. The scanning visor at the apex of its blunt cone shape had a full circle view from this vantage point, and it watched carefully for any movement in the vicinity. After all, a murder had been committed on this site only weeks before, and who knew if the culprit might return to the scene?

Slowly, carefully, Ardra advanced, silently cursing the eddying winds that confounded the direction she was able to draw from the strange scent.

"It's like it's coming from all over," she said. "But now that I'm down low, I'm zeroing in."

She hoped she was zeroing in. To the ordinary noses of the Green Realm, this arid world was thin on odors, but to an Olidan like Ardra, it had a unique rainbow of scents. Unfortunately, there was a confusion of scents in the area—the burnt spice smell of the skeleton tree, the sour leather smell of the fist cactus, and the edgy odor of the sun-baked sand. There was even the odd whiff of something that smelled like orange blossom. None of these drew her to the boulder, though. What drew her was a strange smell that was oily and out-of-place.

"There's no movement anywhere within my visual range," Skrif reported.

No sooner had Ardra grunted an acknowledgement of this report than she flinched. A twinkle of motion under the lip of the boulder stopped her heart for a nanosecond, but, fortunately, the culprit was small, barely the size of a finger, and headed in the opposite direction.

"That's a microlizard," Skrif announced when the creature fled clear of the boulder.

"And just look what it shared its crevice with," Ardra mused. "Special pebbles."

There, under an overhang of rock, lay a number of small, pink pebbles in the pattern of an ellipse with a dot in the center. Warily, Ardra leaned in closer and tasted the air.

"That's it," she pronounced, relieved that nothing else moved in the area. "That's the odor that was out-of-place. It's not the pebbles, but smudges of some oily organic substance on their surface. I can see the smears." She hopped to her feet and dusted off the knees of her field coveralls. Then she spoke to the audilink on her collar.

"Wythian to forensic flies. Deploy to my location."

From the open cargo boot of the PKF Lancer Ardra had parked nearby, swarmed half a dozen small globes. Buoyed by antigravity and propelled by tiny jets, they hurried to her side for detailed direction. Then they closed in on the protected overhang and deployed. Lights and cameras recorded a perfect holographic image of the pebbles in situ, then switched wavelengths and catalogued further details.

"Murder!" grumbled Ardra as she watched the PKF globes at their work. "It's primitive. It's unworthy of us. In spite of all the awesome traits that have evolved among the descendants of the

Great Dispersal, every race knows murder—even the Thalians admit to it. Why haven't we evolved beyond it?"

"An unfathomable mystery," said Skrif, from its watchful position. The robot estimated that the question had been rhetorical, but it was poised to give a more detailed answer if needed. Conversation with a human of any race was always a dance without choreography.

Alone yet together, the Olidan human and her companion robot surveyed the desolate patch of desert immediately around them on the newest planet to join the Realm, Planet Wanderer. Four Standard weeks ago, Surveyor Cara Stine had drawn her last breath here just before an unknown murderer wrapped a garrote around her throat. Now there was only hard packed sand, wind scoured rock outcroppings, and a few desiccated desert plants to mark the spot.

"It's empty. Like death," said Ardra.

"Yes," said Skrif, now confident that the conversation was not literal.

Their job of recording the pebbles and their pattern complete, the light globes winked out and withdrew with the cameras to the boot of the Lancer. A larger globe settled to the sand next to the boulder, disgorged an evidence keeper, and extruded a thin metallic arm. With meticulous care it transferred each pebble from the sand to the evidence keeper, then sealed the keeper and marked the seal.

"The wind's swept away all the sand tracks since the crime and the original investigation, but it couldn't carry off those tiny stones," said Ardra. "I'd call our trip out here a success. A rightful thing. I wonder if there's anything more."

Using her nose and a grid search pattern, Ardra discovered two more patterns of pebbles. A pair of mirror-image esses lay in a sheltered nook between the trunk of a skeleton tree and the shoulder of a fist cactus. A triangle with two concave sides was tucked in the shadow of another undercut rock. They were all located just outside the area documented by the original crime scene analysis, an analysis that pre-dated Officer Wythian's assignment to Wanderer.

"The locations of the pebbles form three points of a triangle and the triangle surrounds the murder scene, so they must be connected to the killing in some way," Ardra said. "And where did the pebbles come from? They're pink, flecked with white intrusions, not like any of the boulders and stones in the area. Someone brought them in."

"Quite," agreed Skrif, who immediately connected with the Repositor and indexed out the appropriate data.

"The boulders and outcroppings are composed of pseudomonsonite and, based on their appearance, the pebbles are granite," Skrif reported promptly.

"They must have been brought here from another location."

"They must."

"I wonder where they came from. Any data on that?"

"Only a tiny percentage of this planet's habitable areas have been . . ." Skrif interrupted itself and simplified its answer. "There's no record of granite like this, so far."

"Whatever the smudges on the pebbles are, they smell like nothing I've studied in scent identification."

Back at the PKF station, a full chemical analysis would identify the oily smudges and who knew where that might lead? Any evidence, any information, any scrap might be the key to solving the crime.

This crime. There had been two murders on Wanderer in the short time since the handful of planet surveyors arrived. As murder rates went in the Green Realm, it was astronomical.

"I hate this," Ardra muttered. "I hate the emptiness and the wildness. Most of all, I hate what happened here."

Skrif searched its linguistic pathways for a suitable reply and selected silence.

"Well, standing around staring at nothing won't undo Stine's murder," Ardra said finally. "There's nothing more for us here. Let's head back to the port." She returned to the missile-shaped Lancer, ordered its boot shut, stretched her body along its pilot rest, and grinned as it locked onto her riding harness and shut the cowling around her back. Her booted feet automatically found the power pads and her arms slid easily up the attitude sleeves, her means to control every dip and turn of the vehicle.

"Power up," she commanded and the Lancer's antigravity unit responded with a buzz and a hum. "Cruise minimums," she said and the Lancer wafted itself to a two meter height above the ground. With her right foot, she applied a dab of thrust then she cocked her left hand until she brought the Lancer around 50 degrees, ready to head back to the spaceport.

All she really had to do was give a "retrace" command and the Lancer would take her back automatically, but that was no way for a Wythian to ride.

"Hey Skrif. Look how those skeleton trees on the plain line up to make a slalom course," Ardra said; her words were captured by her collar audilink and boosted through the cockpit's multiplier. Of course, the plants in question didn't merit the designation of tree. Ardra had seen real trees as a child when her parents took her to visit Olid, the ancestral planet of her race. These leafless, drooping twig clusters didn't qualify. They were barely twice her height.

"Slalom?" Skrif responded. "But why would you . . ."

"I'll wait for you at the base of the foothills on the other side of the plain," said Ardra. "It's payoff time." This was her payoff for having the galactically bad luck to be drawn in the lottery for colony duty, she decided. It was payoff for her trouble-shooter assignment to Wanderer, for the backwater that was Chelidon, for Haley and the aching hole his loss had left in her heart. Here, she could make a Lancer howl in ways never permitted back home on Planet Metro.

"Disengage safety margins," she commanded, then added, "Confirm" even as the Lancer queried.

"That's dangerous!" Skrif cried. The robot hadn't been with Officer Wythian as long as with some of its previous owners, but it had known her long enough to realize such a protest was futile. It would be ignored. It was.

Ardra spiked the power, leaned to her left, tilted her left palm, and cocked her wrist. The Lancer leapt forward then curved into a banking turn. Together they carved a smooth arc around the first skeleton tree.

"Too tame," she decided. She pounded the power and banked right for a closer pass around the next tree. If she could go fast enough, apply enough thrust, maybe she could outrun the lack of evolution from humankind's murderous ancestry. Maybe she could generate a time tube to what should be.

In the wake of the Lancer, Skrif fine-tuned its own antigravity and applied minijet thrust. Slower than the speeding Lancer, the robot could only hurry after it and try to control its projection thoughts.

"Don't think about the potential consequences," Skrif scolded itself. "Don't think of the forces that could result if she clips, ricochets off, or collides with one of those skeleton trees. Think of chess gambits. Think of fabric care. Think of anything else. Everything else." Skrif knew well how fragile humans were. Despite that, some of them were dreadfully reckless.

Ahead the Lancer screamed, tore at the air, and ripped it aside. It arced around the trees, faster, closer, lower. Finally, it completed the line.

"Disengage bank limit," Ardra ordered, then she cranked both hands fully right and the Lancer spun in a celebratory helix as it shot forward.

"Acute!" Ardra exclaimed. Not even the most extreme thrill rides in Placidon's party domes could compete with a real-life slalom run.

Eventually, Ardra squared up the Lancer, re-engaged the limits, and slowed. But as she let the Lancer idle along, as she looked for another worthy grouping of skeleton trees, she acknowledged she hadn't gone fast enough. Surveyor Stine was still dead, forever etched in holoevidence as a staring corpse, ebony fingers frozen at the cord around her neck.

"Was it a murder of impulse?" Ardra mused aloud. "Whoever did it only used a scrap of tagging cord from the surveyors' equipment, not something brought to the scene. What if her trio of surveyors violated some sacred ground and one of the native Wanderites came across them, was outraged, snatched up a bit of cord, and killed her?"

"Perhaps the killer placed the pebble symbols to appease sacred spirits," Skrif replied through their audilink. "But why would a Wanderite use a cord when it's said they're all armed with lances?"

"Good question. And apart from the pebble symbols, there was nothing ritualistic about Stine's murder. The Wanderite as a suspect is weak, but it's an angle we need to explore. I can't believe the symbols surround the murder scene by chance. Maybe we should . . ." Ardra bit off the end of her sentence when a sudden warning squeal focused her attention on the Lancer.

"Failure of primary antigravity systems," it announced. "Emergency landing initiated." The Lancer automatically fired braking thrusters and adjusted the level of backup antigravity to lower itself to the ground. The descent was sedate down to the last few fingers when all systems disengaged and the machine thumped rudely onto the sandy surface.

"Oof! Grime!" Ardra exclaimed. She ordered the vehicle to repower, but it responded no more than would a lump of circuitless conplast.

"Boiling Jahan!" Ardra yanked her arms out of the attitude sleeves and hammered one fist on the manual restart sensor. Insensitive to her attack, the machine remained inert. Hidden from disapproving eyes by her isolation and the enclosing cowl of the Lancer, Ardra gave rein to her frustration and pounded on the sensor with her fist until the cockpit echoed like a drumming chamber.

Finally, she reasserted control, manually unclipped her restraint harness, and laboriously cranked open the cowling over her back. The cramped cockpit of the Lancer was efficient for streamlined acceleration but it offered little elbowroom for manual operations. Ardra cursed out six unwarranted collisions between her elbows and the cowling before it had retracted enough that she could squeeze out of the rapidly heating oven that imprisoned her. No power, no cooling system.

"Skrif?" Ardra queried as she emerged. No response. Frustration surged through her body yet again, but she managed to confine her response to a thorough kicking of the sand under her feet. It was no surprise that Skrif didn't respond to her hail. She had been using the Lancer's system to boost her collar communicator rather than wear the multiplier pack from her equipment belt. Now she would have to dig it out of the boot. In the near distance she could make out the blunt shape of her companionbot as it hurried to join her.

From the moment the Lancer went down and communication ceased, Skrif's worries intensified. Should it raise an alarm? If Officer Wythian had been injured, help must be summoned immediately. But the Lancer had looked to make a reasonable landing and a false alarm could mean serious repercussions for the companionbot. Skrif had borne dreadful consequences of acting on its own initiative with previous owners. Not that long ago in the lifespan of a robot, it had worn the scarlet letters F L A W E D on its side. If only its minijets could produce more speed.

"Peekay, it's hot!" Ardra grumbled as she tussled with the manual latch on the Lancer boot. There had been a whisper of a breeze for relief back at the murder site, but out here on the plain, the air stood motionless. The one risen sun of Planet Wanderer seemed to be pouring Jahan lava on her black Peace Keeping Force coveralls.

"What idiot supplied this planet posting with black field coveralls?" she seethed. "It's not like the PKF doesn't have a desert issue white."

By the time Ardra had won her battle with the boot latch, her companionbot was within hailing distance.

"Are you injured?" Skrif cried. "Shall I alert rescue?"

"Well, what do you think?" Ardra snapped back. She took off her riding harness, hurled it into the Lancer boot, and put on her equipment belt.

"Wythian com, contact Retro vehicle hangar," she ordered. The weight of her belt felt good. Even better was the re-established function of her communication system. "We're in the middle of nowhere," she thought.

"Hi-ho from the hangar," sang a voice through her belt squawk. "Zill, here."

"This is PKF Officer Wythian," she said. "Gotta problem for you . . ." She described the actions of the Lancer as it failed and how she had tried to revive it. For the moment, she left out details of the way she had been flying shortly before the problem. Her flight record would show what she had done, how she had raced through the makeshift slalom course. Perhaps the extra forces had shaken something loose. Would her new sergeant blame her?

"Better a breakdown happen now than during a PKF chase," she decided. She had been dressed down before. It was the price of initiative and a small price indeed for the rewards. Initiative and a bit of luck had won her early promotion from the rank of Patrol to Officer. She already had her sights set on Sergeant and, one day, one day not long in the future, she would wear the crescents of Director.

"W'got nothing to send for you, Wythian. Everything's out'n'bout or in service," said Zill. "Y'be best to start striding."

Walk? Ardra bit back a protest.

"Zill, I'll be back in port before you can blink," Ardra bragged via her audilink. "Wythian com, hangar over."

"Oh dear," said Skrif.

"Grime, grime, grime," Ardra muttered. Back home on Planet Metro, if her patrol vehicle, her Beast, broke down all she had to do was step into the nearest commute station. And she didn't have to watch for slithery, scaly things there, either.

"One thing we know, stay clear of the dire lizards," Orientation Officer "call me Kip" Myro had warned. "The dire is a knee-high lizard that eats anything it can catch—smaller lizards, insectiles, multipedes, or each other when one wins a fight. Fortunately, humans are too big for them to hunt, but they'll attack if they imagine they're being provoked."

"They actually eat each other?" Ardra had asked.

"There's a fight to the death whenever they meet up, male or female, it doesn't matter. It's amazing the species survives. They don't mate directly, they kind of spawn. The female digs a moist pit near an oasis, lays soft-shelled eggs in it and sings a mating croon. Then she heads for the horizon. The nearest male arrives in a hurry, deposits a mixture of sperm and shell hardener on the clutch, buries the result, and clears out like an adulterer who overslept. Hopefully, he leaves before the male from the next closest territory shows up in answer to the mating croon, otherwise one of them will be fastbreaker."

Just remembering that conversation made Ardra homesick for Metro and its orderly skyscrapers and manufactured air. The nastiest thing on that planet was the common pinkrat and it was only a problem because it chewed on supercables.

But wishes weren't commute stations.

"How far are we from Retro?" Ardra asked Skrif as she rooted out the Lancer's small emergency pack and made space in it for the critical evidence keepers.

"As the hoverjet flies, it's almost five klics to the port. But those foothills intervene . . ."

"It's a hop and a transfer," Ardra snorted. "Five klics is nothing. Let me tell you about my survival test on Planet Brumal."

But the tale of Ardra's adventures on the ice planet was told before the pair even reached the foothills.

"Rise or set, but get the Jahan out of my eyes," Ardra Wythian snarled at the half-circle of sun now on the horizon. It glared remorselessly into her squinting face as she peered toward the cleft in the hills that stood as landmark for the spaceport. Stupid, unpredictable sun! And it was only one of the two that governed the planet's erratic orbit. When she allowed herself to think of it, Ardra felt only horror that a planet could exist in such a configuration.

"Even chaos has its own stability," Kip had told her when she voiced her concerns during her orientation session. His words were meant to soothe but were visually contradicted by his Eifen mannerisms of nervous tics and incessant hand wringing.

"But there's nothing to stop the planet being sucked in or booted out at any moment. Is there? And how can the two suns stay stable so close?"

"It's been stable enough to support human life for thousands of years since its Great Dispersal race landed. Not only that, but it's developed its own plant and animal life. That means it's been going strong for billions of years. Odds are outstanding it'll keep on."

"Odds are?" Ardra never trusted odds. Her life was dedicated to beating the odds, even the long ones.

Better not to think about it. For a moment, Ardra paused in her trudge to the foothills, turned her back on the hot white stare, and indulged in a mouthful of water from her echoing canteen. Though it felt generous in her mouth, when she swallowed only a trickle ran down her throat.

"Is the water sufficient?" Skrif asked. "I could hurry ahead and fetch more from the port."

"It's plenty." Ardra had been shocked back at the Lancer when she found a crack in the water reserve vat. It had been damp inside but contained nothing pourable. All she had for the hike back to Retro were the contents of her canteen. Why did anyone need to kill anyone else in a place like this, she wondered. Surely the primitive conditions would kill them all soon enough.

Coarse sand grated under her boots as Ardra turned in a slow scan of their surroundings. She and Skrif were still in the flat plain, a landscape dotted with withered grey growths that ranged from lumpy, ankle-high knots to the twiggy, leafless wonders known as skeleton trees. Surrounding the plain stood a series of slumped hills, none with the backbone to reach defiantly for the stars.

Desolate and alone they were, save for the odd flicker of movement from one of the reptiles that called this wasteland home. There were small ribbon-like creatures and larger blocky creatures, each uglier than the last. They were all impossible to see until they moved and they were always darting into the shadows of the desiccated plant life and freezing into an immobile non-existence. To Ardra, their combined scent smelled reminiscent of nervous armpits.

"What am I doing here?" she muttered.

Skrif recognized the question as rhetorical and remained silent.

The simple answer to Ardra's question she already knew. As soon as she'd been able, Ardra had joined the Peace Keeping Force and served as a beat cop on her home planet of Metro. Both her parents were cops and many of her aunts, uncles, and greats, too. A lot of hard work and a little luck earned her a place at the Wythian Academy on Planet Placidon where she received advanced training.

On Placidon she had also borne the mixed envy and admiration of fellow cadets when they discovered how closely she was related to the hero for whom the academy had been named. Gil Wythian, her mimilo, or great-uncle on her mother's side, was retired from the PKF but still active in the family on Metro. No doubt he had dug deep for credits when the family bought Skrif. Ardra was still awed that her extended family had marshaled the funds necessary for such a purchase.

So Ardra was a PKF officer. She was an officer with a job to do.

"Let's keep it going," Ardra said. She tucked the water canteen back into the shade of her pack, reslung the pack over her shoulder, and turned once more to face the staring sun. Head bowed, she watched as drops of sweat gathered force on the tip of her nose, then pulled loose and plummeted to draw small dark circles on the sand that fled under her boots.

Finally, the flatness beneath Ardra's feet began to slope upward; she had reached the hills. Deciding the event earned her a short rest and another gulp of water, she moved to the broken shade of a skeleton tree. She carefully avoided the barbed thorns of a hookbush then scrutinized the sand and pebbles under the tree. She had been impressed by Kip's colorful warning about bubble cactus and had no desire to repeat his mistake.

"They look a lot like pebbles but they're perfectly round and easy to spot if you check," Kip had said. "That's the key, you've got to examine the ground before you touch it with anything but your booted feet. When a bubble cactus is ripe, the slightest touch will trigger it to erupt, firing its tiny arrow-like seeds in all directions. On my first foray out of town, I flopped down for a rest on top of a cluster and they all fired right through the seat of my coveralls into my butt. I launched, howling, into the air and at the zenith of my leap I remembered the cautionary memo Botanist Cullen had sent around. It still stings, I swear."

As far as Ardra could tell, the area under the skeleton tree was clear and she thumped her pack to the ground and dropped down beside it. Skrif settled close by, powered down its antigravity unit, and streamlined its power consumption.

Ardra eyed her companionbot. It wasn't much to look at, a cone of grey durmet half her height and broadly flared toward the base. At the blunt tip of the cone sat a smoky green cap, its visual scanner, capable of a full circle horizontal sweep and a quarter arc of rise or dip from level. Two skinny, multi-jointed arms were attached, one on each side, near the base of the robot. Now at rest, they lay clockwise in the groove around its flare. Just above the left arm socket gleamed the robot's only decoration, the PKF crest, which featured a spouting sidearm and an open palm.

Skrif examined Officer Wythian's face and reassured itself that, as long as the human continued to sweat, there was no medical emergency due to heat exhaustion. However, the dark and light olive patterns on her face were more pronounced than usual and that could indicate many things in an Olidan—simple exertion, extreme anger, even physiological shock. The first two, exertion and anger, it had seen on more than one occasion.

"What if she suffered internal injuries?" Skrif worried silently. "In my current configuration, my antigravity unit doesn't have the lift capability to carry her."

"Conventional thinking would suspect one of Cara Stine's surveyor team," Ardra said suddenly. "They were right there. Grime, I wish I could interview them myself and see if either has a pebble fetish. Sergeant Rosil should have put more pressure on them in her interviews."

"Do you think the encampment was near enough to Retro that someone could have come out from the port?" Skrif asked.

"With premeditation, I guess. An A-pad would make for a quiet approach and the dungsnake who did the deed would have had plenty of time to slip away before morning. However, it assumes the culprit knew where the team was camped. Then there's motive . . . we need motive."

A sudden whiff of an orange blossom scent made Ardra look around at a nearby spiky bush and a fist cactus, then up into the twisted branches of the tree. If anything was blooming she saw no evidence of flowers.

A flicker of movement to the right caught her eye and she snapped her head around to face an elongate reptile. It had a yellow snake's body the length of her forearm and four stumpy legs. Its red eyes gleamed up at her. Ardra's stomach knotted and she glared down at the creature; her fingers twitched toward her sidearm.

Then she felt the most bizarre sensation, as if an invisible hand drew a cold finger through her brain. Before she could react, before she could formulate the thought, "What's that?", the feeling was gone. Just as quickly, the yellow ribbon flicked and vanished back into the shadows, and the young Olidan struggled to relax the tension in her trigger finger. Ardra shook her head to clear it and told herself to stop overreacting to every little thing.

"I wonder if there's any evidence the forensic flies missed at the second murder site," she said. "We should have a look when we get back to Retro."

"Is there any chance the same individual killed both victims? Is that possible?" asked Skrif.

"The timing of the two murders, right after each other, that's suspicious as a coincidence," said Ardra. "But each of the murders involved a different method of killing. Surveyor Stine was strangled and Forecaster Lesting was clubbed. That's a big difference and it grates at my sense of order." The brutality of both murders had grated on her, too.

Back at Eagle III Station on Blooh, she had seen Lesting. The man lay sprawled, his arms and legs were twisted askew, and spatters of blood drew lines over the sand beneath his body. The back of his smooth-shaven head was crushed like a red eggshell.

It wasn't real, of course. It was only the reconstructed holographic image of the second murder victim and Ardra had studied it while she still had access to the advanced equipment of the Eagle III Station. When she had glanced up from the control panel and caught her first glimpse of the newly formed image, she had felt as though her stomach suddenly was being sucked down a vortex.

Leaning back, Ardra gazed up through the limbs of the skeleton tree into Wanderer's pale sky. Up there, beyond the glare of daylight, there were stars, and somewhere among those distant points of light was home. The Olidan closed her eyes for an instant and smiled. At least her physical reaction to gore wasn't as strong as her mother's; she chuckled at the thought.

Then her smile faded and a small sigh slipped out. If it weren't for that wretched lottery for colony duty she could be with them right now. In two Standard weeks, Olidans around the Realm would celebrate Eternity with traditional dance and tongmusic and feast. If she were still working a beat on Metro, her off-duty hours would be filled with preparations.

"Enough!" Ardra muttered; she gathered her pack and sprang to her feet with resolve. There were puzzles to be solved, perhaps even lives to be saved. The sooner her feet carried her back to the spaceport, the sooner she would be off this sandy, chaotic rock and back to a planet that behaved in an orderly manner. On this and any other planet the PKF powers threw at her, she would serve her colony duty and get back home. Then she would never leave Metro, never again.

Skrif snapped out of its conservation mode and lifted off the ground to follow Officer Wythian, the human that finally, after a string of dissatisfied owners, seemed to be the right one. The companionbot still marveled that Officer Wythian hadn't sent it for correction after that unfortunate incident on Chelidon when the robot had decided to defy orders.

"I'm not flawed after all," Skrif reassured itself silently.

The pair's route now led uphill, the sun frying down from above and the rocks radiating up from below. Drops of sweat formed on Ardra's skin, gathered into trickles, and matured into streams, which explored the contours of her face, scurried down the furrow of her spine, and slithered between her fingers. She continually blotted her forehead with a sleeve and still the liquid found a way into her eyes until they burned and stung. To make matters worse, the heel of her left boot had begun to chafe the moment she started going uphill.

She distracted herself with a mind game she had played as a cadet during endurance runs. In this game, she imagined her didactic training officer in a dozen different torturous scenes: mired in a bottomless tar pit on Tithe and struggling futilely to lift even one foot; clinging to the crumbling lip of a lava blister on Jahan, the cauldron below spitting red rocks at his dangling feet; here on Wanderer, inadvertently stepping on the tail of a dire lizard. The game was to see how many original scenarios she could create. The reality was that if her training officer were ever really in trouble she would probably do something stupid and heroic to save him.

"Heroic and dumb, those two words are synonymous, aren't they?" Haley had often asked her in their time together. She'd always agreed.

Skrif watched the sweat intensify on Officer Wythian and held an internal debate.

"I should remind her that I have the lift capability to carry the pack."

"She hates to admit any weakness."

"But it's sensible for me to carry the weight and she'll perspire less if her load is lessened."

"She might get angry."

"Furthermore, if the pack is removed from her back there will be more cooling airflow."

"She might even lose her temper. And her temper . . ."

"Is more like a Kelpan than an Olidan."

Skrif held its silence and considered that Ardra's temper had been less volatile during her time with Haley, the young entomologist she had lived with on Planet Chelidon. On Chelidon, Haley encountered a giant creature similar to a heritage dragonfly. Remarkably, this species of insect had the intelligence to learn a simple tapping code and to communicate with this code.

When conditions fell to pieces on the planet, Haley decided to save as many of the dragonflies as possible. His noble purpose had gone badly, though. Planet Chelidon had taken a terrible toll on them all.

Finally, Officer Wythian and Skrif crested the hill on Planet Wanderer and looked down over its golden flank to the cluster of blocks and circle of apron that marked the spaceport, Retro. To Ardra, it looked close enough to kiss and, if she only had the gliding membranes of a tiffin, she could unfurl them right now and swoop into town. But she didn't have wings, it felt like her sock was starting to stick to her left heel, and an honest estimate said walking was going to take at least another hour.

It did.

Ardra was hobbling by the time she reached Main Street, not an original name but every spaceport had standard street names so travelers could learn one pattern and always be oriented. Its official offices were also in standard locations and painted standard colors. They were standard colors to the ordinary eye, that is, but known to planners as Sunny Blade, Gentle Smoke, and Aqua Glow. For her part, Ardra passed the green vehicle hangar where she had gotten that wretched Lancer, then she limped by the grey cafeteria. Up ahead, a figure darted out of the blue administration building and she recognized him at a glance.

Orientation Officer Kip Myro was an Eifen and typical of the race, tall and emaciated, always twitching with nervous energy. Eifens had reflexes that were so fast they were a blur, which was an advantage when a drillbug needed to be swatted, but they had a hard time relaxing.

Ardra made a practice of memorizing a person's physical characteristics, mannerisms, and scent clusters on a first meeting. Now Kip's hazel eyes and hooked nose seemed as familiar as her own image in a mirror with its emerald eyes and narrow nose.

"Well found, Kip," she called out, trying to overpower her limp as she and Skrif approached. She marveled at how dry and cool the man looked. As an Eifen, he probably found the day cool with only one sun to warm the air.

Wringing his hands, Kip danced from one foot to another before her. "Sergeant Rosil needs to see both of you immediately," he said.

CHAPTER 3

Dark Encounter

"First day on Wanderer and you're already scoring points on the home wall," Rosil grumbled the moment Ardra and Skrif entered the sergeant's office in Retro's PKF station. Seated behind an expansive workdesk cluttered with volleywar memorabilia, Rosil scowled up at Ardra and added, "That was our only Lancer before you killed it, Wythian. What's your excuse?"

Ardra came to a halt in front of the workdesk and Skrif settled to the floor next to her. From this position, Skrif's scanning visor was just high enough to see over the desk. The companionbot wasn't sure if it wanted to be noticed or ignored; in Skrif's experience, attention from an authority figure was rarely favorable.

"The Lancer's primary antigravity malfunctioned and . . ." Ardra began to explain.

"Just what the Jahan were you doing out of town? Your assignment's in Retro later today. Nightwatch."

"I thought it would be useful to visit the Stine murder scene before my shift so . . ."

"I covered the encampment crime scene with the forensibots weeks ago. Were you planning to have a psychic moment?" Rosil snickered.

Ardra took the time for a silent count to ten, not trusting her voice to reply with an even tone. As she counted, Ardra contemplated her new supervising officer.

As a member of the Kelpan race, Sergeant Rosil had a short, powerful build, skin as grey as fog, limp brown hair, and muddy green eyes. Kelpans were renowned for their quick tempers and the flaring light in Rosil's eyes told Ardra the sergeant was true to her genetics.

Ardra assessed the lines on Rosil's face and the strands of white in her brown hair then assigned her the designation of middle aged—80 or 90 Standard years old. That was old to be nothing higher than a sergeant, but perhaps it explained her presence on Wanderer. Who better to assign to a survey crew of less than 50 people than a mediocre officer? Surely under normal circumstances, such a posting would be a routine, even slack, assignment. There would be no sense in wasting top-notch personnel on a mundane posting, Ardra concluded.

"The forensibots missed something at the Stine murder site," said Ardra to Sergeant Rosil in her best attempt at a neutral tone. "Until the bots are calibrated to recognize normal versus abnormal for a given planet and region they can miss certain . . ."

"You have new evidence?" Rosil snapped. "Why didn't you say so? Where is it?"

Ardra slipped off her pack and dug out the evidence keepers. Rosil surged to her feet and snatched them.

"What's this? Pebbles?"

Ardra explained about the oily scent and the symbols and the fact that such stone didn't occur naturally in the area of the murder scene. Rosil opened one of the keepers and sniffed deeply. Ardra flinched at the sight; as an Olidan, she would never draw so much scent from an enclosed space. Just the thought of such an act made her sinuses ache.

"Hmm, it's mighty faint and nothing I recognize," said Rosil. "Are you certified for scent identification?"

"It's nothing I've studied and it's not characteristic of the plain or foothills," Ardra replied, refusing to react to the suggestion she, as Olidan and PKF, might not be certified. "It's definitely organic and I'd guess it's something the Wanderites use. Skrif and I speculated the survey crew might have violated something sacred to the local population."

"Whoa, time out!" said Rosil. She re-seated herself and plopped the keepers onto the desktop. "I'll want you to keep that kind of speculation to yourself. Both of you. The last thing we need is to spook the survey crew about the Wanderites. Apart from the few that hang out in town they're seen so seldom the townspeople are already uncomfortable about them and pointing fingers. Yep, outside Wanderite sightings are as rare as a defensive double in a championship match. Their behavior does nothing to calm people, either. I don't want to have to deal with a mob determined to do some lynching."

"A lynch mob? Here? Aren't surveyors screened for stability?"

"And in a perfect Realm, the screening would be impartial. Remember, somebody killed Stine and somebody killed Lesting. What better way for either murderer to cover their crime than conjure scapegoats in the Wanderites and instigate a bit of vigilantism? After all, there's a streak for vicious, bloody revenge in all of us."

"Surely not!" Ardra blurted.

"Heh, heh, you are a young one," Rosil chuckled and followed up with an order, "Rosil desklab up." With a click and a hiss, the left side of her workstation opened and an ident tower rose and claimed the space. The sergeant placed one of the evidence keepers on its intake pan. "Rosil desklab, analyze for surface evidence," she said.

While the tower drew in, extracted, and contemplated the offering, Rosil leaned back in her seat and examined Ardra through narrowed eyes. "You're not on Metro anymore, Wythian," she said. "Out here on the bleeding edge of the Realm, initiative like your joy ride this morning can get you killed. That's not what you're here for, understand?"

"Yes, sergeant."

"You were barely out of orientation and you took off on your own. You hadn't even seen me for your first briefing."

"You were unavailable and I . . ."

"Let me be clear," said Rosil. She leaned forward and deepened the resident frown on her face as she spoke. "You didn't request permission to leave Retro with the Lancer today and in future all such acts must be approved by me."

"Yes, sergeant," said Ardra. She wanted to argue that the trip had been made on her own time but there was the matter of the official Lancer she had used. A sticky detail, that.

"Analysis complete," reported the ident tower.

"Do you have dress uniforms with you?" Rosil asked, ignoring the tower.

"Dress? No, I didn't expect I'd need dress blacks for a temporary posting to a survey port," Ardra replied.

"Uniforms impress the Wanderites and black is a color of power for them," Sergeant Rosil explained. "At least, that's the official word from Anthropologist Udell, who's studying their culture, trying to study their culture. It's not easy because most of them stay out of touch." While she talked, the sergeant's eyes strayed to the ident tower on the left then jerked away to rest on a replica InterStellar Volleywar trophy on the right.

Ardra suppressed a smirk. She had never met a Kelpan who wasn't passionate about the ISV league. She hoped Rosil's love of that rigorous sport was the only stereotype the sergeant fit; a boss with an explosive temper would only add to her misery. The two eyed each other warily.

"Black's a brutal color for the climate," Ardra said. "Is it that important to impress the natives with dress uniforms?" It didn't make sense to her. According to the preliminary planet report, the Wanderites' highest level of technology produced polished copper tips for their lances. Only a handful of the native population had been seen by the surveying team and only three locals frequented the block of buildings planted next to the launch and landing circle. It was tragic that one of the Great Dispersal races had sunk so low and never recovered over the millennia before Reunification.

"Of course it's important we wear dress black for them. Wanderer is their planet, their home. It's the least we can do. Can't you city cops handle a little heat?" Rosil demanded.

Ardra held her tongue. Just as Skrif had concluded that Ardra's question about murder and evolution had been rhetorical, so she concluded that Rosil's question demanded no answer. Indeed, it seemed to insist on silence.

"There's uniform stock down the hall," said Rosil. "I want you wearing dress black on your shifts."

"Yes, sergeant." Ardra looked pointedly at the ident tower and Rosil looked pointedly away from it. From the right side of her workstation, the sergeant picked up a miniature version of a volleywar ball, barely the size of an orange, and tossed it from hand to hand.

"The results?" Ardra suggested.

"You should probably get ready for your shift," said Rosil. "Get cleaned up, have a nap, whatever."

For a moment, diplomacy struggled against assertion. Assertion won, as usual, and Ardra asked, "Aren't we both on the same team here?"

"Right, you've got it exactly," Rosil nodded. "I'm the halberd and you're the water dipper. Understand?"

Ardra blinked. "Er, yes sergeant." The young Olidan understood but didn't like the way some people in the PKF got territorial. No doubt Rosil wanted the glory work and its payoff. No doubt the sergeant expected the new arrival to manage only the petty problems of daily life among interacting humans. "We'll see about that!" thought the new arrival.

"Ardra Wythian . . ." Rosil snorted " . . . as in Wythian Academy on Placidon, the elite training college for PKF officers. I understand you're related to the man it's named after and have a pedigree of peace keeping heroes that would stagger a Names of Renown editor."

Ardra swallowed a retort, which forced itself back up her throat. She coughed.

Then Rosil put down the ball, leaned back in her chair, and let the corners of her lips turn up in a thin smile that failed to reach her eyes. "Of course, I'll add these ident results to Stine's file. In good time."

Propping an elbow on the arm of the chair, Rosil contemplated the gold glitter on her fingernails. The color complemented her black uniform, Ardra thought, but it wasn't regulation. She held her tongue.

"So what did you think of the encampment scene?" Rosil asked.

"There was plenty of cover in the rock outcroppings around the camping site so an outsider could have lain in wait without being seen." The blister on Ardra's heel started to ache from the continuous pressure of standing. She gritted her teeth and refused to favor it.

"Outsider? Huh!" Rosil snorted. "It had to be one of her campmates, Blaze Myro or Cliff Sennett. It's just a question of figuring out which one. Trouble is, there's no real motive. Cara Stine, the victim, was Retro's ray of sunshine; she was a friend of everyone and always looking for ways to help. She was optimistic and bubbly, a Carrian through and through. The whole town took it hard, her death."

"Do those shapes formed by the pebbles have any significance to the Wanderites that you know of?" Ardra asked.

"Never heard of such a thing," said Rosil. "Don't waste your time worrying about the Wanderites as suspects. It's ludicrous. Trust me."

"The symbols seem to be the kind of thing a Wanderite would leave behind, don't you think?" Ardra pressed.

"Huff! It's a great way to throw blame their way. Besides, there's no telling when they were laid out. Could have been years before or days after the murder." Rosil's eyes snaked across the room to a small side table where a leaf-shaped lance tip winked up at the ceiling light. "You're dismissed, Wythian," she said and, for the first time in the meeting, Rosil looked directly at Skrif. "You too, Daisy," she added.

"Yes, sergeant." Ardra snapped to attention despite a yelp from her left heel. Skrif powered its antigravity and rose into the air.

"Full issue dress blacks," Rosil repeated.

"Right!" Ardra strode out of the office, spun around the corner, then hobbled down the hall. Skrif glided alongside. Both held their silence until they were out of human earshot.

"Well, Rosil's going to be a challenge to work with," Ardra said through her teeth. "What was it she called you? Daisy? What made her call you that, I wonder?" Ardra shook her head.

"A number of Standard years ago, I worked for Mayor Nechako of Coeur Southcenter," said the robot. "For a time, the mayor called me Daisy. Later she called me Dax. But my name has always been Skrif. I suppose the information about Daisy exists somewhere in a stray data thread."

"I don't believe the useless grime we save as data."

"It's odd the sergeant came across the reference."

"She probably dug for it. You know, my family tree isn't part of my PKF record so that means she ran an outside trace on me. She's envious, that's certain. Here I am, a young officer named Wythian with a PKF-certified companionbot and the whole future of my career in front of me. What's she got by comparison?"

"Rosil has the rank of sergeant, the wisdom and experience of many decades as a PKF member, and absolute command of the PKF on Planet Wanderer," Skrif responded.

"Well, that's blunt enough." Ardra jerked to a halt.

"Oh dear." Skrif reversed minijets. "Did I answer a rhetorical question?"

"Never mind." Ardra paused and shifted her left foot in its boot, trying to find a position where it wouldn't rub. "So the locker room's this way, isn't it?" she asked. "Are we headed the right direction?"

Although the survey crew on Wanderer was small, some of Retro's buildings had been put together with optimism to accommodate a subsequent wave of colonists. The PKF station had hallways and rooms far in excess of the needs of two cops and one bot. Skrif consulted the Retro-specific map it had acquired from the Repositor and confirmed their direction.

"If only I'd mustered a suitable reply after the orientation session this morning," Skrif thought as they entered the locker room. "If I'd dissuaded Officer Wythian from visiting the murder site, we wouldn't have found disfavor with Sergeant Rosil."

In the morning, after they'd parted company with Kip, Ardra's first question outside the administration building had been "Is there a PKF vehicle free?" When Skrif checked and confirmed "A Lancer" she said, "Then there's nothing to stop us checking on the

Stine murder site, is there?" Skrif searched every area of data available but was unable to find any reason. Not one.

"But I haven't had time to shake out your clothing. There's unpacking to be done," Skrif had said. It wasn't much of a reason, it knew, and if it objected too strongly, Ardra might insist on going alone.

"Skrif, you're a PKF-K9 certified bot now. You're not a valetbot. You don't have to worry about trivial things like clothes anymore."

Skrif was not as knowledgeable as the Repositor, but it did know clothing wasn't trivial. Not at all.

"Peekay! There's only two sizes in here," said Ardra, her head and shoulders buried in the stacks of black uniforms on one of the locker room shelves. "There's one size fits none or a cut that would fit a tree stump—tailored for Rosil, no doubt."

Ardra backed out of the shelf with one of the generic-sized uniforms, then shed her field coveralls and tried it on. The uniform tunic was short in the arms, ballooned at the waist, and fit snugly around the neck. The trouser cuffs crept up toward her shins when she squatted to buff the tips of her boots with one of the sleeves of the spent coveralls. She straightened and tugged for slack around her neck; this tunic reminded her of the Academy when she had mercilessly starched her collar to earn maximum uniform points at classes.

Dilli, her study mate for forensics, had worn his collar soft and laughed at those who chafed. "How many points can you get?" he challenged. "Maybe ten for uniform, one or two for collar, and that's out of five hundred for the year in all conduct and study areas. I'd rather drop the two points for the benefit of being able to concentrate in class. It's worth more than two points in fact acquisition."

Ardra grinned at the memory. Those extra two points had been enough to see her finish the first year at the top of her class, with Dilli placing a close second. He had been a challenge the next year, too.

Ardra stopped smiling as she turned to stare at the cartoon cop in the mirror on the back of the locker room door. Its billowing middle and stubby sleeves seemed incapable of impressing anyone. Behind the unimpressive figure she saw only an empty expanse of lockers. It was nothing like a Metro locker room filled with bustle composed of an overlayer of ribaldry and an underlayer of camaraderie. A deep sigh echoed through the under populated room.

"This room even smells empty," she said. A flicker of movement over the shoulder of her mirror image caught her eye and she spun around.

"What was that? Did you see that?" she asked. Before her were two banks of lockers and a long bench. Nothing stirred.

"I detected a tiny reptile on the wall above the lockers," said Skrif. "It moved into concealment."

"Lizards! Like I didn't get my fill of lizards when my parents dragged me to Olid. My ancestral planet. Huh! My ancestors can have it, I say."

"Shall I check with the Repositor to see if there's a species name for the reptile?" Skrif asked. "Perhaps it's a common one that's already been classified and named."

"This is really pathetic," Ardra grumbled. "On Chelidon we had chitinous creatures everywhere and here we've got beasts with scales. Why can't modern technology design a door with the brains to keep wildlife out of our buildings?"

"An unfathomable mystery?" Skrif wavered.

Ardra grinned at the robot's reply, but the smile vanished when she turned back to her image in the mirror.

"I could make alterations to such a uniform," said Skrif. "But it would be a compromise."

"I wonder if I'll be posted on Wanderer long enough to have them send my storage cube out on a supply ship. Then I'd have my own."

"Perhaps I could glean material from two uniforms to make one of a suitable fit." Skrif knew Ardra wasn't ready to deal with certain items in that storage cube. Not yet.

"It's worth a try," said Ardra as she de-equipped and bundled up the sweat-dampened field coveralls. "Wythian hamper open," she commanded and a brown chute next to the lockers yawned wide. She leaned over and crammed the coveralls into the chute.

"I'm the halberd and you're the water dipper," she cursed out Rosil's words as she straightened. Only the twinge of her blister kept her from kicking the nearest locker.

"Why don't you head to the barracks and get started on the alterations?" Ardra suggested as she strapped her equipment belt over the new uniform and clipped the audilink to the tunic collar. "I might stop over at the clinic and see if I can get my blister patched."

Skrif happily selected and draped two uniforms over one arm while Ardra manually slid the locker room door open and peered out, up and down the hallway. It was empty so she favored her blistered foot as far as the outer door where the companionbot passed her, minijets pressed for acceleration. Ardra paused and straightened before marching evenly out into Main Street.

Two paces from the door, Ardra stopped and stared. It hadn't seemed like she and Sergeant Rosil had talked that long, yet, here it was, pitch dark. Giant lamps standing at intervals along the street dropped orange pools of light on the dusty ground and broad fingers of shadow reached out from between the buildings.

"Wythian data, what time is it?" she ordered.

"Realm Standard time is fifteen oh six," replied her belt.

"That's mid-afternoon," she muttered.

"Oh, you'll get used to the sunlight and darkness having nothing to do with day and night here on Wanderer," Kip had told her during her orientation session. "Just eat when you're hungry, sleep when you're tired, and align yourself with the clock rather than the two suns."

"Hoof! Hoof!" something beyond the lights made a deep chugging sound and the hairs on Ardra's neck bristled. She brushed her hand against her sidearm then forced out a chuckle as she commanded her hand back to a position of relaxation. For a moment, Ardra contemplated the welcoming face of the town tavern directly across the street from the PKF station. The curves of its turquoise sign spelled out its name, "No Limits", and its iris door was a pulsating bull's-eye of orange light.

"That might take the sting off the day," she thought and followed along as her blister led her across the street. By the time she reached the other side, though, her boots turned left in the direction of the clinic.

Just as she came to the gap between the tavern and the administration building, a human-shaped shadow flitted across the alleyway. Ardra slowed and watched it without turning her head. It froze in the hollow of a wall and seemed to coil with attentiveness. Ardra paused, gazed casually up the street, hitched her equipment belt, and strolled on. She could go to the next alley, dodge in, and double back to see who it was, or she could speak directly to the form. Still weighing the alternatives, she continued forward, eyes and ears and nose on full alert, fire starting to pump through her veins.

"It's you!" the shadow whisper-hissed as she drew abreast. When she turned her head to look at it, the shadow shrank back.

"PKF Officer Wythian," she identified herself. "Did you want to speak to me?" In the silence that followed she searched the breeze for a scent but the stranger was upwind and all she could smell was dust from the street and citron fabric softener from her new uniform.

"We could flap gums, somewhere," the shadow spoke this time; the voice was low-pitched.

Male, she decided, probably a local, a Wanderite. Kip had mentioned they'd been quick to learn Standard and spoke an extremely slang version of the language, filled with roughly translated idioms from their own tongue.

There was a chance this man was an informant and would yield valuable information. There was a chance he was a murderer and wanted to lead her into a dark corner.

"Where is somewhere?" she asked. As long as there was only one of him she felt sufficiently armed and trained to go anywhere— senses on full alert, of course.

"Follow the leader," he said, backing away from her.

"All right," she agreed and pressed the manual trigger on her belt to activate her audilink. Then she stepped into the dark gullet of the alley. The stranger turned in a fluid motion and glided into deeper shadow toward the back of the building. He was shorter than Ardra and lithe, but it was too dark to distinguish coloration and features. Now in his footsteps, she was almost overpowered by the reek of scent from him in which sweat warred with rootsmoke. The shadow before her slid down the alley, flowed around the corner, and swung to face her, tucking his back against the wall.

"And who are you?" she asked.

"I am myself."

"Do you have a name?"

"Yes."

"What is it?"

"They call me Kafka."

Ardra made a mental note to be careful of the literal meaning of things she said to him. "I'm pleased to meet you," she measured out her words and extended a hand. Kafka lifted a narrow arm and lightly touched two fingers to her palm. The arm retreated.

"Your wisdom will stop the killing?" he asked.

"Ah, well . . ." she began, then paused. This was the first time anyone had granted her the status of wisdom. After all, she was just a cop and young on a relative scale of such things. Certainly, her new boss hadn't credited her with such a talent. "I'm here to help Sergeant Rosil determine the cause of the murders—who did them and why. Then we'll see that justice is done." No matter what Rosil said, Ardra planned to be involved in the investigations.

"Does justice stop the killing?"

"Whoever did it will be stopped, yes," she replied.

"The prophecy awakens." Kafka's shadowy head nodded solemnly. He raised his left hand and stared at his wrist. "No," he said to it. "I must flap gums."

Ardra looked for a communication device on his wrist but it was bare. Then Kafka dropped his arm and spoke to her again, "It's you. You are the Avenger and you will purge the land and the people."

"I'm not an avenger, I'm a cop and anything I do will be in line with proper PKF procedures." Ardra found herself favoring her blistered foot and re-set her ready stance. "What do you know about the two murders? First there was Cara Stine, a surveyor who was strangled at a camp site south of the low hills, then there was Les Lesting, a town worker, who was beaten to death behind the tavern."

"I know nothing," was the reply.

Ardra started to sigh, then reconsidered. Perhaps the phrasing was wrong and the word "know" implied too much. She tried again. "Where were you at the times of the two murders?"

"I was where I was."

A hand of heat slid up the back of Ardra's neck and she counted to ten, then pressed on, aiming for simplicity. "Do you see things that happen in town?"

"Yes, I see whenever my eyes are open."

"Good. What did you see when Lesting was killed behind the tavern?"

Kafka sucked a noisy lungful of air in through his nose and expelled it in a singsong, "Two suns threw two shadows and my feet led me between the two shadows. Ivy stood over two shadows and her face was lost. There were ten in a circle and everyone looked down."

"Who's . . ." just as Ardra was about to ask who Ivy was, she remembered that Sergeant Rosil's first name was Ivy. There ought to be a way to get better information from this fellow. "What did you see before you saw Sergeant . . . I mean Ivy?"

"I saw the suns rise in the sky and I saw a flight of eagles and I saw the ground run in rivers."

"Did you see someone hit Lesting?"

Kafka dropped his head, spread his hands and stared at their shadowy blackness. Ardra counted seconds until one minute passed, then two. Finally, Kafka muttered, "I see nothing when my eyes are closed."

"What are you afraid of, Kafka?"

The man lifted his face slowly, placed one hand over his heart, and whispered, "Everything."

For a moment Ardra struggled to find meaning in Kafka's words. How could Rosil's face be lost? What river?

"Were you in the plains when Cara Stine, the surveyor, was strangled?" Ardra opted to stay with reality.

"I was where I was!" Kafka insisted. "I saw the ground run in rivers and I knew."

"Knew what?"

"The prophecy must be answered. You must answer the prophecy."

"Can't you help me answer the prophecy? What did you see?"

"The cat bites my tongue and my back turns yellow." With a twitch, Kafka pulled away from the wall, then he glided along the back of the building to the mouth of the next alley. "Thank-you, Avenger," he called out before vanishing.

"Wythian audilink off," Ardra ordered. She stared at the blackness where Kafka's heels had vanished and her mind searched for meaning in his words. What had the man been raving about? A flight of eagles? Kip hadn't mentioned any large flying creatures on this planet. Ground running in rivers? There were no surface rivers around Retro and she'd seen no evidence of landslide in the hills. Was Kafka a mad refugee from a nearby clan or was he so twisted on rootsmoke that he couldn't express himself properly?

"You and I are definitely going to talk again," Ardra muttered at the shadows that had swallowed him. She was certain he knew a great deal and equally certain she could coax it out of him.

"Ardra the Avenger," she chuckled as she turned back toward the main street.

CHAPTER 4

Lights and Fights

Retro's clinic, like the PKF station, had been overbuilt for the town's current population. The structure was a perfect cube, two stories high and externally rose-colored, a shade the designers called Pulse Pink. Ardra winced as she walked up the clinic's approach ramp; the angle of the ramp rubbed her heel exactly the wrong way.

"Wythian audilink on," she ordered. Even though Ardra's purpose was the repair of her blister, there was no telling what question might slip out of her mouth while talking with the doctor. No telling what answer might slip out in return. With the audilink on, Skrif would be able to monitor her conversation and file anything worth later review.

The clinic door sprang open at her approach and Ardra stepped into a reception bay the shape of a half-moon. Only a quarter of the moon was functional, the rest was cluttered with scraps of slaptogether and stacks of cargo crates. A mixed string of formchairs and armlounges stood along the wall in the functional part of the room.

"Rrrrgph, ssssseeee." Sprawled on his back on one of the armlounges lay an Olidan male, limbs askew, jaw limp, snoring. He looked no more than her age, Ardra decided, maybe younger. The olive mottlings on his face leaned diagonally left above his mouth and swirled to the right over his chin. They were nothing like the smooth, contour-following markings of Haley.

Ardra advanced into the room, covered the only strip of carpet in three paces, and set boot to bare conplast floor. At the first click of heel, the young man snorted and snapped to a sitting position. In one blink he located and focused on Ardra.

"Doctor?" Ardra asked.

"Clais Sethline, that's me. You must be our new arrival. Here to save us all, are you?" he said with a grin. Ardra recognized his name; she had skimmed the team list before her arrival. She also noticed that, unlike Rosil, Sethline's smile went straight to his eyes, his glittering emeralds.

"According to a strange fellow I just met outside, I'm an avenger foretold in myth and legend. Actually, I'm Officer . . ."

"Ardra Wythian. Right. The town's already abuzz over you. Did you injure yourself when the Lancer crashed? Maybe I should check you over. Come in, come in, my examining room is . . . just follow me." Sethline hopped to his feet and breezed toward one of a dozen doors at intervals along the arc of the reception bay. With a muted shriek of machinery, the door accelerated open. Doors always sounded alarmed by anyone moving faster than a stroll.

"Actually, the Lancer's emergency antigrav did its job and set me down without a scratch," said Ardra, following at a stride that annoyed her heel but kept up appearances. "I just developed a bit of a foot chafing problem on the walk back to town. Don't ask me why, I've done more vigorous hiking than that in these boots and never gave birth to a blister before."

The room they entered was clean, bright, and fully finished. It smelled fresh and pure, no doubt thanks to the whispering extractors in the ceiling. There was also Sethline's scent signature in the air, a delicate odor reminiscent of crushed leaves.

"A blister? Wonderful. I thrive on cases like this. It's not life threatening and the treatment is completely effective. No side effects, either. Stuff like this actually makes me believe I'm a healer." Sethline beamed as he activated the room's workstation and ordered Ardra's medical history, part of the data that had arrived with her on the supply ship. After a brief perusal of the information, the doctor gathered equipment onto a tray and puffed anticontaminant powder on his hands.

"Hop on and bare the beast," he said with a nod toward the room recliner.

It was only when Ardra was well seated and reached to unlatch her boot clamps that she realized her timing could have been better. Why hadn't she gone back to the barracks to cleanse and change before coming to the clinic? Too late now, she decided and whipped off her boot then delicately peeled away her sock. The skin of her blister had broken away and a circle of raw flesh wept at its loss.

"It doesn't look like much," Ardra said. "It ought to be twice the size and bleeding according to the fuss it's been making."

"Best to catch it when it's young," Sethline replied. "I've seen neglected feet—infected, eroded—bad news." He ordered the recliner to the right height and position then moved in close and sprayed a mist of de-infect over the wound. Between the anticontaminant powder and the de-infect mist, the room's smell evolved from fresh and leafy to medicinal.

"I went into the PKF station this afternoon in daylight and came out in darkness," said Ardra. "It threw me for a moment. I hadn't expected it."

"Dark in the afternoon, yep, that fits with today's light forecast," said Sethline. "Some people schedule their day by the forecast but most of us run on Realm Standard time."

"How are people coping? It's not like the races of the survey team have evolved with unpredictable light and dark."

"True, true. Random intervals of light and dark create a situation we've never had to cope with before," Doctor Sethline agreed as he snipped out a patch of nearskin and sealed it onto Ardra's heel. "Except for the Wanderites, all the Great Dispersal races developed on worlds that orbit a single sun. Even during the second colonization after space tuck, we've only settled on globes with one principal star. Naturally, we're all accustomed to predictable and regular intervals of light."

"Who would think the sun could have such a powerful effect on us?" said Ardra through teeth gritted against the searing chill of the treatment. "After all, most of us are used to living and working by the clock."

"It should be so simple!" Sethline laughed. "Actually, a direct neural pathway runs between the retina and the biological clock, located in the hypothalamus. Bright light inhibits the secretion of melatonin, a hormone normally secreted at night, and long periods of darkness can trigger depression and withdrawal in certain individuals. When that happens we try to counteract it with light therapy, which isn't always practical. Then there's something called wide-eye from too much light. It's a common problem for immigrants to Kelpa. You're done now." Sethline stepped back, cocked his head, and admired the even transition from real skin to nearskin. He ordered the recliner back down and Ardra reached for her boot.

"You should give it ten minutes or so before you do any extended walking," Sethline said.

"I'm just headed to the barracks."

"Hmm, I could offer you a refreshment in my office. I don't want to find myself replacing that patch after your next shift."

"We're in harmony on that," said Ardra. She swung her legs off the recliner then stood on her good foot. Gingerly she tried the sore one; there was a numbness to it but no pain, so she pulled her sock and boot back on.

"Would too much or too little of this hormone you mentioned make a person violent?" she asked as she followed Sethline through a side door that opened into an office dominated by a pristine workdesk. To one side stood a small counter covered with family holoportraits, evenly arranged.

"Sleepiness and withdrawal from others is a more likely reaction than violence."

"There isn't a yes or no answer to my question?"

"Anything's possible, isn't it?" The doctor shrugged and flopped into the chair behind the desk. He waved Ardra into one of the two chairs across from him.

"Could this erratic light and dark situation be the reason the Great Dispersal race here on Wanderer deteriorated so badly? After all, they arrived with space age technology and now they carry spears."

"Well, there's a lot of regression in all our histories, and each race reclaimed civilization at its own pace. It's hard to say if the light cycles are the problem here on Wanderer. It might explain why the Wanderites retreat underground for periods of time. At least that's where we think they go when they vanish. Perhaps it's an attempt to allow their biological clocks to rediscover their own rhythms. Still . . . hmm . . . I don't think it can explain the way they've regressed. You'd learn more about reasons for their regression by talking to Anthropologist Udell in the surveying team."

They were interrupted by a low squealing sound as a squat, flat-sided hostbot entered the room.

"Do you believe this?" Sethline muttered. "Top of the line sealed robot and it spits sand regularly. I'm going to have to restrict it to the building, I guess. Every time it makes a trip to Provisions, it comes back dragging a wheel. No sooner do I get it fixed but it starts dragging on a different corner. Of course the units with antigravity instead of wheels cost a galaxy and a half so that's out of the question on my earnings here. I'm sure looking forward to getting back to civilization once my colony tour is over."

"You're due back soon?"

"Well . . ." Sethline's olive mottlings paled in an Olidan blush. "Actually, this is my first posting and I've barely begun."

These last three words echoed for a moment in Ardra's ears and she did a quick calculation of the duty time she'd already worked on Chelidon and the time remaining in her two year obligation. Idly, she wondered if the few weeks she spent on Eagle III while she awaited assignment would count against the total. Probably not, but even if it did, she had barely begun.

The hostbot finally screeched to a halt before Ardra and, taking advantage of the pause in the conversation, spoke. "How may I serve you, honored guest?"

"Spring water," Ardra ordered, wishing she could let herself have something more powerful—a booster or a silver screw could work wonders.

"One spring water," repeated the robot, then it swiveled and, left rear wheel dragging noisily, circumnavigated the desk until it faced the doctor.

"Iced gudday," commanded Sethline. He sighed as the hostbot made its noisy exit. "I couldn't believe my bad luck when I graduated and discovered Wanderer, a planet only in the process of its initial survey, would be my posting. Of course, the League of Colonization paid for my schooling and I knew I'd have to put in time somewhere other than an advanced planet. But I'd hoped to spend a few years at a major center before serving my time. Even then I'd hoped to draw a planet that was well into the colonization phase, not one this raw. It's so primitive and empty."

Ardra nodded slowly. "I know what you mean. I'm from Metro."

With its noise having evolved from squealing to scratching, the hostbot returned bearing beverages on its flip-down front tray. First it stopped before Ardra and she lifted a sturdy goblet from the tray. As the robot swiveled and headed for the doctor, Ardra caught a whiff of overheated circuitry in its wake. Still, it made its second delivery and exited without mishap.

Their eyes met over the smell and Sethline wrinkled his nose and shook his head. "Take my advice and never own a robot," he said. "Repairs are a constant drain on resources."

"Too late. I already do. And I know what you mean," said Ardra. She sipped from her goblet, realized she was dehydrated, and drank deeply.

"Retro's a strange posting," said Sethline. He covered a long yawn, then continued. "At first the town was maddeningly quiet. Its small group of workers selected, in part, on the basis of their good health, didn't need me for much of anything. The native Wanderites wouldn't come near my clinic. I was actually working regular hours and sleeping huge solid blocks every night. But now, everything's happening—falls, brawls, and homicides—all in a string. I haven't slept more than two hours in a row for weeks."

"When did the fights start? Was that before or after the first murder?" Ardra asked.

"Hmm, just before, I guess but I don't know if it's related if that's what you're getting at. Maybe it's the way things go in a new town. First everyone's polite and on their best behavior and later they settle in and frictions develop."

"It's a thought," Ardra mused. She gulped more of the spring water, hoping to drown a growl that was forming in her stomach. She took a moment to wonder if she'd missed a meal somewhere.

"Even worse," Sethline continued. "Now a few of the Wanderites have had a taste of the more exotic recreational drugs served up at Retro's tavern and they're mad for more. It's as if they have no concept of excess. They'll sell anything—heirlooms, information, or their souls if anyone would buy them—all to scrounge the price of another indulgence of rootsmoke or blast. It's ghastly. They're brought to me twitching and wheezing with overdose and showing reactions that I've never even heard of."

Ardra gestured to a twisted purple gourd on the floor near the counter of holoportraits. "A souvenir?" she asked.

"Yeah, I buy the odd trinket from them. I'd rather they had the credits for certified hits at the tavern than see them downed by street mix." Sethline rubbed his face and smothered another yawn.

"Who'd sell street here? There's only a few dozen professionals on planet and they wouldn't need the money."

"Someone must be dealing in it. I've seen the physical reactions in the sorry Wanderites brought in to me. It doesn't happen often, but it's there. That's all I can say."

Ardra made a mental note to query the bar manager about it. Sometimes barkeeps sold cheap grades of intoxicants on the side. "I understood that very few of the Wanderites ever came into Retro," she continued.

"Yeah, I guess that's true but these days they always seem to be in my clinic in the middle of the night and in the midst of a seizure. Then, when I pull them out of it, they act like my treatment has defiled them and they can't get out of my presence fast enough. One of my specialties is addiction mediation but the surveyors don't need it and the Wanderites avoid me. It's not terribly fulfilling. Hah, understatement! If I hadn't been under obligation to serve here on Wanderer I could be working with Doctor Archet, THE Doctor Archet, at Placidon's University Clinic."

"What a shame," Ardra murmured.

"That sounds selfish, I know," Sethline sighed. "Why can't I be like the surveyors? They want to be here, they volunteer for it."

"Was there anything unusual about the bodies of the murder victims that you didn't feel belonged in your forensic report?" Ardra asked. She didn't bother to mention that she wasn't a volunteer either.

"Nothing. Cara, the intrepid surveyor, was strangled and died quickly while Les, our sunlight forecaster, had his skull crushed and died as the result, sometime after he was struck and before he was found behind the tavern." Sethline paused and frowned. "Of course, there was . . . no, it's stupid."

"Anything, any impression you may have had could be useful," Ardra insisted. She placed her empty goblet on the workdesk and fought against the feeling that her body had been infected by the doctor's yawns.

"It's just that when I was called in to see Les on scene behind the tavern, one of the Wanderite townies—I don't remember who—was hanging about on the outskirts of the crowd and it seemed to me that he was telegraphing some kind of message with his eyes. That's crazy, though. This place must be getting to me." The doctor shifted in his chair and scratched the bridge of his nose.

"Was it Kafka?"

"Mmm . . . maybe. I was distracted. I mean my attention was on the deceased."

"Who was on the receiving end of the telegraph?"

"I don't know. I would have said he was mostly looking at Ivy Rosil, the town cop. But she wasn't paying any attention to him. I can't believe I even mentioned this."

On the other hand, Ardra was pleased that he had mentioned it and she thanked the doctor for the first aid to her foot and the drink, and walked evenly and painlessly out of the clinic.

"Wanderites," she mused silently. "Did a different Wanderite murder each victim or was it the same individual? And what were the motives? Is Rosil involved?"

Outside, the afternoon was still dark but now there was action in the street. A couple held hands and strolled through the orange pools of street light toward the cafeteria. Four single figures walked angles between other buildings.

Ardra stood for a moment and looked up and down Main Street. She wondered what excuse she could find to speak with Anthropologist Udell about the Wanderites. Then, overcome by a yawn, she decided it would be unseemly to solve the murders on her first day and she headed toward the barracks to catch a quick nap before her shift. As she passed the tavern its door opened to admit a coverall-clad figure and to exude the sounds and smells of boisterous recreation. Ardra yawned again, open and shut, in synch with the door iris.

Just beyond the tavern stood the barracks, a rectangle of conplast and slaptogether no bigger than necessary to house the first residents of Retro. Later colonists would construct their own dwellings, though from what Ardra had seen of the planet so far, she didn't expect there would be any rush of immigrants.

"Pathetic crate," she muttered as she entered the barracks and scuffed down its mud-brown central hallway to door number eight. She vocalized for the lock, "Room eight, admit Wythian," and the door slid back to reveal the shoebox she and Skrif would inhabit for the duration of their stay. It took the logic of a town planner to build offices out of all proportion to the first wave of surveyors, yet scrimp on barracks because they would be replaced by bungalows when the colonists arrived.

"Welcome home," said Skrif.

"Such as it is," Ardra replied. "I can practically touch all four walls just standing in the middle of the room."

Skrif measured the dimensions of the room with its scanning visor and compared the amount to the human's arm reach. A gross exaggeration, the robot concluded.

"It's no bigger than a premium berth on a Hyperspeed liner," Skrif acknowledged. "It's unusually small for a living space on a planet."

Ardra took half a step into the room. To her left there was a closet where she deposited her tunic and equipment belt. Next to the closet was the entry to a small bathroom. The remaining corners of the room were filled with a bunk, a tiny workdesk, a counter, and a storage cubby. Skrif sat on the counter, locked into a charge pad and surrounded by strips of black cloth.

"Is the alteration hopeless?" Ardra asked. She sat on the bunk then unclamped and kicked off her boots.

"Not at all," said Skrif. "I'm just dropping the cuffs for length, then I'll add false cuffs for show. No one will see the join when I'm done."

"Did you hear Sethline's take on what light does to humans? It sounds like the Wanderites might have been warped by this place, doesn't it? Imagine what must have happened to them over the generations living in such chaos." Ardra yawned and fell back on the bunk.

"Yet Sergeant Rosil seems certain the Wanderites are blameless," said Skrif.

"Why are you still charging?" Ardra asked. She let her eyelids fall closed.

"Unfortunately, this charge pad is a MultiLowfunction Unit, designed to charge simple devices, not robots. Perhaps an upgrade would be useful."

"Sure, why not? What else is there to spend credits on out here anyway?" Ardra sighed. Although the PKF paid a good percentage of Skrif's maintenance and repairs there were always extras. No doubt a special barracks charge pad would be considered extra.

"After you finish the uniform, you'll hibernate, right?" Ardra asked. "That'll help speed the process."

"How many functions should I hibernate?"

"Everything."

"If I go into deep suspension I'll be sufficiently charged by nightwatch."

"Good. I'll trigger you when I'm ready to go out the door. You haven't seen any lizards in the room, have you?"

"No lizards."

Ardra felt her body begin to drift. "Wythian room wake-up call," she ordered as she rolled over.

"Time, please," the room answered.

"Nineteen forty-five. Lights out."

The light in the room dimmed and blackened around a human already asleep. From its perch on the counter, Skrif continued to scan its work, unaffected by the loss of light so necessary to the Olidan. Held captive by the weak charge unit, Skrif had to delay its wish to unpack for Ardra, its wish to set out her anchoran in the hopes she would pick it up and play. She hadn't sounded a note since Chelidon.

"Ping . . . ping . . . ping. It is nineteen forty-five," the room called, its tone evenly modulated and hateful. Ardra cracked one eye and cleared her throat.

"Time verify," she croaked.

"Nineteen forty-five."

"Errrff. Lights up." The ceiling glimmered faintly and rose to a glow, filling the room with a mock daylight. "Wake-up reset to music," she said.

"Specify music."

"Bloohan throat songs, random selection."

"Wake-up reset to Bloohan throat songs, random."

"Wythian bathroom. Face cloth," Ardra ordered as she swung her feet down to the floor and stared over at the counter, the silent companionbot, and a crisp dress uniform.

"Acute," she whispered then jumped to her feet and shed the rest of the ill-fitting uniform she had slept in. Just as she finished her strip, the bathroom gave a chirp so she took two steps to the right and ducked into the narrow room. She seized the steaming cloth that slid out of the toiletry unit and buried her face in its warmth, cleansers and moisturizers; it was scented with the lightest hint of Celestian fern spice. At least someone had been clever enough to program the room for an Olidan.

In final preparation she filled her mouth with toothscrub and held it to the count of ten while it foamed and sizzled around her teeth and gums. Then she spat it into the liquids basin, wiped her mouth and examined her face in the mirror. There it was—narrow nose, angular cheekbones, alert green eyes. Her face looked wide awake and ready to pounce on every detail of her job. But her head felt like it was full of unfulfilled sleep bubbles and her eyes were dust dry.

Ardra dropped the face cloth into its tray and was back in the outer room before the wall had sucked the cloth in for reprocessing.

Her internal clock ticking, she dressed quickly in trousers and tunic, now perfect fits. She snapped on her boots, then stepped over to the closet where she verified the charge on her blaster and its spare power clips, and ran a self-test on her belt's Lifeline unit, which checked out the locator and communication functions. Then she transferred her audilink to the new, non-strangling tunic collar. It was a routine she didn't have to think about and she hardly registered the motions of her hands as they strapped on the belt.

Finally, Ardra returned to the counter and pressed the heel of her hand against Skrif's access panel. A dot of green light appeared in its visor and swung around the circumference, faster and faster until it formed a smooth line.

"Nightwatch time," Ardra announced. "Let's fogee."

As the pair departed barracks room number eight and traveled down the hall to the outside door Ardra thought about the pink granite pebbles and Kafka's fear.

"Those pebbles are important, I'm sure of it," she said aloud.

"On our trek back to Retro you suggested we should check the area where Forecaster Lesting was murdered," Skrif said. "The forensibots missed the symbols at the first murder site so they might have missed something of similar importance at the second site."

"Brilliant. Just what I was about to remember," said Ardra. "What say we start our nightwatch with a stroll around the tavern?"

When she stepped out into Main Street Ardra caught herself breathing a sigh of relief. It was dark. It would feel good to work a night shift in the dark.

"Wythian com, contact PKF station," she ordered.

"PKF Retro Main Station," snapped her belt. It was the supervising computer at the station, of course; even if Rosil were still on duty she wouldn't waste time answering standard log entries.

"Officer Ardra Wythian reporting for duty. Time check."

"Confirm Wythian on duty. Time check nineteen fifty-nine."

The PKF team of Olidan and robot didn't have far to go. They walked across the face of the barracks then turned up the alley between it and the tavern. Once they were past the influence of the street lamps, Ardra pulled a handtorch from her belt and activated it so she could see and avoid the clutter left by construction. Soon they turned the corner and were behind the building.

"What a mess," said Ardra. She flicked her light over drifts of scrap slaptogether and discarded packing crates. "The crime scene holo didn't take in all of this." Then Ardra circled downwind of the area where Forecaster Lesting had been killed and began to search the warm night breeze. She worked in a wide circle, bending low to peer under debris, to sniff.

"What's this?" she exclaimed. "A familiar smell, new but familiar." Once again she found smudged pebbles formed into the same three symbols and hidden in three locations.

"Incredible. The two murders are connected after all," said Ardra after she completed her olfactory search of the area. "It must be a Wanderite, maybe more than one. What was it Doctor Sethline said about them wanting to get away from him?"

"'Then, when I pull them out of it they act like my treatment has defiled them and they can't get out of my presence fast enough,'" Skrif repeated.

"Right, right, we must offend them somehow. We all ought to be back on our own planets."

"All the other races of the Realm celebrate Reunification," said Skrif. "Aren't all humans family, no matter the race?"

"Well, maybe it's not Wanderites in general but a particular Wanderite who is offended. That's what I meant."

"Shall I fetch equipment and secure the evidence?"

"Good idea. I'll stop in at the tavern and see if the barkeep has anything to say about street mix in town."

Ardra and Skrif parted company; the companionbot darted across Main Street to the PKF station and Ardra lingered in front of the tavern. Just as she was about to walk in its pulsating bull's-eye of a door, a shriek and a booming shout from down the street spun her around.

"You stinkin' thievin' worm!"

"Aieee, my hands are clean!"

Two figures, two men, tumbled out from the alley next to the cafeteria and the larger figure hurled the smaller down to the dust of the street then raised a foot to kick at the man who had fallen.

"Hey, PKF! Back off!" Ardra yelled as she sprinted toward them. From her belt she seized a small intervener globe and threw it ahead of her. The globe initiated its antigravity and its jet, and homed in on the heat signatures in its path.

The taller man, startled, raised his face at Ardra's shout and the street lamp nearby glared on his thick features and leathery skin. He wore surveying coveralls, crumpled, with one chest pocket torn and dangling, and his kick went astray at the interruption. The man on the ground lay huddled with his arms clutched over his head; he looked more like a heap of rumpled laundry than a human.

In her skim of survey team names, Ardra had paid particular attention to those most closely associated with the two murder victims. In fact, she had studied their images as well, looking deep into their faces, their eyes, trying to spy the dark flaw. Thus, she was quick to recognize the man glowering under the light. It was Survey Tech Cliff Sennett, a Lavarite with a Lavarite's typical deep voice and thick lemon-yellow skin, which formed folds at jaw and chin. He had worked with Cara Stine. He and Blaze Myro were the two most obvious suspects in her death.

The intervener globe arrived first and beeped a warning to the combatants and a readiness to the PKF officer following in its wake. The Lavarite frowned at the intervener and held himself in check; no sensible citizen of the Green Realm wanted to experience the noxious fog such a globe would exude on command.

"What's the problem here?" Ardra demanded when she finally skidded to a halt near the men.

"Arrest this wallet-snatchin' pebble brain!" Sennett pointed a vibrating finger at the motionless lump of clothing on the ground.

"Calm down and tell me what happened."

The fallen man raised his head. "I am driven snow," he said.

"I'll drive you . . ." Sennett lunged forward to grab at him again, but Ardra stepped between them.

"That's enough! You, Sennett, go stand next to the cafeteria door and wait for me. Don't move from there. And you . . ." Ardra stooped to pull the other fellow to his feet. "What's your name?"

Now that the man was standing under the light Ardra could make out his features. He was short and wiry, with a button nose and a cleft chin; his clothing consisted of a hooded sweatshirt many sizes too large and worn inside out, and a pair of expedition trousers, which were rolled up at the cuffs but still dragged mournfully in the dust around his bare feet. Ardra grimaced at the reek of him, a week of unwashed sweat and the rotted cabbage smell of one addicted to booster. As she registered the fact that this man was another Wanderite, Ardra wondered if he would be as obtuse in his answers as Kafka had been.

"I am called Vincent," he replied.

"What happened here, Vincent?"

"The other raged," he nodded toward Sennett.

"What did you do?"

"I fell."

"Did you take his wallet?"

"I am a lamb."

"Why did you run from him then?"

"Evil shadows poured from his eyes."

"Evil shadows? You don't say. OK, why don't you stand right here under the lamp while I go talk to Sennett? Don't move." Ardra parked Vincent against the post and plucked the intervener globe out of the air. "Wythian intervener off," she ordered as she snapped it back onto her equipment belt. Then she walked over to Sennett.

"What's your story?" she asked.

"He picked my wallet," Sennett growled. "I was just goin' into the caff when he lurched out of the corner there and bumped into me and took off. Knew he was up to no good so I ran him down."

"And your wallet?"

"He must'a dumped it while I was chasin' him. I'll press charges, so go ahead and arrest him."

"My fingers do not stick!" Vincent called out from his posting under the lamp.

"They ought'a be broken, both hands," Sennett bellowed back.

"Are you sure you had your wallet with you?" Ardra asked. "It could be hard to press any charges if we find your wallet was back in the barracks all along."

"Of course I'm sure. Wouldn't be any use goin' to the caff without my ID creditab to do the payin'. Now, are you goin' to arrest him or am I goin' to break his face?"

"I'll tell you exactly what's going to happen: first, I'll put Vincent under restraints, second we'll search the areas you chased him to see if we can locate your wallet, and third you are going to button up those threats or I'll put you in restraints too. You're not going to break any part of this man or I'll have you up on charges faster than you can blink. Understood?"

"Hmpf."

"Understood?" Ardra stepped closer to Sennett, looked down into his grey eyes, and raised her voice. One of the advantages of her Olidan blood was her ability to stand taller than most of the other races.

"Mmm, all right. It's just that he got me seein' red. Hey, I'm a Lavarite and we don't beat on people. It's not in our nature. I was just lettin' off steam through my voice box."

"Good." Ardra walked over to Vincent who was already holding out his hands for the cling bands. As she slipped the bands onto Vincent's wrists Ardra considered that Sennett was correct in saying that Lavarites didn't have a reputation for violence. However, they also had no reputation for temper. Despite all that, Sennett had been shouting and striking at the Wanderite when Ardra interrupted them. "So much for generalizations," she thought.

"Let's all take a stroll," she said aloud and they set off around the outside of the cafeteria; Sennett drew a torch from a pocket and stomped along in the lead, Vincent drooped in the middle, and Ardra cast about at the rear with her own torch. As they passed the first corner she caught a whiff of orange blossom from the shadows. Strange place for flowers, she mused.

They found the wallet tumbled up against the back wall of the building. Using her finger-sized evidence reader Ardra made a quick scan of Vincent's hands and the surface of the wallet where the instrument found his prints.

"You're a lamb? Hah!" Sennett muttered. "What're your little lamb fingerprints doing on my wallet then?"

Vincent, now mute, hung his head.

Ardra coded and registered the prints then handed the wallet to Sennett. "Anything missing?" she asked. They moved back out under the street lamp and the surveyor pocketed his torch and flipped through his wallet, which held half a dozen flat portraits, his ID tab, and a novel chirp.

"Mmm, nope, it's all here."

"Well, now that you have your wallet back there's no harm done to you. Perhaps if you don't pursue the theft charges, Vincent won't feel obliged to file assault charges."

"No deal!" Sennett boomed.

Ardra sighed and turned to Vincent. "How about an apology? Would you apologize to Survey Tech Sennett?"

"My tongue doesn't fork," Vincent muttered. His head hung down and one toe traced an ellipse in the dust, over and over. Ardra watched for him to mark a dot in its center but he never did.

So Ardra shepherded her charges up the street to the PKF station for processing. She decided it was going to be a long shift and was soon to discover length was the least of her problems.

CHAPTER 5

Temperamental

"What are you doing here?" Rosil's voice demanded the instant Ardra and her charges walked through the door to the PKF booking chamber. Ardra peered over Vincent's head and saw her superior seated at the registration counter, leaning back in its chair with her feet propped up next to the data terminal. The soles of her boots showed little wear and tear.

"Just a snatch and run," Ardra replied as she steered Vincent over to the counter. She felt a frown pull at the edges of her mouth as she wondered what the sergeant was doing here this late in the evening and in this room. How could Rosil look like such a slacker yet put in such long hours?

"Vincent, Vincent, Vincent," Rosil said as she swung her feet down to the floor and leaned forward. "I thought we'd had a good little talk about this business of keeping your hands off things that don't belong to you. You're a member of our clan now and you can't take things you want from other members. Those are our rules, remember?"

"What's mine is yours, what's yours is mine," Vincent replied.

"I know you're used to taking what you need but you can't do that here. It's not our way. You understand, yes?"

"Yes. I'm sorry. I will not take again."

"Good. Now apologize to Tech Sennett."

Vincent turned toward Sennett and lifted his face. He squinted, tilted his head to one side and said, "My heart weeps."

"Mmm, well . . . I suppose it's all right, no harm done." The surveyor stuffed his hands into his pockets and shrugged.

In stunned silence, Ardra stared from the Wanderite to the Lavarite. She reminded herself that Vincent had refused to apologize to Sennett out in the street. In return, Sennett had been adamant he would press charges. Had something come over them on the walk to the station? Had the bright lights in the building acted to bring them to their senses?

Rosil got to her feet and leaned out over the counter as she peered into Vincent's face; one of his eyes was beginning to puff up. Looking from Vincent's eye to Sennett and back again, Rosil cleared her throat. "You don't really want to press charges here do you Cliff?"

"I guess not."

Struck wordless, Ardra slipped the cling bands from Vincent's wrists. She then watched, amazed, as the two strolled back out the door together. Sennett clapped a hand on Vincent's shoulder and offered to buy a round at the tavern.

"Incredible," she remarked after they had left.

"Indeed," Rosil replied as she settled back into the booking chair. "That's the sort of incident you should be able to handle in the field. Really, I oughtn't to be clearing up such small matters for you."

Ardra cleared her throat then busied herself with resetting the cling bands and putting them back into the appropriate slot on her equipment belt. Forward and backward she reviewed the incident, but she couldn't see what Rosil had said to the men that she hadn't already put into words next to the cafeteria.

"I learn quickly," she finally said. "It won't happen again."

"I hope not," Rosil sighed deeply and leaned back to swing her feet up onto the counter again.

Ardra turned to leave then stopped and faced Rosil.

"Has Skrif brought in the new evidence from the murder site yet?" she asked.

"What? What are you talking about?"

"We took a look behind the tavern and found the same three symbols formed with pink granite pebbles where Forecaster Lesting was killed. I guess there's an outside chance we have a serial killer on our hands."

"The same type of pebbles?" Rosil dropped her feet to the floor with a thump.

"I don't suppose Vincent is anything more than a petty thief," Ardra mused aloud. "He wasn't able to put up much of a fight against Sennett. But maybe the Wanderites in town are here because they're weaklings among their own kind. Maybe the killer is . . ."

"It's not a Wanderite," Rosil insisted.

"I met another fellow called Kafka," Ardra continued. "He's small but he flows like a shadow. With the element of surprise he might have caught each victim unaware."

"Kafka?" Rosil erupted into a laughter that rose and fell like a siren.

"I'm just speculating . . . brainstorming . . ." Ardra muttered.

Rosil gasped for breath and wiped a drop of liquid from one eye. "That's so funny," she said. "That's like saying the Bloohan chess champion might challenge the Kelpan hand wrestling champion to a finger tussle." Rosil indulged in a few more snorts of mirth.

"I should get back to my rounds," Ardra said.

"Have you shown the collar in the tavern yet?"

"No, I was just headed that way when I encountered Sennett and Vincent scuffling. It was . . ."

"Well, get on with it!"

Ardra's spine stiffened into a steel rod, a rod that should be rammed up . . .

"Yes, sergeant," she said, then spun and stalked out the door.

"Skrif?" Once outside the station, Ardra hailed her companionbot via audilink.

"I'm in the evidence room," Skrif responded. "Shall I join you in the tavern?"

"No, I think we should split up and patrol more area. That scuffle by the cafeteria might be only the beginning. When you're done in the station, start your round at the port and its warehouse. Once I'm finished in the tavern I'll work my way along the west side of Main Street. You work the east side and we'll swap over and alternate."

"It sounded like Survey Tech Sennett has a temper."

"He does. I wonder if Forecaster Lesting said or did something to set him off. That beating Lesting took was all about fury."

"And Tech Sennett was one of Surveyor Stine's camp mates. Perhaps she triggered his anger and he killed her."

"The problem is, Sennett's record is spotless. Someone with a violent temper turned murderous should have tallied at least one assault on his PKF record."

"There are many pieces to the murders and none of them like to fit together. Perhaps it's too early in the investigation to draw inferences."

"Rosil certainly seems to think so. She acts as if she's expecting the culprit to stroll in and confess."

While Ardra marched across the street to the pub, she tried to shake the notion the sergeant had set her up to look bad. Did Rosil have an agenda? The sergeant naturally knew everyone in the town; she had been living closely with them for several months. Just suppose she arranged the whole incident with Sennett and Vincent to make her look good and Ardra look bad. Maybe it was her idea of a practical joke. Ardra had paid her dues as a rookie back on Metro. She had endured the pranks and chuckles and shaking heads, not to mention being yelled at on principle, even when she had done nothing wrong. Was it starting all over again?

"No," she thought. "There's the way of paranoia. I'm not going there."

Finally, Ardra presented herself to the orange bull's-eye of the tavern door; it swept open with a musical flourish and exuded tantalizing whiffs of indulgence. Despite the building's rectangular exterior, the room she entered was round. The central floor was sunken and vast, crowded with tables and chairs, which, this early in the settlement, stood mostly vacant. In the exact middle of the room, two overall-clad technicians tinkered with the mechanisms of a platform.

A segmented bar ran around the circumference of the room. Plush stools ringed the bar on the outside so their occupants had their backs to the wall and faced the platform. Ardra noted Vincent and Sennett on two of these stools; Vincent sat tilted sideways and clung to the bar with both hands.

A hostbot whisked up to Ardra. "How may I serve you, honored guest?" it asked.

"PKF Officer Ardra Wythian, on duty," she replied. "Bug off."

"Certainly, Officer." The hostbot hurried back to its charge station, a pedestal that overlooked the room; its visor line glowed red and green as it scanned the tankards and pipes on the bar and tables, ever watchful for any need of a refill.

There were five people scattered among the tables and one, which Ardra identified by behavior as the manager, who stood at the inner side of the bar. That made a total of ten on the premises, unless there were others tending to biological needs in the pit rooms. The space, huge in anticipation of later settlers, swallowed them up.

Ardra walked over to the man standing on the inner ring of the bar and introduced herself.

"Pubkeeper Trudge," he responded and grinned at the introduction, showing a line of gleaming silver teeth. His scent cluster carried undertones of metal and lubricant.

By his name alone, Ardra realized she was facing a digger, a freelance prospector. Diggers were a special breed; they were individuals with a need to live on the edge. They would work their way onto a planet (sometimes legally, often not) as soon as possible after it was opened. Once there, they scattered into the wilderness to find the mother lode, that elusive strike to make them obscenely wealthy. It did happen, but rarely. The big mining cooperatives seized the most promising regions of new planets and competition among the diggers for the leftovers was intense and occasionally violent. They were solitary types and always among the first to be exposed to the new beasts and diseases of a colony planet. Life expectancy was low.

"You're the new collar in town? No problem, I run a clean joint. Do," Trudge said.

"Nice place," Ardra nodded, looking around again. Overhead, huge filter units sucked rising smoke out of the room and sent the cleaned air through pipes to vent at floor level. No wise bar manager wanted customers getting high on anything they hadn't paid for. "When will your holostage be ready?" she asked and waved one hand toward the platform in the center of the room. "Wish I knew. The techs are hopeless and it's bad for business. Is." Trudge shifted on his feet and Ardra heard the sigh of prosthetic hydraulics; she wondered how much of the man was real—his teeth had been replaced, his lower jaw had the smooth look of a reconstruction job, and both his legs hissed when he moved.

"Are you doing double duty here, Trudge?" Ardra asked. "Bar keeping and prospecting?"

"My digger days are over," said Trudge. "I'm retired now and hardly even speak the language anymore. My machine bits are reliable enough for town living but can't be counted on when things get rough. They're not up to the life or death days of real living."

"That's a shame."

"Is."

Trudge went on to explain why he retired. It had happened on the planet officially named Cauldron and called Jahan Junior by the diggers because of its stinking rivers of lava and expanses of barren plain that turned out to be brittle crust over hidden lava lakes. The place was a mini version of Planet Jahan, but without that world's regions of fertility.

"A beautiful place, Jahan Junior," Trudge said with a wistful sigh. Trudge was a Jahanite by birth and early rearing and, like others of his race, loved the rigor of home planet with an intensity that shocked races from gentler globes. To the non-native, Jahan was a horror of noxious gases that leaked from steaming cracks and ground that melted or exploded unpredictably.

But no natural disaster had ended Trudge's search for precious gems and metals, it was a claim feud. He and a woman known as Slither had happened on opposite ends of a short vein of double diamond crystals at the same time and neither was prepared to yield the find or share it. Negotiations between the two took the form of sabotaging the other's mining equipment. Trudge's grin spread wide as he recounted the time he rigged Slither's crack

impacter so that it beat itself to pieces when she went to use it; the
smoke it gave off in the process sent her to her bedroll for the best
part of a day.

At the time, Trudge had a few grains of ignite, a tremendously
powerful explosive—illegal, of course. One day during the dispute,
when Trudge set his pack on the ground it blew. Maybe it was an
accident, maybe it was sabotage. Slither won, Trudge lost, and
that's the way life was. The digger was philosophical about it and
even spared a bit of admiration for his rival. In his opinion, anyone
who would risk rigging ignite for accidental detonation deserved
the win. Besides, Slither had found him, carried his bleeding body
to a solid area and set up a beacon for emergency medical evacuation.
This was an act few diggers would have performed.

After the accident, the miracles of medicine had saved Trudge's
life by replacing or rebuilding most of his body. Now he was barkeep
on the newest planet of the Realm and here he would stay until
the true colonists moved in or a newer, wilder planet was found. It
was life as close to the edge as he could get.

"I suppose, since he was killed out back, Forecaster Lesting
used to be a regular customer here. Was he?" Ardra asked when the
digger's tale concluded. She and Trudge continued to regard the
reputedly hopeless technicians at their work on the holostage.

"Les was a customer, sure, but he spent most of his time holding
down a chair and watching the steam over his tankard as it cooled.
Nothing pleased him. He had a bad mouth and he put people
off."

"Bad for business?"

"Not good."

"Who did he drink with? Did he have any buddies?"

"Drank with Cara for a bit. Then he put her off. That must've
taken a lot. She knew how to get along with anyone, I'd say. She
was a sunbeam, always cheerful, always looking for the best in
everyone, and seeing it, too. Anyway, after Cara and Les split he
was always by himself, a vile shearfunnel sitting with his back to
the wall furthest from the entrance and nursing one lousy drink
for hours. Hours."

"How about feuds?"

"Nobody liked him—after Cara, I mean. He rode his workers at the forecasters office, rode 'em hard, especially that little guy, Tech Murl Daly. Saw Les screaming in Murl's face one evening when the poor bugger was trying to unwind with a pipe. Les just marched up to him and cut loose for no reason. He used to badmouth my hostbot too. Now that's pretty stupid because it's programmed to ignore anything that isn't an order that's part of its normal duties. Some waste of breath, that. Might as well swear at a stone."

"Did you get along with him?"

Trudge's teeth glinted at the question as his lips peeled back to form a sneer. "He had an attitude about people who didn't have the right job titles. Digger and slime were like the same word to him and he told me so right in my face. And he couldn't stand the townies so bad he was always blaming everything on them. He tried to organize a lynch mob after Cara was killed out in the wastelands, figuring the only good Wanderite was a dead one. Put them out of their crazy misery, he'd say. It was him that was always stirring up talk of the locals being who'd murdered her."

"Do you think he could have been right about the murderer?"

"Don't think he was ever right about anything. Don't."

Ardra fell silent for a few moments and assessed the information she had accumulated. Two victims more unlike would be hard to find in any typical serial murder case. Cara Stine was a friend to everyone and liked by all, while Les Lesting was a person who made enemies as quickly as he alienated friends. Still, if a Wanderite such as Kafka had killed Surveyor Stine at the encampment, then Lesting's reaction and finger pointing was a workable motive for his death. But why kill Stine in the first place?

"Trudge, have you heard of any areas sacred to the Wanderites that the surveyors might have violated?" she asked.

The retired digger sucked air in through his teeth and clicked his tongue before answering the question. "Couldn't say for sure. They have lots of superstitions about sunlight and shadows but it seems that their way about things is to share most of what they've got or just to help themselves and expect others to do the same. The only place that's special to them is a loony pillar on a hill that's way off from Retro. Need a hoverjet to get there. It's just a column of stacked rocks going up and up, not part of a building or whatever. The locals won't go anywhere near it and don't even like to talk about it. They say it built itself at the beginning of time and when it finishes toppling rock by rock to the ground then time will end. There's a pretty story, huh?"

"It should be so simple to explain time and the universe."

"Should."

A thump interrupted the conversation and they turned to see that Vincent had listed a fraction too far and fallen from his bar stool. Sennett, sitting on the next stool, ignored his fallen companion and even seemed to be masking a satisfied smile in the leathery folds of his face. When Ardra looked directly at him, he said, "There's more than one way to put'm on the ground. Still . . ." Sennett glanced down at the heap of trembling clothing on the floor, then sighed, rose to his feet and leaned down to scoop up Vincent by the scruff of his shirt and the belt of his trousers. " . . . like they say, one sour note spoils the chorus, and I'm not lookin' to be Retro's sour note."

"In the back," Trudge grunted, jerking his head in the direction of a door on the other side of the room. As Sennett dragged his charge around the bar toward the door Trudge explained to Ardra, "I let the townies sleep it off in a storage room. There's nothing but extra chairs and serving supplies in it and they've got nowhere of their own to go. Except for Kafka, that is." Trudge looked sideways at Ardra.

"Where does he go?" she asked.

"Around . . ." Trudge grinned. "Must say, it's a pity only men have drifted into town so far. I'd be some interested to see what their women are like. Some interested."

"Did Cara Stine get along with the townies?" Ardra asked. "The Wanderites, I mean."

"She practically adopted them. If they were having the shakes she'd buy them a round of smoke to take the edge off and if they'd oversucked she'd personally carry them over to the Doc. Always talked to them like they made sense, too. At first I thought their craziness was a reaction to the rootsmoke or that we just collected the mad ones here in town, but from what I've heard from Elya—that's Anthropologist Udell—it's normal for the Wanderites to have a conversation with a stool or to swat at bugs that nobody else can see."

"They all act that way? Amazing," said Ardra.

"Yep," said Trudge. "It's hard to believe that we all descended from the same ancestor. I guess it's easy to understand you sniffers developing a keen sense of smell on Olid, needing it in the first few millennia to pick up early warnings of empress lizard packs and it's easy to understand leathers developing a tough yellow hide on Lavar so's they'd survive the needle storms. But what's about this place that would make people go crazy to survive? That I don't figure. Don't."

"The erratic comings and goings of the suns, maybe."

"That's no problem. You're new here so you feel it some but it don't bother me in the least. I enjoy it, never knowing what'll be there for light when I step outside. This's what new planets are all about."

"I hope I will get used to it," Ardra said. Wanderer is very different from my last posting, a planet called Chelidon. We had to evacuate when its atmosphere turned unstable."

"Chelidon? I heard tell that globe's dripping with blood reds. Dripping."

"Still interested in gems?" Ardra asked. "I thought you'd retired from prospecting."

"Hmm . . ." Trudge chuckled and leaned lazily against the bar. "I'm retired, of course, but that don't stop me keeping my ears cocked. Folks get real relaxed and talkative in taverns. But I figure you know that."

"I've worked a few taverns and giggle bars in my beats." Ardra grinned. "By the way, what have you heard regarding street mix here on Wanderer?"

"Street? There's none of that here yet. Who'd be selling street with so few people landed? I run a clean joint. Do." Trudge's legs hissed as he pulled himself erect. His face struggled to look innocent, offended, and shocked, all at the same time.

"Well, Dr. Sethline told me he'd had Wanderites in his clinic showing reactions typical of street mix."

"Young Clais? Ahh . . ." The bar manager relaxed and leaned back against the bar with a snort. "That young pup don't know his lips from his hips. Don't. He's the last person to go recognizing a body writhing under bad street."

"Hmm . . ." Ardra reserved judgment. It did seem unlikely that anyone would smuggle and sell the cheap forms of popular drugs on such a new planet. Still, the place had more people than the few dozen surveyors and an opportunist might hope the Wanderites were numerous and possessed of significant wealth. Tavern managers were notorious for dealing on the side.

"After her split with Lesting, was Stine seeing anyone else?" Ardra asked.

"Hard to say. Plenty tried." Trudge clicked his silver teeth together then grinned again. With a wink, he added, "Might have been something quiet . . . someone bonded." The digger chuckled then fell solemn and looked at her sideways, as though he was checking on her gullibility.

"Looks like you're quiet here," Ardra said. "I suppose I'll take a cruise around the town. Maybe I'll stop in later."

Trudge nodded and flashed his silver teeth again; then he moved along the bar until he reached Sennett, now returned from carrying Vincent to the storeroom. Ardra noted that the two technicians and two of the customers had left so only three people occupied tables now. On the far side of the room someone slumped, head flat on the tabletop, arms dangling toward the floor. Closer to the holostage, two people sat erect. The man was visible only from behind and Ardra couldn't recognize him from this angle but the woman's face was fully in view.

"Coordinator . . . Hesty," Ardra reminded herself silently. Hesty was a Lavarite, like Sennett, but much older than the surveyor; her skin folds were twice as deep. She had dropped in on Ardra and Kip Myro during orientation, introduced herself, and stressed the urgency of solving the murders. Planet Coordinator was a polite title for Local Boss.

A yawn sneaked up on Ardra and jolted her to motion. With a nod to Trudge and Sennett she walked through the break in the bar circle and stepped out the door. She stood for a moment with the light from the bull's-eye running up and down her uniform and she wondered about the digger, Trudge.

Perhaps he was retired from prospecting officially but not in fact. He might have come to Wanderer in the capacity of bar manager as a means to gain access to its resources before the mining companies and prospectors were allowed to land. He would have a jump on everyone. Maybe he had done some illegal digging and Cara Stine had spotted him. If she had threatened to tell, he would have a motive for killing her. From his contact with the local Wanderites, he might have learned that they used the pink stones. Perhaps he had collected a few to make the strange symbols and throw suspicion elsewhere.

"It's a theory," Ardra thought. "But . . ." But threats probably weren't in character for the all-friendly Stine. And why would Trudge want to kill Lesting? Maybe he worried that Stine had told Lesting about his prospecting or perhaps the pubkeeper had no patience for being called slime by the forecaster.

Ardra suppressed another yawn and realized that walking a straight path would do nothing to keep her awake. She decided to loop figure eights around the buildings as she worked her way down the west side of the street.

"Skrif, do you have anything to report?" she asked when she reached the alley between the administration building and the clinic.

"Nothing. There's no human activity on the port apron or in the warehouse."

"The tavern's emptying out, too. It could be a quiet night."

"How fortunate," said Skrif.

The companionbot finished its internal patrol of the warehouse and exited a small door near the southeast corner. Apart from an assortment of small reptiles and darkmoths, nothing had stirred

the air of the building. The door's lock chunked behind the robot
and reset. It would open only to certified codes of robots or voice
commands of authorized humans.

A movement on the flat ground behind the warehouse caught
Skrif's attention. In less than a second, the robot identified the
source as a cluster of short-legged snakes that moved as one over
the sand, from due south to due north. "Nothing significant," the
bot concluded and it headed for the next building on Main Street.
There were seven hours and thirty-two minutes left in the
nightwatch.

Normally, Skrif looked forward to games of chess with robots
of similar intelligence at the end of work. While humans slept,
companionbots were quick to link together on dormant com
channels and vie for wins. So far Skrif was the only companionbot
on planet but there were two hostbots in Retro and hostbots could
be a challenge as long as they limited the number of concurrent
games they played. If they were inexperienced with the game, Skrif
might spot them a pawn.

Unfortunately, the charge pad in barracks room number eight
was inadequate and Skrif would have to sacrifice its chess time
until the pad was upgraded. However, the robot was determined
to delay its next charge session long enough to unpack the rest of
Officer Wythian's belongings. It was time.

CHAPTER 6

Interlude

"One thousand," said Ardra as she finished her walk around the spaceport landing circle and headed back down Main Street. It wasn't really her thousandth trip down the street. Then again, it might be. She felt like she'd scuffed along the street at least that many times.

Although she hadn't counted the trips, Ardra had counted her strides and she now knew exactly how many paces there were between the space pad at the north end and the science building at the south end of the dusty road. Like her father always said, it never hurt a cop to embed every corner and nook of a beat in her subconscious. There could come a time when such familiarity would give her a reaction advantage. Her father had worked some of the toughest beats in Coeur, the capitol of Planet Metro, and always bragged on coming home "without a scratch" every shift end. He never mentioned that he didn't count bruises.

As the town timepiece on the administration building advanced toward morning, Wanderer's second sun rose to sit low on the west horizon while the first sun, which had claimed the sky hours ago, crept toward the hills in the east. Numb with boredom and fatigue, Ardra glared at her ghostly twin shadows and walked.

Apart from her encounter with Vincent and Tech Sennett, there had been few highlights during the nightwatch. Trudge had waved goodnight to her after he closed the tavern. Ardra had broken all records for vertical distance jumped into the air when she rounded a corner of the hangar during the dark hours and an unidentified creature bolted out of the shadows. Fortunately, there were no human witnesses to her alarm and she didn't fire her weapon, drawn in reflex.

"That skittering beast was more terrified than you were," she'd assured herself as she reswallowed her heart. She tried to block the sight of the monstrosity from her mind. Had it scampered on extra legs? Had it waved claws in the air? One aspect she wasn't able to block from her memory was the reek of sour onion mixed with cesspool that it left in its wake.

At four in the morning, a contraption had emerged from the hangar and hummed up and down Main Street. It was rectangular, wide, and low to the ground; narrow fingers of metal stretched out of its belly to comb and rake every wisp of trash from the sand. Ardra had stood in the lee of the administration building and watched. "Here's yet another highlight of the shift," she thought.

It was then she released Skrif from the beat.

"Everyone's tucked in," she had said. "Nothing's happening. Why don't you finish the unpacking in the barracks room and set up a workdesk for me at the station. You can monitor me while you're at it."

So Skrif had bustled off, leaving Ardra with even less company on the walkways of the town. Now, on her thousandth trip down the street, people began to emerge from the barracks and thus break her solitude. Singly and in pairs they wandered out onto the street, stretched, tucked in shirt tails or hitched coveralls, yawned, and checked the sky for signs of weather.

Then the smell of real food drifted out of the cafeteria and Ardra followed the trickle of early risers in for a meal. The Nutritube supplement she had choked down at intervals during her shift demanded reinforcements.

In contrast to the subdued grey of its exterior, the interior of the cafeteria gleamed with chrome fixtures, mirrored tables, and tusk-white walls. There were eleven people in the large room, almost invisible in a space that could accommodate two hundred at one sitting. Ardra marched up to the meal dispenser, slipped it her identitab and ordered a regular fastbreaker. While the room-sized chefbox behind the dispenser hummed and glopped, Ardra looked around for familiar faces.

"Rosil isn't here. Good. Neither is Sennett. Hmm," Ardra mused as she scanned. "Ah, there's Kafka all by himself and nursing a mug of hot gudday."

"Ping!" The dispenser chimed, snapped open its flat face, and pushed out a tray. The mingled odors of the food momentarily turned Ardra's knees weak.

"Will Kafka bolt if I try to join him?" Ardra wondered. "He might not and it's worth a try. He knows something." She picked up her tray and walked casually and obliquely in the Wanderite's direction.

Rather than run or even flinch, Kafka turned worshipping grey eyes up at the Olidan when she came to his table. "Avenger!" he said.

"Kafka, I'm Offic . . ." Ardra curbed the urge to re-introduce herself. The man knew her name. If he chose to call her Avenger, she would answer. She wanted him to feel at ease. "I'm hungry this morning," she said and sat across from him. "Are you hungry?"

"The wall does not dance for the star children," said Kafka, eyes wide and sad above his button nose.

"Wall? What wall?"

"The Avenger is brave. The Avenger is here and brave."

"How about you, Kafka? Are you feeling brave today? Can you tell me what you saw when Cara Stine or Les Lesting were murdered?"

Kafka hid his face with the mug. His throat twitched as he swallowed and swallowed. Ardra shrugged and began her meal. Bites of legume loaf fell into warm, tangy crumbles on her tongue, and mouthfuls of grilled bokstem melted in creamy sweetness around her teeth. She saved the scrambled ayduck eggs for last. They were their usual peppery, buttery ecstasy. The taste was even better than the smell.

From her experience on Chelidon, Ardra knew food like this was the early feast after the visit of a supply ship, the supply ship she had ridden to planetfall. As time passed before the next ship, food selection would narrow and fresh choices would vanish. Crops wouldn't be raised on Wanderer anytime soon and no one knew yet if the agri-strains of the Realm could cope with the erratic light situation. Any long-term settlers on this world might have to resort to the hydroponics techniques perfected on Planet Kelpa.

Chelidon had been early in the agricultural process, too, during Ardra's stay, even though early colonists had moved in. Ardra remembered the first native Chelidon fruit cleared for human consumption. She remembered its crimson flesh, its creamy flavor, and its juice on her chin. When she first tried it her eyes had closed with pleasure and they'd opened again to see Haley's gentle smile.

"Tell me what you saw," Ardra demanded of the Wanderite across the mirrored table.

"I see nothing," Kafka replied. He stared sadly into his empty mug. Ardra swallowed the last of her food and examined the man. He seemed different today. How? Was he more lucid?

"Can you show me the dancing wall, Kafka? I'd like to see the wall." Maybe the surveyors had violated this wall in some way.

Kafka picked up his mug and inverted it over his left hand. Then, elbow planted on the table, he let the forearm and its mug hat sway to and fro and front and back. "Well found," he said, looking down at the mirror image of his hidden hand in the tabletop.

Nope, Ardra decided, he's not more lucid. She picked up her tray, wished Kafka a good day, and followed the lead of other diners who were carrying their own trays back to the dispenser.

"No hostbot here?" she asked a mutually besotted couple ahead of her.

"The caff hostbot's in traction. It had a crushing encounter with a crate loader when the caff was still in set-up."

"Brutal," Ardra thought. "The planet, the people, the conditions. It sure isn't Metro." Metro was another word for paradise in her opinion. Some people considered Planet Celestia to be paradise, but Ardra knew better; there were wild unknowns on Celestia.

At the door to the cafeteria, Ardra encountered Sergeant Rosil on her way in. The sergeant looked crisp in her dress blacks and she walked with the bounce of the well-rested.

"You can sign off now, Wythian," said Rosil. "I'm in control."

"Thanks." Ardra stepped aside so Rosil could pass through.

"I trust you're not planning any field trips today," Rosil tossed back over her shoulder. She didn't wait for a reply but sailed on toward the dispenser.

Strangling on a retort, Ardra whirled back to face the door. Already half-closed, the door was slow to react to her sudden approach so she disciplined it with a shadow kick and counted to ten in Olidan. "Me, da, ai, al, oh . . ." the words reminded her of an Olidan lullaby and she hummed a few notes in an attempt to calm her flare of temper.

"I wonder if Doctor Sethline celebrates the Festival of Eternity," she mused, as a swirl of homesickness eddied through her irritation.

Outside the cafeteria, the street glowed scarlet on one side, struck by light from the setting of the first sun. The air smelled of hot sand and, at that moment, Ardra realized Kafka had washed since they'd last met. That was the difference.

Ardra turned north on Main Street and allowed herself a satisfied burp. The food in her belly was already generating a radiant warmth that spread through her torso and into her limbs; gradually it chased away the remnants of her annoyance.

When Ardra reached the south corner of the administration building a Tithenite woman spurted out of its entrance, stopped, stood on tiptoes, and craned her neck to peer up and down the road. She spotted Ardra and darted toward her, the excess folds of her stylish showbiz wrap fluttered and flapped in the breeze of her motion. Three hovering globes followed her in tight formation.

"Acute," Ardra murmured. "The media have arrived." Then the woman's round face rose before her like a pink moon.

"You must be Officer Ardra Wythian," she said. "It's a pleasure to welcome you to Retro. I'm Lead Journalist Jal Sumner." Sumner reached out a hand and Ardra extended her own, which the journalist pumped vigorously as she examined the PKF officer with wide, pale crystal eyes. The pupils in those eyes were contracted to near invisibility in the harsh light, a necessary defense for Tithenite eyes, renowned for their excellent night vision.

The woman's scent aura assailed Ardra's nose with a wide range of odors that included spiced shampoo, floral skin cream, citron fabric softener, berry nail paint, a trace of swilk, and a delicate and subdued personal scent cluster. Ardra tried not to wrinkle her nose at the warring odors. She put on her best official smile, the one that said, "I'm all about cooperation with the media."

Handshake completed, the journalist turned her head and barked at the hovering globes, "Sumner imager, deploy for interview." One of the globes fragmented into a dozen smaller spheres, which scattered into positions encircling the two people. The other two balls deployed slightly right and left and, with a click and a hum, ignited into glaring suns.

"I'm just coming off shift," Ardra protested, convinced she must look even more tired than she felt, despite the revitalizing meal. "I'm afraid I don't have any new developments to report on the investigations." Her protest was weak, though. If this interview could make it onto an interstellar news bullet then her family would have view of her sooner, cheaper, and in higher quality than personal mail.

"Tut!" Sumner waved the objection aside. "I'm not looking for hard news right now, just a few words on your impressions.— Sumner imager, record!—This is Lead Journalist Sumner talking with PKF Officer Ardra Wythian. Officer Wythian arrived yesterday from Eagle III Space Station of Blooh and has now experienced almost one full day on Wanderer. What are your first impressions of this planet, Officer?"

Ardra swallowed hard and mentally kicked at the corners of her mind for the words to form a good reply that would be neutral for political reasons, but with a daring edge to make it broadcast-worthy.

"The chaotic patterns of light and dark here are incredible, as are the flora and fauna I've seen so far," she said and stifled a sigh. She would have to say something bolder than that to win a place in the crowded news feeds of Metro. Did she dare say the suns were weird and the wildlife was weirder? Not a chance.

Sumner bobbed her head encouragingly and spoke again, "Of course, there's more to this planet than its suns and our small survey outpost. Wanderer is home to a race of descendants from the Great Dispersal. Have you met any of the Wanderites yet, Officer?"

Ardra felt beads of sweat gathering at her temples. Media relations had been her weakest subject at the Academy on Planet Placidon. What to say? What to say?

"I have met a fellow by the name of Kafka but, as I understand it, he no longer lives in a traditional manner. He's taken to living here in Retro."

"And did you talk with Kafka?"

"We spoke briefly, but his dialect of Standard is new to me and I've had some difficulty extracting meaning from his words. I do hope that will change soon, though. I'm sure there's much of value we can learn from him and his people. After all, they've been here for thousands of years and I only showed up yesterday."

Journalist Sumner went on to ask Ardra a few questions about her PKF background and what it had been like on Planet Chelidon, her last posting. Finally, she ordered the imager off, and the hovering flies consolidated and retreated to lurk behind her shoulder. Sumner's eyes now seemed to be trying to see beneath Ardra's skin. After a few moments, she nodded and spoke. "Off the record, you might like to know that I'm doing a little investigative work on our two murders."

"Really. Any progress?" Ardra asked.

"I confess I did a check on you," Sumner said. "Impressive. You really rose to the challenge on Chelidon. I'm hoping you'll be interested in our working together, unofficially of course. I have some early crime scene holo of the Les Lesting murder and there's . . . well . . . an interesting aspect to it that even I can pick out. Most of the holo run was edited out in the report that made the news bullet, but I still have the original file."

"I didn't see any reference to it in the case notes. Hasn't Sergeant Rosil seen it? Why haven't you offered it to her?"

"I think you'll understand after you've viewed it."

"You don't say . . ." Ardra said aloud and thought, "So I'm not the only one questioning the way Rosil's handling the cases. How should I handle this? I need time to formulate a plan."

"Of course, the PKF will accept cooperation wherever it's offered," Ardra continued. "I'd like to see the holo you're talking about. But right now I've just finished my night shift and I'm headed for bed." Inside, she wavered. Should she seize the moment? What if Rosil saw her go into the building with Sumner? What could she use as an excuse for visiting the news office? Did she really need excuses to investigate the murders? Maybe if she had another word with Sergeant Rosil . . . Then she realized Sumner was talking to her.

" . . . quite right. Stop by any time. My office is on the top floor of the administration building. Sleep well." The journalist gave Ardra's hand another vigorous shaking then trotted off down the street in the direction of the science building. Ardra signed off with the station computer then headed to the barracks.

"Skrif, where are you?" Ardra asked as she passed the tavern, still tightly closed.

"I've located an operational K-9 charge pad in the station," Skrif replied. "I'm charging and I'm preparing a spare uniform for you. Do you need me?"

"No, I'm just going to catch a rest bar or two."

"And I'll recharge."

"Does the Repositor have anything on a special wall built by the Wanderites?"

"The only Wanderite structure on file with the Repositor is the tower of stones that Barkeep Trudge mentioned last night."

"Even with his weird behavior, it's hard for me to see Kafka murdering anyone. He seems like a gentle, harmless fellow. And fearful, too. Same goes for Vincent."

"According to the registered schedule, the surveyors who worked with Cara Stine are about to depart for another field session."

"I want to talk to them. And Lesting's co-workers, too. The copies of Rosil's interviews with them reveal nothing. There must be something she missed."

Ardra contemplated plans of action as she walked to the barracks, entered, and ordered her door to open. Eyes already starting to close, she stepped inside and promptly tripped over a power extension that snaked from the side wall into the bathroom.

"Identify yourself!" demanded a voice from the blackness that was the bathroom. With a hiss of hydraulics and a rumble of castors, the source of the voice appeared at the entry; its beady red sensor pulsated as it scanned her.

"PKF Officer Ardra Wythian," she responded. "Check your file with the Repositor. You should know that I'm working nightwatch and just got off duty."

There was a long pause while the janitorbot contemplated. This was the largest of the serving robots; tall and cylindrical, it bristled with working arms.

"There's no record of Officer Wythian working nightwatch," it finally replied.

"Well, add it. And when you work in my rooms turn on the ampin' lights."

"Acknowledged." The bathroom glared with sudden illumination. "Do you wish me to leave or complete today's cleaning?"

"Oh, finish it off." Ardra waved a weary hand at the machine and stumped over to the bed, which the janitor had already freshened. She dumped her equipment belt on the chair by the workdesk.

"Acknowledged." The janitor returned to the bathroom and scrubbing sounds soon followed.

Ardra flopped onto the bed and stared up at the ceiling. It was too bright but she didn't want to order the room to dim the lights after having just demanded the opposite of the janitor. Rapid reversals of command always made the serving robots pause for contemplation; they were actually verifying the change by running a check of their memory and logic, but to Ardra it felt like the pause and stony silence of disapproval. Besides, in the simpler-minded servants, such reversals could cause a system crash, which left them inert and in the way.

So Ardra contemplated the minute ripples and ridges of her synthetic sky as she fantasized about Skrif reverting to valetbot functions. The bot would pull off her boots and massage her feet. "Which would be a total waste of talent," she admitted.

A low whine signaled the final phase of cleaning and the janitor emerged from the bathroom. From its belly a hose reached to the floor where a squat box with a flashing red eye ran back and forth like a hyperactive shimpuppy on a leash. A faint rattle in the hose indicated that it was finding sand tracked in by her feet. With each new click of sand the bead of red on the box seemed to glow brighter. Watching it, Ardra remembered the red eye of the snake-like lizard she'd encountered under the skeleton tree. The bed underneath her twitched as she shuddered; back then, it had felt as though the creature drew an icy finger through the center of her mind.

"Any requests, Officer Wythian?" the janitor asked as it retracted its belly hose and used a five-jointed arm to snap the lower box into a slot near its armpit.

"How about a foot massage?" she suggested.

"That function is not in my programming."

"You're no fun at all."

"I'm a janitor."

"Yeah, right. You can go now."

"Acknowledged." The janitor rolled over to the hall outlet, snaked its five-jointed arm down to the auxiliary power cord Ardra had tripped over on the way in, and tugged it out. Then it sucked the cord in like a fat strand of black spaghetti. The outer door opened to its silent command and the silver cylinder breezed out of her chamber.

Ardra found herself on her feet, pacing from the foot of the bed to the bathroom doorway and back. Six steps. That was the extent of her main room and the walls seemed to be constricting as she watched. Five paces. Four strides. Finally, she reined herself in and sat back down on the bed to drag off her boots.

"Grrr . . . ime!" She wrenched the one boot off and tossed it to the floor near the chair. With a sigh, she flopped back on the bed and stared, wide-eyed and numb, at the ceiling.

"Wythian room. Time check," she ordered.

"The time is eighteen minutes after eight in the morning," the room intoned.

"Yeah, tell that to the suns," she muttered. "One of them just set."

"Please repeat your command," the room responded.

"Disengage."

"Disengaged."

Ardra sat up again and tugged at the second boot, slowly separating it from her foot; her feet must be swollen, she decided. The second boot tumbled to join the first. Staring down at her dangling feet and the neutral brown of the floor, Ardra weighed the benefits of a cleanse before sleep against the less demanding plan of going straight to bed. She lifted her eyes and noted evidence of Skrif's earlier visit to the room.

Evenly placed on the workdesk were three activated holoportraits. On the left was her graduating class at the Academy, a miniature Ardra standing front and center, Dilli and the others forming crisp lines beside and behind her. It was their first day in their Officer First Class uniforms, not the cadet versions, and their faces strained under the force of their grins.

The middle and largest portrait had been recorded at a Wythian family reunion and, despite its mobbing of relations, she kept it because it was the best image she had of her parents. Here, they looked relaxed and happy as she remembered them, in contrast to their usual formality when posing.

On the right was a portrait of "the Imp", Ardra's kid brother. His name was actually Piam and he wasn't a kid anymore, either. By the time Ardra finished her colony duty, he'd be graduated from Basis. He had a terrific talent for holoart and had already been offered apprenticeships on Planets Gavial and Olid. He wasn't a bad hand at anchor music, either, and he and Ardra had never let an Eternity Festival go by without a long duel. Ardra would win with music and Piam would win with his infectious laugh.

Behind the holoportraits stood her anchoran, its polished gold stem and pearl keys glinted at her. "Play me," it teased.

Ardra pulled the audilink from her collar then slipped off her tunic. She got up and took it to the bathroom hamper chute, checked her trouser pockets, then added the bottom half of her uniform and her bodyvest to the chute.

Back on the bed, under its single sheet, dressed in a sleepsuit from the freshly filled cupboard, Ardra ordered the lights down and closed her eyes. She imagined that Cara Stine had traveled with gaggles of family and friend holoportraits, enough to cover her workdesk and her counter. Just as Ardra drifted into sleep she glimpsed a black-eyed mother weeping over a holo of Les Lesting.

CHAPTER 7

Pebbles and Planets

"Do you think it was a guilty slip when Tech Sennett called Vincent a pebble brain yesterday evening?" Skrif asked. The companionbot and Ardra were headed down the street on their way to the administration building. It was mid-afternoon under two low suns and the hours of freedom before nightwatch held infinite promise.

"He said that? I didn't notice at the time. Too much going on." Ardra felt restored and powerful after her time of sleep. When she rose, she'd been careful to dress in civilian clothes, an ivory jumpsuit and cushioned sandals. She planned a series of social visits and casual chats to introduce herself to people. Nothing official. Nothing to upset her sergeant.

"Interesting, interesting . . ." Ardra continued. Sennett's shaping up to be a lead suspect in Surveyor Stine's murder, isn't he? He was close by when Stine was killed, he showed a violent temper with Vincent, and he has pebbles on the brain. What about those oily smudges on the stones? Do they connect him? Has the analysis been put in the file yet?"

Skrif checked with the Repositor and responded, "The main component of the material was identified as a triacylglycerol, type unknown. It is perhaps residue of an oil extracted from a plant native to Wanderer."

"Grime! That's gets us back to the Wanderites again. Did the analyzer have any luck piecing together fingerprint fragments?"

"No luck. The pebbles were too small and too rough."

"I suppose we'll have to entertain the notion the stones were something a Wanderite placed after the initial crime scene investigation," Ardra sighed. "Maybe they were laid out to chase off evil spirits after the fact. I wonder if there's any point asking Kafka about them and hoping for a direct answer."

"Perhaps Wanderites would give more sensible answers in their own language," said Skrif. "Unfortunately, the Repositor has no records of their vocabulary or grammar. Not yet."

"Well now, here's a bit of good fortune just coming out of Provisions," said Ardra as she spied Tech Sennett dressed in fresh coveralls and tucking a swilk bar into a breast pocket. The afternoon breeze carried his scent cluster to her; it was tinged with the odors of soap and the delicate confection he had just purchased. No amount of protective wrap could keep the smell of swilk from eager nostrils.

"Afternoon snack?" Ardra asked as the trio came together and halted; she nodded at the bar in his pocket.

The street boomed as Sennett laughed and placed a protective hand over the bar. "My biggest vice," he said. "I buy one a week and ration myself a bite or two each day. Can you imagine life in a Realm that didn't include Planet Simblo and its swilk-producin' gossamers?"

"I'd rather imagine a Realm where swilk didn't cost a ransom. How are you and Vincent getting on today?" Ardra asked.

"We've been avoidin' each other and that seems to work well for both of us." The surveyor squinted up the street then dropped his eyes to scowl at a fat orange beetle, the circumference of a human palm, waddling a direct line to the wall of the store.

"I'd hate to see Vincent get hurt again," Ardra persisted. "How do you feel about that?"

"He's so crazy he does it to himself. He does that kind of stuff, just ask around. I heard he was hittin' himself with a rock once. Look at that stupid bug."

The beetle had reached the wall and scrambled with its front legs as it tried to scale the smooth face. However, its fat rump refused to budge from the ground despite all desperate flailings of its bony forelegs.

"Give up and go around!" Sennett muttered. "Even the insects are crazy on this planet."

"Maybe we put up the building on an old migration route and the pull of instinct is too strong for it to resist," Ardra suggested. As her words hung in the air, she realized that they sounded like something Haley would have said. Apparently, she hadn't always tuned out when Haley and his colleagues talked thrips and theory over an evening get-together. Ancient history, she scolded herself. Get over it.

"Everybody and everything around here is nuts." Sennett lifted a booted foot and stomped it down beside the beetle, but the ensuing micro-earthquake did nothing to deter it. With a snarl, the surveyor lifted his boot again and moved it over the scrambling creature.

"Leave it be!" Ardra shouted. "Sennett! It's not hurting anything. Just ignore it."

Sennett withdrew his foot and peered at her. "I heard you were from Metro," he said. "Since when does someone from a barren rock littered with cities care about dumb bugs?"

"I . . . I don't," she declared, squaring her shoulders. "But if you squash something that big its inner slime might squirt out in any direction and I don't want to wear it on my clothes or, worse, my face. Do you?"

"Suppose not."

"Anyway, I wondered if you'd tell me your version of what happened when you, Blaze Myro, and Cara Stine were coming back to Retro on the day Stine was killed."

With a flick of a shoulder, Sennett launched into a recitation of events. The day was unremarkable and his version of how their heavy-duty Carrier had started to cause problems matched that in the report. But his description of the sleep time caught her interest.

"I fell right off to sleep, which is unusual for me. Usually, I spend an hour or so starin' at the cover on my sleep pod and worryin' about when I'll get to sleep and whether I'll get enough that I won't be draggin' my feet all the next day. We all have sleep problems off and on. Sometimes Blaze and Cara would be so restless they'd get up and go out of the shelter so not to disturb me. They'd go some ways off and sit and talk. I'd hear the distant murmur of their voices like water over stones and it'd help lull my mind to sleep."

"Were they restless that night?" Ardra asked.

"Can't say. Can't say at all. I winked out so fast I don't even remember snappin' the pod cover shut."

"Cara and Blaze were good friends, do you think? Did you ever see them argue?"

"Not what you'd call argue, exactly. Survey teams are always workin' in new and unpredictable situations and equipment breaks down or things don't work out the way they're supposed to. Tempers fray every now and then. We were a good team, worked well together and generally coped with things when they fell apart. Sometimes Cara's good cheer in the midst of chaos would get to be too much and Blaze, figuratively speakin', would bite her head off. Ten seconds later they'd be laughin' at it together." A sigh overcame Sennett for a moment.

Waiting for him to continue, Ardra reminded herself that the other surveyor, Blaze Myro, was a Jahanite, a race with long limbs and often a lanky build. By contrast, a Carrian like the victim, Cara Stine, typically had the build of a brick. Idly, Ardra wondered whether a Jahanite would have the strength to overpower a Carrian. No doubt, there would need to be a powerful and empowering motive.

"Blaze and Cara were close friends," Sennett continued. "I suppose they each knew all the other's secrets."

"Speaking of secrets, I guess it's no secret Cara Stine was a popular woman in many ways. Were you trying to get to know her on a more personal level?" Ardra paused and studied the thick folds of the Lavarite's face; they could have been chiseled from sulfur rock for all the movement her comment inspired.

Sennett shrugged. "After Cara dumped Les she was involved with someone else. I think she got involved first and that's why she finished with Les, but only she and the mystery lover know for sure. She was just about the most beautiful woman in the Realm.

Her eyes were blue as an Eifen rain cloud and her skin was black as hot gudday. She could have whoever she wanted. I figured it was worth a try to get her interested in me; you can't score if you're not in the game. She never rallied to my advances, though. It happens."

"She rejected you. Are you trying to tell me you weren't angry at being rejected?"

"It's not the first time. It won't be the last."

"Any questions you want to add, Skrif?" Ardra asked.

"Do you collect pebbles, sir?" Skrif asked.

"Me? I got no use for rocks. Blaze is the geo in our team, Cara was the bio, and I'm the tech. I fix, I calibrate, and I keep stuff runnin'. Tools are what's worth collectin'." Sennett's face showed only puzzlement at such a question. He shrugged as if to say, What more could you expect from a robot?

Suddenly, Sennett sighed and looked down at the ground and the fat, orange bug. "It was terrible findin' her that way," he said. "Who'd do that? No cause." The Lavarite reached out with the toe of his boot and nudged at the beetle, urging it to the left. It waggled its rump furiously and returned to its original path up the smooth side of the wall.

"I try to sing myself to Center," Sennett continued, "but these days the notes stick in my throat." He nudged the beetle to the side again. Mid-push, the insect suddenly raised its pear-shaped butt into the air and fired a red spray. Both humans jumped back at once, but not before the spray coated the near leg of Sennett's coveralls as high as the knee.

"Gagstick!" Ardra was the first to respond to the accompanying smell.

"PeeYoo! That smells like the rottin' boils in the Infinity Bogs." Sennett snatched a bandanna out of his hip pocket and clapped it over his nose and mouth. Then he started to chuckle. "There's just no tellin' what's under the surface, is there? Here's this pretty orange bug lookin' innocent as can be and it turns around and lets me have it. My pant leg will probably rot and fall off now. So I suppose it's your job to go around pokin' at people until you find out who has a sac of poison under a shiny coat. I didn't kill Cara and if I knew who did I'd see justice done. One way or another." Shaking his leg at intervals, Sennett hurried off down the street to the barracks, a change of clothes, and a cleansing.

A sudden sneeze rattled Ardra to her bones and she backed away from the area shaking her head. The beetle had returned to the wall and showed no sign of losing interest in the impossible climb.

"Oh dear," said Skrif. "The Repositor has no record of such a beetle so there's no information on the toxicity of its spray. Did your sneeze indicate that you inhaled some of its mist?"

"I sneezed to clear the stench."

"Perhaps we should hurry to the clinic and have the doctor check your status."

"I feel fine. We've got more important things to do than bother the doctor over nothing. Besides, I've got you watching my every twitch. If I develop symptoms you'll catch them earlier than any human."

"I'll watch you closely."

"You always do."

"Thank-you."

"I guess you noticed Sennett didn't react to your pebble question," Ardra said as she and Skrif angled across the street toward the administration building. When they reached the foot of its entrance ramp their approach scared up a tiny lizard, green, polka-dotted with brown. It shrieked, reared onto bony hind legs, and sprinted away.

"Weird," said Ardra. "And it smells familiar . . . it smells like an Eifen beet. Ugh!"

More than any other building in Retro, Administration had been constructed on a grand scale. Its five floors and wide stance loomed over Main Street; broad ribbons of windows glared with reflected sunlight. When Ardra and Skrif approached, the entry door slid back to reveal an empty lobby shaped like a half moon. A powder blue floor gazed blankly up at a cream blue ceiling and six hallways fanned out from the back like wheel spokes. The partitions between the halls were covered with rough slaptogether and the floors were uncarpeted. Though the exterior of the building gleamed, the interior awaited a few more supply ships.

"No escortbot. Not even a human receptionist," Ardra said. "Which way to the forecasting office?"

Skrif queried the Repositor but the response was unsatisfactory. "Unfortunately, that information isn't registered yet," the companionbot reported.

"Peekay! How can people stand so much disorganization?" Ardra stomped along the curve of the half moon and peered down each hall, looking for clues and wondering where they would find the forecasting office. Unfortunately, Kip Myro hadn't given her a tour of the building when he led her to the orientation office on the second floor.

"Simple logic suggests sunlight forecasters would work where they could see out a window," she said. "They might like to confirm their reports."

Walking over to the left-most corridor, Ardra leaned into it and called out, "Forecast office?" The question bounced down the hall until it grew too feeble to echo and faded into silence. Where was everyone? Where was anyone?

"Grime!" she vented a sliver of her frustration and moved to the right-most corridor where she called again, "Anybody there?" Just as she took a breath to curse anew, a mop of straw poked out of a doorway half way down the hall.

"You must be Officer Wythian," said the head with the straw-yellow hair. "Well found. I'm Veray Beld, junior . . . no, senior sunlight forecaster here on Wanderer. Come on in and we can talk while I run up some graphics for the evening beam." The head vanished.

As Ardra wandered down the hall she reviewed names and titles. Les Lesting, the man who had been beaten to death behind the tavern, had been the senior sunlight forecaster so this woman she had just glimpsed, Veray Beld, must have been his junior forecaster. By default, she had been promoted. Was such a promotion motive enough for murder?

The forecast office was a triangle with one long side formed of windows, which stretched from floor to ceiling. An assortment of impressive instruments Ardra couldn't identify lined the non-window walls of the office. In each of the three corners of the room sat a workdesk heavily stacked with data cubes and surrounded by a number of half unpacked cargo crates. In the center of the room stood a graphics easel over which the senior forecaster hunched, a second worker peering over her shoulder.

Forecaster Beld was tall. Seated at the low easel, she was still as tall as the worker who stood next to her, and her short yellow hair was so thick and dense it almost stood on end from the crowding. Her veins, visible through transparent skin, drew blue lines along her bare arms. Ardra guessed the woman was part Bloohan, by her coloring, and part Eifen, given her height.

The man who stood next to Beld was short, square and ebony, a Carrian like the late Surveyor Stine. The man's coveralls glowed the same carrot-orange as his traditional crown braid. The two humans were discussing their work.

"If we bring solar B up this way that would give the effect of partial dawn," said Beld.

"But it's inaccurate," Daly replied.

"We're not doing this for a conference of forecasters, this is to help the public visualize the situation."

"Hmf. Don't like the idea."

Ardra cleared her throat and they both looked up. "I'm Officer Ardra Wythian, but you seem to know that already," she said as she walked forward to stand on the other side of the easel. "This is Skrif."

"Everyone knows everyone here on Wanderer," Beld laughed, reaching out to shake Ardra's hand with a grip that melted under pressure. Her eyes were the dense pink of a pure Bloohan. "And when someone new like yourself is going to be brought in, it's big talk all up and down Main Street. By the way, this is Tech Murl Daly." She cocked her head to the side where the Carrian stood and he nodded to Ardra while she nodded back. His blue eyes were steady and he made no move to shake hands. Carrians of faith believed such casual contact clouded the Light.

"I'm sorry you lost your co-worker, Forecaster Lesting," she said.

There was a pause while Beld and Daly exchanged a glance, then Beld said, "It was shocking, even though we didn't know him well. This is our first survey posting, Murl and I. First Cara then Les. Ghastly."

"Then you only knew him the three months this survey outpost has been in operation? Or were you here during the preliminaries?"

"Three full months," said Daly, stressing the "full".

"What was he like?"

Again, there was a pause and a glance.

Forecaster Beld finally spoke; she hesitated as she talked and seemed to test her words as she selected them. "Les was a seasoned survey specialist and had served on many outposts. He was both a perfectionist in method and a traditionalist in thinking."

"Sounds impressive. So how was his sense of humor?" Ardra asked with a wink.

"His what?" Beld jumped, then laughed shakily. "I'm sorry, I feel like such a prime suspect that I hate to say anything negative about him. After all, I've been promoted to his position and some people would consider that to be a motive, which it is not, I might add. And he was rather a tense person to work with because he was closed to new ideas, which he considered radical, and he often demanded precision where none was possible." Beld's words tumbled out, a rushing waterfall of sounds.

Ardra glanced the question at Daly who shrugged and muttered, "I've worked with worse."

"I think Murl can work with anyone," Beld added.

"Did you notice anything different in his behavior in the days before he was killed?" Ardra asked. "Was he withdrawn, nervous, agitated in any way? Did he mention any problems?"

Ardra's suspicion sensor clanged as, yet again, the two exchanged a glance. Then Beld dropped her head and examined the graphics stylus in her hand while Daly chewed on his lip. But Ardra knew the routine and held her tongue; eventually, someone would feel forced to break the silence.

Finally Beld cleared her throat. "You have to understand that Retro is a small community, population forty-two."

"Forty-three, now," Daly interjected.

"Yes, forty-three now that you're here, Officer. People see things and people talk and part of it is just rumor and part of it is knowing private things about others that we really have no business knowing." Beld flicked power to the stylus on and off, on and off. "Cara, poor Cara, was terribly outgoing and friendly and, for a while, she and Les were seen together. I don't know if they were involved, but just before her last survey trip she was being seen more with other people, and Les seemed more intense here at work and even less talkative than usual, which pretty much left him issuing monosyllabic commands. Nothing we did was good enough for him."

"How did he react at her death?" asked Ardra. She wondered why Beld hesitated over the involvement between Stine and Lesting. It seemed to be established fact to the rest of the town.

"His reaction? That's hard to say. I didn't really notice, I was so shocked. We all were. Shocked. On a new planet like this you're braced for deaths among the survey team, but you expect the cause to be a wild animal or a new disease or even a rockslide, but not murder. I mean, the locals are weird, but mostly they stay out of sight and the ones who live in town seemed so harmless up to that point, and now everyone is looking over their shoulder. Myself, you won't get me out of town on a bet or a dare."

"Unlike before," Daly chuckled. Beld's face blinked scarlet then drained as quickly.

"How about you, Tech Daly," Ardra asked. "Did you notice his reaction to Surveyor Stine's death?"

The Carrian's smile vanished, and he shrugged and shook his head. His jaw muscles turned so rigid, Ardra wondered if his teeth were about to shatter from the clenched pressure. She shrugged and wandered over to a bank of instruments where she paused to examine their silver faces and twinkling readouts.

"What does this do?" she asked over a shoulder.

"Murl can tell you anything you'd like to know about any of this equipment," said Beld. "Not just what it does but how it does it and what can go wrong and how to fix it. He's the best."

Daly joined Ardra and ran a finger over the shiny surface before them. His tone relaxed as he spoke. "This is the coordinator in our satellite series. It takes the information from the decoder, checks for anomalies, and directs the data to the appropriate crunching programs. If there's a problem with the signal it'll send a correcting command to the satellite or, if that doesn't work, it pages whoever of us is on call."

"Does that happen often?"

"No, not at all."

Beld snorted. "Hah. He says that because it hasn't paged him after bedtime when he's on call. One or two pages in a person's deepest sleep and it seems to have happened more than often. Of course, the second time it dragged me out of unconsciousness I wasn't on call, I was second call. That was because Les was first page but he wasn't answering and, after I checked on the problem, I found out why he hadn't picked up the page. Someone found his . . . that was the night he was killed."

"Both suns were up then, weren't they?" Ardra asked as she recalled Kafka's mention of two shadows.

"I couldn't say. I remember it was bright and when I got up I felt grateful that at least I wasn't fumbling around in the dark. Beld station, display solar cycle for month nine day seventeen, full screen."

Part of the window panel silvered, then a projection of the computer's readout formed and sharpened on it. It was a graph of sorts; at the center was a time line with the planet's day marked out in standard hours. Curves of yellow arched in from either side, sometimes touching the center line, sometimes retreating far from it.

Beld looked over at the graph and nodded. "You're right. Both suns were up about the time he was found."

"What was the problem that caused you to be paged?"

"It was some kind of a short in the controller. As soon as I figured out that it wasn't a command or reception problem, or anything else that I knew how to fix I had to page Murl out of his bed to repair it. The machinery itself is nothing but a black box to me because I'm all theory and interpretation, so when I realized it wasn't anomalous data I handed the problem over to him and went looking for Les to find out why he hadn't answered the page.

"It was as I was heading to the No Limits that I noticed a crowd of people around the back. That is to say, it was a crowd for Retro. There was our doctor with his pajamas sticking out from under the cuffs of his straights, our cop with her tunic hanging crooked, the three townies each looking completely blasted or smoked or twisted according to their drug of preference, poor Piper emptying his stomach into the nearest composter with small comfort from his bond, and Barkeep Trudge with a bored this-happens-all-the-time expression on his face. When I saw what they were gathered around I went into shock and nothing after that is clear."

Ardra nodded. "I understand. I'm sorry you had to find him that way." She glanced over at Daly. "When did you find out?" she asked.

He shrugged. "After I fixed the controller I went looking for the two of them. Veray had told me she was going to look for Les and she hadn't come back to tell me what the problem had been. I thought it might be some reception malfunction in his pager that they would need me to fix so I went off to see if I could find either one of them. Even as late as I arrived at the tavern, they still hadn't covered the body." Daly's face turned grim at the memory.

"You both headed for the tavern first from the sound of it. Did he spend a lot of his time there?"

"Yes."

"No." The two spoke in unison, then exchanged an anxious look, reopened their mouths, and froze. They seemed poised to agree with each other but had no prearranged game plan.

Beld sank her chin into her hands and sighed. "We must sound like idiots. Ivy never asked awkward questions like that. I guess that's why they've sent you in, so there'll be someone to ask tough questions.

"You see, Les never let his drinking interfere with his work and he was a dedicated professional and I never would have wanted to say anything about what he did on his own time because some people in charge of Survey Assignment have narrow opinions about such things." Beld paused for a deep breath. "Besides, some people don't need as much sleep as others and who am I to judge whether a person should be sleeping eight hours every rotation or five hours or two or whatever."

"What did you think about it?" Ardra asked Daly.

Daly's shoulders spasmed in a shrug and a tic pulsed in his jaw muscle. Ardra wished she could question them separately, then remembered that, officially, she wasn't here to question them at all.

"Actually, I stopped by to ask if you could explain this crazy planet to me," she said. "I keep expecting it to dive into one of the suns or shoot off into nowhere. It bounces around like a volleywar ball, doesn't it?"

"We're accustomed to planets that orbit in flat planes so Wanderer's movements are hard to visualize," Beld said. "You might think of the way an electron orbits a nucleus, rather than a typical planet around a sun. Mind you don't take the analogy too literally, though."

"It's fascinating," said Daly. "Totally new. It's one of those times when our science doesn't explain, can't explain, what we observe. It's like the gossamers. We analyze their wings and say they're the wrong shape and too thin for flight. But there they are, flying all through the meg forests on Simblo. When the rules we've set up don't explain what we observe, it doesn't mean the phenomenon can't exist, it means we need to rewrite our rules."

"Yes," Beld agreed. "It's always a thrill when something exists that our current models and formulae say is impossible. What's more exciting than a paradigm quake?" The forecaster sat tall, her hands lay still on the easel and her eyes shone.

"So how do you forecast the day and night periods and what's your accuracy?" Ardra asked.

Beld rubbed her palms together and leaned forward. "To start with we try to avoid use of the words "day" and "night" and use light and dark or sunlight and darkness, plus twilight for the in-between side of things. That way we avoid "dawn" and "dusk". Are you familiar with chaotic mathematics?"

"Er, just the low mentor basics."

"We're on the cutting edge of new theory here and we've been pushing at the boundaries of making higher chaotics seem as common as quantum mechanics."

"We?" Daly snorted.

"I . . . I suppose the right thing to say is that this is . . ."

"Your work!" Daly insisted. "And Les was doing everything in his authority to squash it." As abruptly as he had interrupted, the Carrian snapped his mouth shut and renewed his silence. Ardra had never seen a Carrian look so grim; his face was set in the natural scowl of a Kelpan.

"In any case," Beld continued. "As you know, the two suns of this system are in tight orbit with each other. The actions of these two massive bodies, the two suns of Wanderer, force the planet into a chaotic series of movements around and about the stars that rule it. It can't maintain the rhythmic elliptical orbit common to satellites of a single sun. But, using higher chaotic analysis, we've improved our path prediction to an accuracy of eighty percent. The process involves a lot of data and a lot of number crunching. It eats computer time for fastbreaker and that's just to warm up. Still, with a little more refining, I'm expecting the accuracy to rise into the nineties."

"What surprises me, is that the planet is habitable, and it doesn't go from ice cube to charcoal briquette," Ardra said.

"But a chaotic process can give rise to order," said Beld. "The movements of Wanderer are affected by strange attractors. The orbit never strays outside of the bounds of the attractors, it's only the movement within these limits that's unpredictable."

Ardra couldn't help but smile at Beld's enthusiasm; it energized the room in rhythm with the gesturing arms of the forecaster. Words spilled over words as Beld explained and Ardra was reminded of the verbal energy of Kip Myro, an energy that shouted Eifen.

"Your work sounds like a career maker," Ardra commented.

Beld smiled, then ducked her head as another wash of red, so characteristic of Bloohans, swept over her face. "For the whole team. It should have been for the whole team—Murl, me, and Les too."

A trumpet flourish sounded from the wall and the forecasting team straightened. "Twenty-five minutes to the evening beam," a strident voice announced.

"Time check acknowledged," Daly responded.

"We need to finish preparing the light and dark forecast for tomorrow," said Beld.

"I won't take any more of your time."

Ardra sighed as she and Skrif headed back down the hall away from the forecasting office.

"Nothing much," she said.

"Tech Daly and Forecaster Beld both had the opportunity to kill Forecaster Lesting," said Skrif.

"They were both nervous about being questioned, too. We can't rule either of them out if we do rule out the pebble symbols."

As they traveled down the hall, Ardra paused occasionally and peered into one of the empty rooms until the baleful staring of their blank walls wakened a ghostly finger to creep up the back of her neck.

"I don't think these rooms will ever be filled," she said.

"You'll solve the murders," said Skrif. "People will come."

"Someone better figure it out."

"What's next?"

"Let's see if Sumner's available," Ardra declared. "That journalist said she had something interesting to show me. Something about Rosil."

CHAPTER 8

Of Lizards and Eagles

Unfortunately, Journalist Sumner was unavailable. According to the message that answered Skrif's com hail, she and her flies were at the hangar recording a feature on delays in vehicle repair. Ardra did her best to ignore a surge of guilt over the Lancer.

"Maybe we can run into Blaze Myro in the science building," Ardra suggested. "I want to talk to her about her nighttime chats with Stine."

The science building was a compact red cube at the southeast end of Main Street. Its interior was linear, unlike the administration building, and Ardra and Skrif foraged through echoing halls in grids, first on the ground floor, then on the second level.

"Imagine having to search a building to find out who's in it," Ardra muttered. "No one's bothered to set up reception units anywhere."

"Perhaps all the scientists are out in the field," Skrif suggested.

"If they're not too far afield we might root up an A-pad and cruise out for a visit," Ardra said. The notion put an extra bounce in her step; even the relatively slow pace of an A-pad might give her a sense of progress, of getting somewhere.

They turned down a new hallway and saw a lab-coated figure approaching from the other end. It was a woman, middle-aged but with an energy that crackled from her every move. She was a Thalian of silver hair, gold-flecked eyes, and skin like sculpted marble. Thalians thought they were the cleverest of all the descendants of the mother race and they were, on average, extremely bright. Born leaders, every one. Ardra wondered what this woman was doing in the science building rather than the administration edifice up the street. As a rule, Thalians migrated to positions of power.

When they closed to speaking distance Ardra asked, "Is Surveyor Blaze Myro around?"

"You're Officer Ardra Wythian, of course," the woman replied, "and I'm Zoologist Darlis, but call me Chup." She held up one hand in a stop gesture and added, "I know, I know, as a Thalian I should be the planet coordinator, or a high ranking administrator, or a visiting VIP but instead I am living my ambition to explore new worlds and name new life forms. Zoologist, that's me."

"I try not to prejudge people," Ardra said. She also tried not to wrinkle her nose at the smell of formalin that came with the woman's scent cluster.

"Of course, I'm a bitter disappointment to my family and a disaster in the eyes of the Purists," the zoologist continued. "To answer your question, Blaze, Cliff, and Lute whipped out to a promising site for an afternoon field trip."

"Lute?"

"Botanist Cullen. He's supposed to work the labs like me, but he has surveyor blood in his veins and likes to get out in the real world."

"Do you know when Blaze Myro and the others will be back?"

"No idea. Is there anything I can help you with? I suppose you're investigating the murders. Unfortunately, I wasn't that familiar with either Cara or Les. They both recreated at the tavern and I don't indulge."

"I guess you can't avoid the Thalian stereotype completely."

"Good point. We're notoriously sober types. I confess, I haven't shaken free of my heritage. But almost . . ." she paused and looked expectantly at Ardra.

"Meaning?" she cooperated.

"I bonded outside the race. Horrors, of course."

"I've seen it work before," Ardra said. She recalled the grief of a Thalian in the colony on Chelidon who had lost his bond, a Jahanite. But Ardra had nailed the one who'd murdered the woman and she'd nail the culprit here, too.

"It's wonderful to see a new face on Wanderer. You'll have to tell me where you've been and what you've seen. There's so much here we haven't categorized yet. I'm on my way to the floor lounge for a break. Would you like some gudday?"

Ardra and Skrif followed in the woman's wake as she breezed down the hall and led them into a small room filled with formchair circles. The companionbot settled in the center of one of the circles while the two humans relaxed in the enveloping chairs and sipped iced gudday.

"There's no record with the Repositor of a fat orange beetle that shoots a red liquid in self defense," Skrif said. "Is it dangerous? Two humans were standing nearby when one sprayed this afternoon."

"I'm afraid I'm terribly behind in filing my reports with the Repositor," Darlis sighed. "I'm familiar with that species of beetle; Vincent calls it Firesack. It sprays a mild acid, not something any human or reptile would want in an eye. The spray doesn't reach very high so it's not a problem to an upright human. The insectivorous reptiles learn to avoid it, though, and hunt other beetles."

"What about something called eagles?" Ardra asked. "Kafka mentioned a flight of eagles to me."

"Flight of eagles? That's strange. Nothing we've seen so far on Wanderer has developed true flight. There are a few insects and one reptile that have glider capabilities, but there's nothing that can soar or ascend under its own power. Eagles, hmm. Vincent's never mentioned eagles to me. I don't see much of Kafka, but Vincent wanders in for the odd visit when he's relatively dry. Poor dear, he just won't take advantage of addiction mediation."

"No eagles? Maybe he was hallucinating." Ardra was disappointed. Perhaps nothing Kafka said could be used to help solve the murders.

"Maybe he was having a vision," said Darlis. "According to Vincent, Kafka has visions."

"Visions of something that doesn't exist on Wanderer?"

"Well, Standard isn't their native language. They often use only the best equivalent of a word, I believe."

Discouraged, Ardra found herself stifling a yawn and hoped the gudday would help her body perk up. Her internal clock hadn't converted completely to a nightwatch schedule yet and her earlier sense of refreshment had begun to wane.

"I've seen and heard the strangest lizards around town," she said. "Inside buildings, too."

"Yes, it's terrific, isn't it?"

Ardra laughed but not too loudly. "Is it?" she responded.

"Oh yes," said Darlis. "When the prelim team arrived and threw up the town all the wildlife withdrew from the area. New smells, new sounds, strange activities. The reptiles weren't taking any chances. Even after the survey team moved in and things quieted down it took time before a few species grew bold enough to reclaim the territory. Now more and more are moving closer and closer."

"Dire lizards, too?" Ardra tried to keep her voice level as she asked. Why couldn't wild things stay out of the town or at least out of the buildings? She would never understand why some people actually sought out contact with strange creatures.

Back when Ardra was still a youth, her family had visited Planet Olid, their ancestral home, and one day they dragged Ardra out on a nature walk. Midway through the walk, they encountered a batbird, a tiny creature with a melodic whistle but ugly green flight membranes. Everyone stood still at the guide's urging. "It's a portent of good luck if it lands on you," he'd said.

"Not me. Don't land on me," Ardra had wished silently. But of course it had landed on her, on her forehead. It was all she could do not to scream like a shimpuppy when its suction cup feet sucked onto her skin.

"The dire lizards haven't come into Retro yet," said Darlis. "I take it you don't like reptiles?"

"Oh, I don't mind too much as long as they don't jump out of the shadows waving claws in the air."

"Isn't that one fascinating? It has four legs and two dorsal, claw-bearing appendages. It's the only species I've recorded so far with zero incidence of dorsal mites."

"It stank," said Ardra. "It stank like sour onion mixed with cesspool."

"Really? How fascinating. Do you find all the reptiles have such an odor? Whatever it is, it's not strong enough for the rest of us to detect."

"Some of them stink. But they're different. There was a little green and brown thing in front of Administration that smelled like overcooked Eifen beet."

"How exciting. I'll have to investigate. Perhaps they exude pheromones. I wonder what their functions might be." The gold flecks in Darlis' eyes glowed bright and the woman shifted forward in her formchair.

Ardra drained the last of her drink and debated one final line of questions. It could be tricky. Still . . .

"There is one reptile I'm curious about," she said. "I saw it out in the wilds south of town. It's a small snake-like lizard, about as long as a forearm, yellow with red eyes."

"Ahah. That's a NoName."

"A what?"

"Of course, that's just the common name, not the scientific one. I try to match the animals with the labels given them by the native Wanderites. When I described this lizard to Vincent and asked what it was called, that's what he told me—NoName. It's bizarre, but not all the names he gives me are as logical as Firesack. I gave the creature "incognitus" as its species name in deference to the common name. It's a harmless little thing that snakes up skeleton trees and eats its fresh podding buds. It's also been observed munching on the occasional grub but mostly it's a vegetarian. Dire lizards think the NoName is a delicacy and will actually stalk them and hide out near skeleton trees in bud, in the hopes one will descend to move to a new tree."

"This NoName, is it . . . er . . . this will sound silly but . . . is it at all telepathic?" Ardra hated to ask, but her curiosity demanded it. There had to be an explanation for that sensation of a cold finger drawing a line through her brain.

"Telepathic?" Darlis looked like she wanted to laugh but her hand shot to her mouth to prevent it. She moved the hand to scratch her chin. "I've never heard of any such thing, not from surveyors nor from Wanderites. If it is telepathic it's a first for the Realm. What makes you ask?" A smirk played across her lips.

"Oh, it was just a passing notion. Probably brought on by a lack of sleep." Ardra tried to convince herself she didn't mind sounding the fool. Of course she knew telepathy was unproven by scientists, but she'd believed the ice gnomes on Planet Brumal were only a myth until one of them knocked the torch out of her hand in that cave. She could still hear the sound it made, "Tasinggga!"

"Proper sleep is tough here at first, but now I sleep like a baby and you will too, before you know it," Darlis said with an encouraging nod.

Ardra said she would look forward to it and Darlis said she had samples to sort and they parted. The zoologist headed down the empty hallway, humming as though empty buildings and ghost towns were her favorite place to be and Ardra headed out with Skrif at her side.

"Well, the expert said the beetle spray was no problem. Feel better now?" Ardra asked.

"The information was most reassuring," said Skrif.

"Right now I actually feel a craving for a long ride in a commute tube packed with evening rushers," Ardra said when they emerged from the building and turned down Main Street. As she walked, she repeatedly glanced down at the twin shadows that the suns created at her feet. They were insubstantial in form and distracting when she was in motion. She was used to seeing one shadow out of the corner of her eye and the second one made her feel like she was being followed.

"What if Forecaster Beld and Tech Daly colluded for the murders?" Skrif suggested, unable to formulate a response to the commute craving.

"That makes some sense for Lesting, neither of them liked him at all and they were both in the right area at the right time. But what about Cara Stine?" Ardra countered.

"She was killed to throw off suspicion."

"But she was murdered first."

"Clever, no?"

"Clever, yes," Ardra laughed. "We should march right over and arrest them."

"Naturally, we need more information," Skrif added as they arrived at the entry to the vehicle hangar.

The vehicle hangar was a giant green cavern, glaringly lit in every corner; its voracious size sucked them inside.

"Y'back for more?" a voice called out, then echoed back on itself from the high ceiling.

With Skrif on her heels, Ardra picked her way around a dozen metal rods and alongside a brawny Carrier until she stood next to two techs huddled over the Lancer she had crashed in the plain. The entire nose section of the craft had been opened along the top and both workers had their arms buried in it to the elbows. An assortment of probes snaked into the gaping Lancer from a bank of diagnostic machines. There was no sign of Journalist Sumner.

"What do you mean by 'back for more?'" Ardra asked. Her nostrils sorted out two human scent clusters surrounded by a collage of sharp metallic and soft oily odors.

The workers, a man and a woman, both of mixed heritage, tittered and smirked at each other. He was short, round and the color of faded lemon peel with hair that stuck straight out in a shriek of red. He was so hybrid of race he even had the combination of one pink and one brown eye, a pairing Ardra found strangely compelling. The woman was tall and solid with a pale oval face, woolly grey hair and turquoise eyes specked with gold.

"Y'be Ardra Wythian, right?" the man asked. "Y'be the one parked this Lancer out of town. W'hope y'not back wanting another ride."

"Who me?" Ardra opted for diplomacy and laughed along. "I enjoyed the hike back to town so much I might never ride again."

The woman pulled her hands out of the Lancer, wiped them on her coverall towel and extended one in greeting. "Vehicle Tech Zill," she said, "and here's Tech Zill."

"Mates and workmates," her husband added as hands were shaken. The couple giggled again. "She's Tate and I'm Piper."

"This is Skrif," Ardra said and both techs turned admiring eyes on the companionbot.

"Ah, prime!" said Piper.

"W'be bot-certified," said Tate. "Y'have any problems, y'come to us, Skrif. Nothing w'like better than working on machinery that talks back."

"Thank-you," said Skrif as it settled to the conplast floor to conserve power. "I'm currently in top form."

"W'towed this poor beast in last evening," Piper said, as she turned her attention back to the Lancer. "Won't be back in service for a good stretch."

"It had been riding perfectly," Ardra explained. "Then, out of nowhere, it lost antigrav lift and planted its nose in the sand. Do you know what's wrong with it?"

"Had a nervous breakdown, poor thing. Could be a virus got in and crossed up all its circuitry. Could be a factory misroute problem," Piper said.

"That's to say w'don't know yet," his bond added.

"Ah, I see," Ardra replied. Neither tech had mentioned the vehicle's flight record, the slalom run, the helix. Hopefully, they viewed it as a coincidence not a trigger.

Piper plunged his arms back into the workings of the Lancer then asked with a wink, "Was there something else y'wanted to break?"

After the couple finished tittering over the comment, Ardra voiced a question that had popped into her mind when she'd walked by the Carrier. "I understand the Stine survey team had problems with their Carrier and that's why they camped in the plain even though they were within striking distance of Retro."

"Thruster slippage," said Piper with a nod.

"Did they call you about it before they camped?"

"H'called here," said Piper.

"Cliff's a good tech but a generalist, not a vehicle specialist," said Tate. "W'gave him pointers on the problem. H'fixed it, too."

"Did anyone else in town know where they were camped?"

"Might have mentioned it around. Maybe at the No Limits."

"Kip knew already when y'told the group," said Piper. "Blaze commed him the delay. Sh'calls regular."

Ardra tried not to look discouraged. Would nothing narrow the list of potential suspects? "I'm sorry about the Lancer," she said. "Is there any chance you'd trust me with an A-pad?"

"Y'didn't make it sick," said Piper. "If a Lancer can't fly a corkscrew it don't deserve to leave the hangar, no matter what some authority types might think of it."

"W'got more A-pads than people," said Tate. "Help y'self. Anytime." She bent her head in the direction of the north end of the hangar as her hands stayed buried and busy in the Lancer.

Ardra thanked the Zills and headed in the direction of Tate's nod. With Skrif close behind, she threaded among several dozen cargo crates, walked alongside two more Carriers, and finally arrived at the northeast corner of the hangar and a forest of A-pads.

There was nothing glamorous about A-pads. While straddle machines like Lancers had speed and Carriers had weight-hauling brawn, the A-pad could only boast simplicity. Its base was a thick disc that contained an antigravity unit and minijet thrusters. Off-center, an adjustable control rod rose from the base to form a T at grip level.

Normally, the driver stood upright on the base and steered by verbal command or hand controls. Some units also extruded a second rod topped by a hip brace, but A-pads were used most often for quick on-off chores so riders generally opted for just the pad and T. Top speed was no faster than Ardra could sprint as she had discovered on Metro on foot when she ran down an escaping bandit. She had caught the light-fingered culprit just before her lungs and legs surrendered to oxygen debt.

"It'd be useful to know how long it would take an A-pad to get from town to the Stine murder scene. It might help rule out some people," she said to her companionbot. "I could make a test run while you do a charge session."

"You're not dressed for it," Skrif protested. "You're not equipped."

"It's just a joy ride. A quick out and about. I'd take a canteen, of course."

"But what if the A-pad malfunctioned? Sandals are most unsuitable footwear. If you should be stranded . . ."

"You could ferry me a replacement A-pad. That's why your staying in town makes sense."

"You don't have backup com capability to call me if the power to the A-pad com fails." Skrif cast about for a reason, a distraction, anything that could forestall another field trip so soon after one gone so wrong.

"Well . . ."

"I've just received notification that Journalist Sumner is available in her office," said Skrif. It was true. Sumner, in response to Skrif's com query, had indicated she was back in the administration building.

"Right. Good. I should check that out," said Ardra. "The A-pad can wait. You can pick up a secondary com unit and fill a canteen for me while I drop in to see her holo. Let's fogee."

"Oh dear," thought Skrif as it hurried up the street. "I've only delayed the trip. I know she won't just go out and back. She always finds something more that needs to be investigated."

"An investigation is like a game of sticky sticks," Ardra reassured herself as she trotted off to meet Sumner. "You weave and place and anneal and it looks like a pile of nothing. Then the moment comes and you pull up on the keystick and suddenly it's a footbridge or a tower or a glider."

Re-energized and arrived on the top floor of Administration, she poked her head into the newsroom.

"Wythian, here," she called. "Sumner?"

The room before her was a study in precision. While other offices she'd seen had been variously cluttered with crates not yet unpacked and equipment not yet assembled, everything now before her looked poised for action. A dozen workstations sat evenly spaced one from the other in the body of the room. Around the room walls stood data cube racks, mostly lined with yellow, unused cubes.

There was not a single cargo crate to be seen anywhere. From behind one of the workstations a round, pink face bobbed into view.

"Wythian! Here you are," Sumner cried.

"Expecting company?" Ardra waved an arm at the other desks.

"There's barely enough news for one journalist. Still, I like to imagine myself in the midst of a busy workroom, colleagues to the left of me, colleagues to the right."

"Rooms and buildings often feel empty around here. I've noticed that myself." As she spoke, Ardra strolled between desks until she reached the one with an owner.

"May I offer you a cup and a crust?" Sumner asked, the standard welcome of devout members of the Just Order of Believers, who allowed no guest to thirst or hunger. The journalist held out her hands in the host gesture, cupped palms nested together.

As a rookie back on Metro, Ardra's mentor in the PKF had greeted her in a like manner at the beginning of every shift. Once, having skipped fastbreaker, she accepted his offer, expecting little more than a ceremonial cup of water and a dry heel of bread. Instead, he whisked open the chill drawer of his desk and brought out a decanter of buoyberry juice and a vacupack of brittlesnaps. The man's rare smile shone beatifically as she sipped and munched with enthusiasm.

Today, though, food was not uppermost in Ardra's mind.

"No, thanks," she replied. "You mentioned some outedits, I believe. Do you have a free moment?"

"Now's fine. I was just updating the ob . . . er . . . now is fine."

"You were working on the obituary notices, just in case. Don't worry about giving offence, I understand how that works, even though I'm hoping you won't need to use any more."

Sumner lifted her palms in a shrug. "Of course, death is no stranger to surveying teams. I thought it might be worth making up a little something on each of our local Wanderites. They've become part of the town and, if something bad happens to one of them, it's at least news to those of us in Retro. If one of them were murdered now, given the other murders that have gone before, the event would make the interstellar news bullets. Speaking of

Wanderites, I heard you intervened in a scuffle between Vincent and Cliff. What was that about?"

"Hasn't Sergeant Rosil given you an official statement?"

"She did. She gave her usual—'not now, Jal, there's nothing to report.'"

"I'm afraid I have to agree. It wasn't much and it was resolved peacefully. Sorry."

"Is there any chance you could say a few words about how the murder investigations are going?" Sumner gave Ardra the look of a forlorn shimpuppy about to be abandoned by a heartless cad.

Ardra picked her words carefully. "Sergeant Rosil is the senior officer here on Wanderer and she's the one handling the investigations. I've been brought in to assist in general peace keeping duties."

"What about the new evidence you found behind the No Limits?" Sumner asked, suddenly wearing a smile that could melt the shady side of Planet Kelpa.

"What? Who said anything about new evidence?"

"Word is you were seen behind the tavern. Then your bot was seen with evidence keepers. What about it?"

"I . . . uh . . ."

"Is it something that connects the two murders? Word is you've been asking questions like you think there's a connection. Well?"

"I can't . . . It's too early . . . You mentioned some outedits, I believe."

"Hmm, yes." Sumner abandoned her charming smile, slid her chair back, and stood with a sigh. "At least I don't have to worry about another journalist beating me to this story when it breaks. So it's OK if you're tight-lipped about it even though here I am helping you. Let's go into the viewing room where we can get the full surround."

"Sorry. I do appreciate your cooperation." Ardra trailed behind the journalist who led her through the desks and into a domed room. A thousand thousand Ardras and a thousand thousand Sumners in the depths of the walls and ceiling and floor stared back at the two standing in the middle of the room.

Ardra whistled softly and the acoustics of the room seemed to sweeten the tone. "This is incredible," she whispered.

"Top of the line, full surround, holographic viewing chamber," Sumner nodded. "Our network transmits and bullets the highest quality product to its viewers because enough of them have excellent receivers and we need to be fussy about quality from the transmission side of things. So I'm careful to edit out bad image data before it ever reaches headquarters for final prep." Sumner cleared her throat. "Do you want the outedit at one hundred percent or do you want a small clear section for the two of us to stand apart?"

"The full shot. I've stood in an image before so it's not a problem." Ardra took a deep breath and closed her eyes. She didn't mind being in an image or stepping into one that was already there, but it was a bit much when it engulfed her from nowhere. From without, Sumner's voice ordered a file from the computer, rattling off dates and numbers and code names.

Then she said, "It's on. And you're standing in the middle of Les Lesting."

Ardra opened her eyes gradually, the way she always opened gifts, pulling back only a little of the wrapping at a time. Below her, the white legs of her jumpsuit vanished part way down the shin, their reality visually replaced by the silent torso of the murdered forecaster. Calmly, Ardra took one step to the left and her sandals appeared on the sand next to the body; she was at the scene but she would leave no footprints. Then she raised her gaze and found herself within centimeters of Rosil's fulminating scowl.

"Get away there. You! Back off," Rosil commanded and Ardra jumped reflexively, knowing even as she did that the holographic image wasn't speaking to her. She turned to see Vincent slinking back to the outskirts of the image field.

"She's a presence, isn't she?" Sumner said from her position behind the circle of images gathered around the corpse.

Nodding absently, Ardra began to concentrate on the information before her. The press imaging flies were showing more of the area and the people that had gathered than the standard

PKF crime scene holograph she'd viewed at Eagle III. There was Junior Forecaster Beld with one hand firmly clamped over her mouth and eyes still wide with shock, Tech Daly with face rigid and jaw muscles taut, Barkeep Trudge with his silver teeth showing in a straight line—grin or grimace, it was hard to tell. One hand braced against the wall, Tech Zill vomited noisily while his bond patted ineffectually at his back, her eyes riveted on Lesting's bloodied head. Another woman, an elder Jahanite, seemed to be torn between watching Zill's distress and staring at Lesting on the ground. Her black eyes were so wide they devoured her face.

Doctor Sethline entered from one side and briefly inspected the body; he stood and confirmed that Lesting was dead. No one looked surprised. At the outskirts of the image field, Kafka flitted in and out of view; he wrung his hands and cast beseeching looks in Rosil's direction.

"This is fascinating," Ardra said to Sumner as the journalist came up behind her. Then she noticed that this Sumner threw two shadows onto the ground below them. "Oops, sorry," she said, then looked around until she spotted the real person among the images. "It's hard not to talk to them," Ardra remarked.

"It's only to worry if they start answering you," Sumner replied. "Here's the curious bit, just coming up. It wasn't audible at first but I bolstered it and enhanced it with a lip-reading interpreter."

From out of range, Kafka darted in and sidled up to Rosil. The wiry fellow leaned close to the solid Kelpan, a blade of grass bending to contact a cornerstone. He whispered into her ear, "Do your eyes open for this? Another. It won't stop until all die or leave this place."

"Swallow your words, Kafka," Rosil hissed back. The Wanderite flitted back to hover near Vincent.

"Well? What do you think?" Journalist Sumner, the real Sumner, asked. "It sure sounds like a threat to me. It sounds like Kafka knows something and Ivy's covering. Of course, she'll say it's more of his nonsensical babbling but I think it's a threat. The Wanderites want us to leave."

"It could be interpreted more than one way," said Ardra. She hated the vagueness of the man's words. They gave her nothing solid she could use for leverage in the case and they further eroded her faith in her superior.

"One, two, three . . ." Ardra frowned as she counted the people around the body. "That's odd. Kafka said there were ten in the circle but I count eleven."

"His way of counting threw me at first, too," Sumner answered. "When I asked him how many people were in his clan he said ten. Then he started naming them and the list went on and on. So I asked him how many people lived in Retro and he said, "ten". It seems they only count up to nine and anything more than that is ten. Go figure."

Then a hiss of sound from above and a speeding arrow of shadows on the ground snapped Ardra's head back to look up.

"A flight of eagles!" she cried.

"Eagles you say? No, it's just a late shift of surveying hoverjets returning to Retro."

Ardra nurtured a tiny ember of success when she finally left the administration building. One of the many pieces had fallen into place. The eagles were Realm hoverjets.

Unfortunately, she had a new piece to worry over. Kafka's words re-echoed in her mind—"it won't stop until all die". Furthermore, no matter how many times she got Sumner to rerun the images, she saw nothing that could pass for the ground running in rivers.

CHAPTER 9

One Step Behind

"Faster! Faster!" Ardra urged her steed, only to be reminded that she rode a nag. "If only I had a Lancer instead of this A-pad," she thought. But she didn't, and the pad cornered sluggishly, unlike the grey shadow that fled before her, dodging, weaving, and running with the fleet speed of an Olidan empress lizard. It took all Ardra's concentration to watch the terrain, steer the vehicle, and keep track of her quarry.

After an uneventful ride out to the Stine murder site, Ardra had noted the time of the trip then opted for the scenic route back to town. She had circled west into the foothills that ringed the plain and that's where, despite the gathering dusk, she spotted a lone figure. Short, wiry, clad in a smock-like garment and carrying a lance, a male figure had darted behind an outcropping when he realized he'd been seen.

If this area was territory to the Wanderite, he could be a witness or even a suspect. Ardra gave chase. Unfortunately, the foothills were a maze of gullies, washes, boulder jumbles, and clumps of vegetation. The man before her ran like he knew every turn and she followed like she was blind. Wrong turns kept her from gaining on him. Conspiratorial bushes barbed her clothing, her flesh, and bid her tarry. In a flat, straight race, no one could sustain the sprint speed of an A-pad, but this race was neither flat, nor straight.

If she were aboard a Lancer she could rise higher than the terrain and follow him from above by sight or by infrared. This strategy was impossible on an A-pad whose proximity sensor restricted it to no more height above ground than a human could stand to fall. The A-pad also lacked tracking equipment.

Then, as though he had transformed into one of the rocks, the figure vanished.

"Grime!" Ardra cursed. She searched the area where he had disappeared and cursed some more. Stray whiffs of his scent cluster teased her at intervals, but there was no odor trail to follow. She rode the pad to a high rock outcrop and raked the landscape with her eyes.

Anger, her oldest companion, rippled through her body. It began as a vibration in her toes then shuddered up through her bones like the shock wave of an earthquake. In childhood, Ardra's anger would break to the surface as a tantrum, but as she grew she learned to live on the fault line of her temper. In public she could project herself as a pond of serenity. But Ardra wasn't in public at the moment and that was only a small part of her fury.

"I'm at the edge of nowhere on a nothing planet chasing a nobody," she snapped.

"But you can't chase what you can't see," the breeze around her taunted.

"I don't suppose he'd have been much help," Ardra thought and wished she could believe her words. She turned again in the direction of Retro and sailed through intensifying darkness, shakily lit by the A-pad's headlamp. Her head snapped back and forth as every shadow seemed to move with her passage. By the time she arrived back in town, her internal vibrations of rage had stilled.

"You're bleeding!" Skrif exclaimed when the robot met Ardra outside the hangar.

"Just scratches. Some bushes got in my way."

"They should be treated with de-infect at once. Caution must be exercised, especially on such a new planet."

"This morning I noticed you armed the barracks room with a first-aid kit."

"Naturally."

"I can use de-infect from the kit as I get ready for my shift."

Ardra nodded to Kip as their paths crossed in the street. Hanging on one of Kip's arms was a long-limbed woman dressed in the traditional wavecloth cloak of a Jahanite. In passing, Kip introduced Ardra to his bond, Blaze, the final suspect of the survey team. Ardra longed to strike up a conversation, to ask a few questions, to ask the right questions, but if she did, she would be late for her nightwatch.

"Was the trip to the murder scene successful?" Skrif asked Ardra once Kip and his bond were out of listening range.

"More or less," Ardra replied. "Listen, I don't want to record the travel time in the official case file just yet. Rosil might get awkward about it."

"Yes, I fear she would."

"So you keep track of it yourself. By A-pad it takes about three-quarters of a Standard hour to reach the Stine murder scene from Retro. It took seventy-seven minutes, to be precise."

As Ardra entered her room, cleaned and tended to her scratches, and prepared for shift, she wondered about the Wanderite she had seen in the foothills. How would he, part of a primitive race on an erratic planet, measure time? Before Reunification, the different races of the Realm had used a variety of intervals to count their various days and years. Most arcane among them was the system used by the Tithenites and based on the numbers sixty and twenty-four. Awkward, impossible numbers.

In Standard time there were 100 seconds to a minute, 100 minutes to an hour, and 25 hours to a day. One of the traits all of the races shared was a biological clock that ticked to the same rhythm. Therefore, one Standard day was set as the median time of a human day. Straightforward. Sensible. Orderly. All of Planet Kelpa ran on Standard time, as did Spaceworld Blooh. In fact, Kelpa was the keeper of Zero Standard. The other planets used these time measures in relation to their own days and seasons. Planet Metro, for example, had a rotation day length of 26.4 hours.

"I hope I get another chance to talk with Kafka," Ardra said as she and Skrif headed out for nightwatch. "Now that I know what he meant by a flight of eagles I'm keen to decipher the rest of his babblings. He must be the key . . . I hope he's the key. I can't shake the feeling the killer is a Wanderite and Kafka knows who it is. Maybe Vincent isn't the lamb he claims to be. He doesn't carry a lance and the murders involved weapons of convenience."

"Perhaps Vincent and the other Wanderites in town are faking their odd behavior," Skrif suggested. "Perhaps they mean to look innocuous while they infiltrate."

"A conspiracy to drive us out?" Ardra muffled a snicker. "It would be impossible to maintain such a pretence every hour of every day. Impossible for a human, that is."

"Ah," said Skrif. The robot reconfirmed to itself how difficult it was for humans to reprogram their behaviors.

Despite the early rise and glare of one sun, Ardra's second nightwatch began much like the first. She broke up two fistfights, one in the tavern and one on Main Street near the barracks. Judging from the aftermath of the encounter between Vincent and Sennett, all parties involved would be sheepish and apologetic next morning. How did less than four dozen people manage to get on each other's nerves so often?

Just after the tavern closed and the town grew still, the second sun nicked the horizon. Ardra leaned against the corner of the clinic, mostly in shade to avoid being roasted in her black uniform. Skrif was patrolling the north end of the landing apron and their audilink conversation to pass the time had dwindled to empty air.

Ardra sighed and closed her eyes at the futility of the empty, glaring night, the unfulfilled investigation. Then she fell asleep. Standing up.

The dream, when it came, sidled into her mind with the coy suggestion that it wasn't pretending to be real. Ardra was with her parents as they visited Planet Olid for the Festival of Eternity. Dancers with bells on their ankles pranced in circles under a young tree of ages, a variety of spreading broadleaf that dropped a new trunk from one of its branches every century; slowly it would form a grove and ultimately a forest. Ardra had witnessed such a festival for real as a child and, as a child, she had yearned for the chance to dance in bells. However, in the dream she wore her PKF uniform and she searched the crowd with her eyes.

"Ooo . . . ugh . . . ugh . . . ugh!"

"That's the mating croon of a dire lizard," her father whispered into her left ear.

"I know," she answered. "I learned that from Kip at orientation. We should leave."

The fresh green smell of the tree of ages thickened and sweetened and an overpowering waft of orange blossom made her choke.

"There are times when the obvious must be pushed aside or we will never see the truth," her mother whispered into her right ear.

"You always say that," Ardra protested. "You say it so often I don't hear it any more."

"So, this is where the nepotism begins." Rosil's square form suddenly blocked out the dancers and the bells on their ankles fell silent. "Peddling influence is against the law and I'm here to arrest Ma and Pa Wythian."

"You're just a cartoon in a dream," Ardra said.

Rosil leaned into her face and bared her teeth in a victory grin. "Don't you wish," she said. "But only in your dreams."

Ardra jerked awake just as her relaxing body tilted her toward the ground. She staggered erect and cleared her throat. A glance around reassured her that the street was empty and no one had witnessed her standing snooze.

"Well, that's what comes of a day spent socializing in town and sightseeing in the foothills instead of sleeping," she muttered to herself. Even as she squared her shoulders and tugged her uniform straight, she could feel the adrenaline that had jolted her to consciousness wane. A leaden weariness pulled at her joints. Surely a mirror would reveal that even the skin of her face sagged with fatigue.

"Everyone lies about something." Mother Wythian's voice sounded in Ardra's head. "The trick is to discover who's telling lies about trivia and who's bringing out the monster lies."

Was Sennett lying about how he felt when Cara Stine rejected him? If it was a lie, did that mean he wanted to hide a motive or he just wanted to save face?

And the crew in the forecasting office, Lesting's co-workers, were nervous. Why? Did it matter? How could it matter when identical symbols formed of pink granite pebbles marked each murder scene?

"The trick here," Ardra thought, "is deciphering that Wanderite's babblings. Kafka knows something. I can feel it in my gut. Where could he be?" There had been no sign of Kafka since she returned from her trip on the A-pad.

Across the street, something flickered in the side passage between the cafeteria and Provisions. Kafka perhaps? The muscles in Ardra's hands twitched and clenched as she wished for a special strength to shake some clear answers out of the man. There must be a way to get her city butt off this dust ball. If Rosil would just get out of her face, Ardra was sure she would make short work of the murders; she had pulled off miracle resolutions before.

A closer look at the alley revealed a lizard as the culprit of the motion. It was a long spindle of a creature that periodically stretched up on its hind legs and sniffed high on the wall of the cafeteria. After it had sniffed and shifted along the length of the alley it reached up with one foreleg and proceeded to walk up the wall and onto the roof.

"Go back where you belong," Ardra muttered under her breath. "Stupid lizard." She rubbed her hot forehead and realized a fiery coal now throbbed at the center of her brain. On top of that was the disgusting smell of orange blossom; it seemed to follow her everywhere. She glared at the skeleton trees behind the clinic, then shadow-punched the air, just for exercise, and called for a time check. Her night shift wasn't even half done.

Time to walk another circuit of the town, she decided. Ardra stepped out of the clinic's sheltering shade and was jolted to a stop by the fiery smack of the suns and the sound of an otherworldly scream. Another lizard? Too unreal to be human. Or was it?

After a brief pause, Ardra headed in the direction of the sound. Her ears strained for more information but all she heard was her own footfall. She began to trot. If the scream was human, it was desperate. Ardra accelerated to a sprint.

"Skrif, converge," she gasped out as she ran. "Came from the barracks, south side, I think." As she closed in on the building,

Ardra saw windows open, tousled heads poke out, hands rub eyes. She passed in front of the tavern and skidded around the corner. "PKF!" she shouted and brought the scene before her into focus just as a darkly clad body disappeared around the back of the building. As she'd noted before, there was junk on this path, a jumble of discarded slaptogether, a tangle of old clothing. Ardra plotted her course through it and shifted into pursuit gear. Half way to the corner and the disappeared person, she skipped a step as she realized the bundle of clothing was a new addition. It moved.

"Who's there?" she demanded, skidding to a halt. The clothing collapsed into an inert bundle again. Ardra stepped cautiously over to it. Then, spying a pool of blood beginning to form under it, she leaned closer and searched for a pulse. When she pulled back a ragged hood she recognized Vincent who moaned and rolled over to reveal deep slashes across his arm and face. His eyelids fluttered open.

"Avenger!" he whispered.

"You've been talking to Kafka, haven't you," she said as her hands pulled out the clean bandanna she always carried but rarely used. She pressed it to the deepest of his cuts, on the arm. "Hold still," she urged.

"Wythian com. Contact Doctor Sethline. Medical emergency."

"The ground ran in rivers," Vincent moaned. "Where are your caverns?"

"Who did this to you, Vincent?"

"His shadows wouldn't dance."

"His shadows? Was it a man? Who?"

"In the prophecy, the Avenger makes the land stand still. I want to see it. My friend wants to see it."

"Vincent, try to make some sense. Tell me who cut you with a blade. What happened?" Ardra felt the tickle of liquid through her fingers and looked down to see that his blood had soaked through the bandanna. She increased pressure on the wound and looked up to see Skrif swoop into the lane.

"Give chase," Ardra shouted. "Dark clothes, average build. Male, I think."

Skrif reversed its minijets just as a cluster of barely awake humans stumbled around the corner and cluttered the robot's path.

"Pardon me. Emergency," Skrif said but the sleepy, shocked humans were slow to clear a path. The robot redirected its thrust and rose up, up above the humans, up above the barracks. Then it tilted to and fro as it searched the area for a fleeing form.

"Sethline, here," a groggy voice rasped through Ardra's belt squawk.

"Vincent's been cut. We're on the south side of the barracks."

"Are you going to take him over to the clinic?"

"What? This is an emergency. Do you want me to spell the word out for you?"

"Oh, boiling Jahan! I'm not even dressed."

"Right now, Doctor!"

Sethline muttered and cut the connection and Ardra took a few moments to exercise her vocabulary. When the words had run their course she glanced down at her hands and noted that the extra pressure had curbed the bleeding. Then she looked up and saw Sethline hurrying toward her, a blue overcoat flapping open and shut to reveal shiny black pajamas speckled with gold stars. His dark hair stuck out in all directions as though each curly strand were desperate to escape his scalp. In one hand he carried a bright red bag marked with silver initials, C.S.

"Vincent again," he muttered as he arrived beside her and carefully descended to his knees. "If it's not one thing it's another. The man has a death wish."

"This wasn't his doing," Ardra countered. "He's unarmed and I've never seen him with a weapon. Someone took a blade to him and I have a hard time thinking it was his fault."

"Nasty piece of work," Sethline grunted when he saw the Wanderite's face. He pulled his bag open and took out a tiny packet, like a sugar sachet, which he tore open. Then he sprinkled the contents in the gash on Vincent's face. "Magic dust," he said. "It's antibiotic, anesthetic, and coagulant, all designed to operate in a restricted area." The wound fizzed briefly before its bright red line turned dark and gelled.

"I think his arm is the worst," Ardra said.

"I'll get to that in good time. I can see you've controlled the bleeding." Sethline puffed anti-contaminant powder on his hands then rooted out a pack of nearskin. He opened it and pared off a strip, which he delicately placed along the cut on Vincent's face. Finally, he pulled out a skinsolder wand and ran it along the nearskin to seal it in place.

"The blade that cut him was extremely sharp," Sethline remarked. "Do you suppose it was done by one of those razor-sharp lances the locals carry? Probably some ritualistic feud or one of his buddies mistook him for an imaginary monster."

"Whoever it was had the wit to run when I came along. Also looked a bit tall for a Wanderite. I only caught a glimpse, though."

"Hmm. I saw Kafka darting up the barracks spiral to the second floor when I came out of my room."

"Kafka usually doesn't carry a lance either. Did you see him with a blade of any kind?"

"No. But I didn't get a very good look at him."

"What was he wearing?"

"Didn't notice. Here, let me cut the sleeve up one side before you release the pressure on his arm." Sethline leaned in while Ardra tried to tilt the arm and still maintain her grip on the wound.

"Hang in there, Vincent," she said. The man's eyelids fluttered open and closed as he struggled for consciousness.

"When are you going to start taking care of yourself, Vee?" Sethline asked. "I'm sure getting tired of seeing so much of you."

"The light hurts my eyes but the stars are risen."

"There you go seeing things, again," Sethline muttered.

"No," Ardra said. "He's looking at the stars on your pajamas." Sethline didn't reply but the backs of his ears blushed pale as he bent low over Vincent's arm. He pulled out another packet of magic dust and tore it open.

"OK, release the arm. Here, help me peel back the cloth."

Ardra tried to help but her fingers kept going stiff. Blood around a murder victim was bad enough. Blood from a living, breathing, moaning person was too much.

"Hold still, Vincent," she snapped.

"There we go," Sethline said. He finished dumping the contents of the packet along the arm and it fizzed and discolored until Ardra thought she might have to sit with her head between her knees. Instead, while her hands cradled Vincent's arm so Sethline could apply the nearskin, her mind scurried into the maze of the murders.

To begin, she contemplated whether this attack on Vincent was related to the two murders. It might be a wild leap of logic but, given the track record of the planet, such a leap was worth considering. The use of a weapon set it apart from the common fistfight.

A motive for attempting to kill Vincent took a bit of scrounging, though. Greed was out because the man possessed absolutely nothing other than the foul rags on his back. Jealousy? He had been a loner from her observations, but it was worth checking with the town gossip. Fear? That seemed to be the best possibility if he, as a Wanderite, was able to slip in and out of shadows like Kafka. Perhaps he had seen or overheard something dangerous. Now if she could only get a coherent answer out of him. Or Kafka. Anyone.

"Done." Sethline sat back on his heels and dusted his hands. "You'd hardly know what all the fuss was about. If you'll just call over a stretcher we can get him to the clinic and I can get back to bed."

"We'll need a medical report from you for the PKF records while it's still fresh in your mind."

Sethline's shoulders slumped but he nodded in reply. Ardra activated her com and ordered an autostretcher be dispatched to their location. Then something in the shadow under a pile of discarded slaptogether caught her eye. She stood and let the dark corner pull her toward it.

"Pink granite," she whispered after she had bent down and confirmed the sight. Three pebbles lay under the edge; they formed half of a curve of one of the symbols that had been found at both murder sites.

"You're dismissed to your beat, Wythian," rasped a voice from behind her. She turned to face Rosil, forensic flies at her shoulder and etched stone for an expression.

"Excuse me?"

"I've secured the crime scene. File your report before you go off duty but, for now, I want you back on your beat."

"I . . ."

"And get yourself cleaned up. You're a disgrace to the uniform." Wordlessly, Ardra stared down at her hands, covered with drying blood and starting to clench involuntarily. There were also damp spots on her uniform where dust had begun to cling. She lifted her face to look Rosil in the eye.

"There's some interesting evidence under that pile of slaptogether. And Kafka was seen nearby shortly after the attack."

"You're dismissed."

"Yes, Sergeant." Ardra marched out of the alleyway, sidestepped the arriving stretcher, and entered through the front door of the barracks. Other residents trickled back in from the commotion, exchanged a few muttered comments, and returned to their south end rooms. No one had stirred from the north side of the building.

"If the breeze hadn't been behind me, if my nose hadn't been clogged with that oversweet orange blossom scent I might have picked up a scent cluster from the fugitive," Ardra thought. By the time the cloying orange blossom scent had lifted and released her acuity of smell, the area was contaminated by the scents of all the newly-arrived gawkers from the barracks.

"Grime!" she said to no one, to herself, to Eternity. She entered her room and ordered a basin of suds from the bathroom. By the time she had pulled off her soiled tunic, bubbles were popping on a mound of foam in the sink. Behind her, the outer door opened and Skrif entered.

"I have failed," said the robot. "There was no one to be seen in flight."

"It's too bad I had to stop to render first aid," Ardra said as she plunged her hands into the suds and began scrubbing. "We might have been able to work a pincer action on the runner."

"Why did Sergeant Rosil dismiss you from the scene?"

"The attack might be related to the murders. In fact, it probably is." Ardra pulled her hands out of the discolored water and toweled them dry as she explained about the embryonic symbol of pebbles.

"But if the murders are to make us leave, why attack a Wanderite, one of their own?"

"Maybe he knows something. Maybe he can implicate the murderer." Tossing the towel on the counter, Ardra walked out of the bathroom and rooted in the closet for a clean tunic.

"Strangled, clubbed, cut," said Skrif. "Each method of violence is different."

"True. Maybe that's of significance to the killer. There's only the timing and the symbols to tie them together."

"They all happened at night, too. One wonders if that's important."

"Our version of night, that is. We're under sunlight right now and Kafka mentioned seeing two shadows after Lesting's murder. Records confirm that both suns were up then."

"Was it dark when Surveyor Stine was killed?"

"Of course. Er, actually, I'm not sure. The report gave the time of death not the state of sunlight, but I've assumed so in all my questioning to date and no one has contradicted me. What do the records say?" Ardra fastened her equipment belt over her fresh tunic and paused while Skrif communed with the forecasting records via the Repositor.

"Dark. That's confirmed."

"That could explain how an outsider caught Stine by surprise if the murderer wasn't one of her team-mates. It's only Tithenites who have outstanding night vision, not Carrians. I want to talk to Vincent and I want to talk to Kafka. I'm going to the clinic." Ardra headed for the outer door.

"I shall try to locate Kafka," said Skrif.

Outside the barracks, only a few onlookers remained; in a tiny knot they stood quietly near the mouth of the alleyway. A round sentrybot, shock arm extended, hovered between them and the crime scene. Behind the civilians, Rosil presided over a swarm of busy forensic flies. Ardra inventoried the crowd as she passed; she took particular note of Blaze and Kip, each with an arm tightly wrapped around the other.

A whistling lizard, perched on the top of an unlit street lamp, began to sing. On her way to the clinic Ardra looked up and marveled at the silhouette of its neck fan and webbed toes as it raised its front feet to the sky and vocalized. Its voice had the clarity of a pan flute in perfect pitch; sometimes it even seemed to harmonize with itself. Despite herself, Ardra began to hum a counter melody to the lizard's song.

When she reached the level of the clinic, Ardra glanced back up the street. Rosil was still out of sight between buildings and unable to monitor her junior officer's movement. So Ardra turned abruptly to the right and entered the clinic.

"The ground ran in rivers. The ground ran in rivers."

"Quiet, Vincent. Try to rest."

Ardra followed the sound of these voices into the room where Sethline had repaired the blister on her foot. Vincent lay on the examination recliner and what was left of his shirt had been cut off. This article of clothing was now a foul lump in the middle of the floor. On the recliner, Vincent's slender chest, beige in color and smoothly hairless, heaved to his agitated breathing. His head and his eyes rolled from side to side.

"Avenger!" he exclaimed, as Ardra approached his side.

"Well found, Vincent," she replied.

At the counter, a busy Doctor Sethline peered back over one shoulder to eye the center of the room. "Oh, it's you," he said. "I thought he was seeing things again."

"I stopped by to see whether I needed to take special precautions because I'd had his blood on my hands."

"Eh?"

"Well, new infectious diseases or whatever. What's the procedure?"

Sethline turned around and frowned. "Don't worry about it. I'm sure there's nothing to worry about."

The doctor's expression was at odds with his words and ignited a spark of doubt in Ardra's mind. She had asked about the blood as an excuse to enter the clinic and now she was starting to worry like Skrif. Forget it!

"The ground ran in rivers," Vincent repeated.

"Did you see it?" Ardra asked. "What did it look like?"

"It ran. It ran. Kafka saw it. Kafka sees."

"Was Kafka there?"

"The Speaker is everywhere."

"Who cut you, Vincent?"

"The one who sees not."

"Who sees not? What did he look like?"

The Wanderite's eyes rolled back in his head to reveal whites heavily streaked with red lines.

"I know you want to get to the bottom of this, but could you please question him later? I'm trying to get him to rest," Sethline said.

"Sorry," Ardra said. "He's never made much sense before. I don't know why I expected he would be coherent this time."

"He's too much a Wanderite and too heavily addicted to booster. Let me know if you feel odd at all," the doctor said as Ardra made her exit.

"I haven't felt normal since I got here," she muttered back over her shoulder.

"The ground ran in rivers." Vincent's wail followed her out the front door.

CHAPTER 10

Questions

"Rainbows!" Ardra cursed under her breath as she stomped up the street. Flashes of magenta and peach and lime stabbed in her memory. Rosil had abandoned the gold-flecked polish for the latest in color streaks and her nails had flaunted themselves at Ardra as the two PKF members confronted each other in the station at the end of nightwatch.

"When are we going to bring Kafka in for an official interrogation into the attack on Vincent?" Ardra had asked with a forced calm.

"There's no cause to bother him."

"He was seen in the area at the time of the attack. Sethline saw him."

"The doctor wasn't the least bit sure what he saw."

"He was sure he'd seen Kafka when I talked to him right after the attack. His only uncertainty was whether Kafka was carrying anything."

"I've had a word with Kafka and he has nothing to add to our investigation."

"Whatever he said should go on the record. He always talks in riddles and, when we figure out the code of what he's saying, we'll probably have the answer to everything right in front of us." By this point Ardra had struggled to keep from shouting and pounding a fist on something. "Didn't you see the pebbles? They were the same as the ones that marked the murders."

"The forensibots found a total of three pebbles, not enough to form even one symbol and not in any recognizable pattern. They were probably strays."

"Strays? How can you say that?"

"You're so young, so naive. You can't possibly believe you were sent here to be of any significance to the investigation."

Then Ardra had to leave, too angry to trust herself. Now she stomped up the street and muttered. As usual, she wondered how her two placid parents had managed to produce an offspring with such a chronic temper. It had been toughest back in the days when anything and everything that didn't suit her mood generated a temper tantrum.

"I won't do it," wailed six-year-old Ardra, stamping her feet in a tap-dance of rage.

"Your room must be cleaned," said her mother in a gentle voice.

"Why can't we get a janitorbot like everybody else?"

"It's good for you. Remember the proverb of our ancestors, 'Without bones, no child stands tall.'"

"I already have bones, see?" Young Ardra stilled her feet, held up her arm, and poked at the bones in her forearm.

"I see those bones," said her mother. "But the important bones are the ones you can't see. To make them strong you'll clean your room for me today so that when you're an adult you'll do it for yourself." Mother Wythian smiled as she spoke. She was so patient, so Olidan.

Back in control by the time her room door slid open, the adult Ardra greeted Skrif in a calm voice that some ears would claim sounded like her mother. The robot was perched on the counter, clamped into the charge pad and plucking microscopic bits of lint off a tunic. Skrif didn't mention the argument with Rosil though it must surely have been monitoring her audilink feed; she hadn't ordered it off before the discussion began.

"We're not getting anywhere in the investigations so I might as well get some sleep," Ardra announced. She stripped, hung her uniform in the closet, collapsed onto the bunk, and pulled the cover over her head. She was asleep even before Skrif ordered the room lights off. Three hours later her eyes bolted open and her limbs thrashed around under the cover. For the next hour she tried to ignore her wakefulness and count herself back to sleep but finally she surrendered and ordered the room light up.

"That was insufficient sleep," Skrif remarked when Ardra sat up on the bunk.

"No kidding," she growled. "I can't get my mind to shut off and all the evidence and testimony and conflicting opinions of the case keep spinning around inside my skull. Something's nagging at me that the answer is in the information I already have. It makes me remember evenings around the meal table at home and my mother would say, for the hundredth time since I'd been keeping count, that sometimes you have to push aside the obvious to reach the truth."

"An accomplished detective, your mother."

"So what's obvious? What shall we push away?"

"In my analysis, all the facts are obvious."

"Maybe the obvious thing that we should be ignoring is a need for motive. Kafka has no motive for the killings and the attack but he also has no alibis, an ability to move more silently than a shadow, and an intimate knowledge of Wanderite symbols and customs. Rosil's been doing such a good job of shielding the fellow, it's a wonder she hasn't obliged him with an alibi or two."

"Isn't he a bit small in stature to be bludgeoning a big man like Lesting and strangling someone as fit as Stine?"

"He's small but he's wiry. Besides, Lesting could well have been taken by surprise and Stine must have been." Ardra flopped back on the bed and stared up at the ceiling as she considered Kafka. On the surface, he looked like the best candidate. But something didn't feel right.

"I'm too hungry to sleep. That's the problem," Ardra finally announced.

"I could fetch you a light snack, suitable for bedtime," said Skrif. "Perhaps a measure of lulltime tea would settle you." The robot disconnected from its charge pad and lifted into the air. It paused expectantly.

"No, don't bother." Ardra was too restless and too hungry, of a sudden, to linger on her bunk. She pulled on a pair of coveralls, pushed her feet into sandals, fingered her hair back, and headed out.

"Perhaps it would soothe you to play your anchoran . . ." Skrif's voice was cut off by the closing door. The robot wavered, wanting to follow, needing to finish its recharge. In the end, Skrif re-assured itself that Ardra would be safe along Main Street and in the cafeteria during the working daytime, and she would need backup more during her nightwatch. It returned to its charge pad, wishing she would wear her audilink whenever she stepped out of her companionbot's presence. What if an emergency arose and she was unable to summon the robot's help? It was too terrible to imagine.

When Ardra entered the cafeteria she was disappointed to see that ayduck eggs were not on offer. Indeed, none of the choices appealed to her. They were nutritious, solid, boring choices. The special of the meal was Eifen beets, fillet of Waddington, and mashed turpeens.

"Beets and turpeens? I'd rather eat dirt," she muttered as a shudder passed through her shoulders.

From behind her, a voice said, "There's always second choice." Ardra turned to see Blaze Myro, hands stuffed in the pockets of dusty coveralls, her ruddy face covered with more dust.

"Nutritional paste is a choice? Not for me, I'm afraid," Ardra replied. "You're here alone? Where's Kip?"

"He's working on orientation updates and I'm on late noonmeal break. I heard Eifen beets were the special. Eifen beets are my favorite."

"As a child I used to think only parents and other masochists liked Eifen beets. Still, they're supposed to be the most nutritious vegetable, gram for gram. I eat them occasionally as a test of character."

Together, Ardra and Blaze approached the dispenser. In turn, they submitted their identity tabs and ordered the main meal.

Blaze requested a double helping of beets while Ardra asked for a half order; there was a limit to how severely she wanted to test her character.

"What are you working on these days?" Ardra asked while the chefbox hummed and glubbed over their orders.

"We're sorting samples brought back from the Century Shield. And we're doing more detailed analyses to confirm mineral richness."

"Century Shield?" Ardra asked, "Where's that?"

"North and west of Retro."

"Ping!" The serving door on the dispenser slammed open and a mechanical arm thrust out two trays of food. Ardra breathed deeply of the steam.

"It always smells so much better than it tastes."

"The beets? Yeah, they do smell good, don't they? You want to sit by the window?"

They strolled over to one of the many empty tables in the cafeteria and sat down facing each other over its mirrored surface.

"So, you were saying the samples were rich?" Ardra asked as she organized her utensils and glanced briefly out at the dark day. Weird.

"All the samples are richer than rich. This planet's no vacation destination like Celestia, but it'll draw miners from every corner of the Realm. Once the diggers hear about it there'll be no keeping them off the planet."

"Does Trudge know how rich it is?"

"Trudge knows everything, I'm sure. But he's hung up his crack impacter, you know." The moment Blaze finished her sentence she packed a fork load of diced beets into her mouth. As she chewed, crimson juice threatened to trickle from the corners of her mouth and she blotted at it with her napkin. Ardra cut a piece from the fillet and scraped a bit of mashed turpeen onto it. Not bad, she decided after tasting it. But it wasn't ayduck eggs.

"If the planet's so rich in minerals, why aren't the Wanderites living in skyscrapers?" Ardra mused aloud. "I mean, the ores would have been easy pickings for the Great Dispersal generation that landed here way back. It's not like they found themselves on a low-ore bog like Tithe."

"Maybe the Dispersal generation had a rough landing. We haven't found any remnants of the generation ship. Who knows what they had to do to survive? If only a handful survived and then they interbred, that could explain a lot. They obviously have nothing like the reproductive technology the Thalians developed."

"Speaking of Wanderites, did you notice . . . ?" Ardra caught herself up with a mental reminder to ease into her questions. She began again, "First, let me say I'm sorry about Surveyor Cara Stine. I understand you and she were friends."

"We were. From the beginning we clicked like we'd been sisters or something in a former lifetime. She was full of zip." Having swallowed the first mouthful of beets, Blaze stuffed in another wad. Ardra cut another bit of fillet.

"Zip can be tedious sometimes," Ardra commented. Blaze shrugged and jerked her head to the side. "Still," Ardra continued, "I haven't heard a bad word about her from anyone. She was well liked. No one seems to know why she and Lesting split up. Do you?"

"She never said, but I think she finally figured out that the good qualities she saw in him at first were only mirages. The man had the personality of a swamp swine." Blaze paused to muffle a burp with her napkin. "They were like night and day, or I suppose I should say darkness and sunlight."

"Then after Stine and Lesting split, Sennett started wooing her?"

"In town he pestered her constantly, but on the job he was totally professional. Bizarre how he could turn it on and off." Blaze's black eyes darted briefly as she spoke. Then she shoveled in more beets.

"Word is she was involved with someone else. Any idea who?"

"Lute. That's Botanist Cullen." Blaze spoke around the beets. "Cara told you?"

"She didn't have to tell me." The Jahanite swallowed her mouthful, became aware that fingers drumming on the table were her own, and stilled her hand.

"I heard a rumor she was involved with someone bonded. Did your bond, Kip, show any interest in Cara?"

"Kip?" Blaze laughed, a short, harsh bark. "Never. People are throwing mud all over the place. I don't know why it isn't obvious to everyone that these crazy locals are behind it all. It has to be something the Wanderites are doing. You know there's more to them than a few town derelicts."

"There's the problem of motive." Ardra pushed the diced beets back and forth on her plate; the tines of her fork turned scarlet. She kicked herself mentally for not wearing her audilink. She would have to remember this conversation and repeat the key parts to Skrif for their records. Then again, sometimes people were less forthcoming when they saw an audilink pickup across from them.

"A motive for the Wanderites?" Blaze mused. "For starters there's the value of deposits on this planet, worth quads by quads of credits, I'd say. But I don't think they need a motive. Once I saw Vincent beating on his arm with a stone. He was just sitting in the dust in front of the No Limits, no expression on his face, pounding away. Well, I took his rock away and carted him over to the clinic, but got no thanks from him and no explanation either."

"Neither victim was killed with a lance and that's their weapon."

"Are you going to eat those?" Blaze had finished her beets and now eyed the mound on Ardra's plate. The officer shook her head and scraped them onto the surveyor's dish.

"I thought Les was right about the Wanderites," Blaze continued. "And I told him so. We were just starting to get some support from the other surveyors when Les was killed. There's no way that was just a coincidence so I'm keeping a low profile. I don't want to be the next name on the native hit list."

"Do you feel you're in danger?" Ardra asked.

"Not as long as I keep my head down."

Blaze packed another wad of beets into her mouth and Ardra looked down to find her own fork pushing her barely-nibbled fillet back and forth on the plate. She had been hungry when she came in, but somehow her appetite had evaporated.

"Did you see any Wanderites around your encampment before or after Cara Stine was killed?" Ardra asked.

Blaze sighed. "No, but that doesn't mean vapor. Who can see

them in the plains or foothills? Vincent vanishes as soon as he steps outside Retro. I don't know how he does it."

"Did you and Surveyor Stine get up together and talk that night?"

"If Cliff said he heard us talking, he was dreaming."

"He said he was sound asleep. Were you up?"

"Wish I had been. Wish I could have stopped it." Blaze turned her face away and, for an instant, was completely still.

"So tell me . . ." Blaze began. Her eyes tried to meet Ardra's but they dropped away and darted around the room. "How's the official investigation going?" One of her shoulders twitched.

"I can't really discuss it."

"But is progress being made? When will we be able to stop checking behind ourselves all the time?"

"Blaze, is there anything you can tell me about Cara's death? Any small thing?"

Blaze sighed and stared down at her empty plate. "It was terrible," she said. "In the morning. We found her." Then the Jahanite jumped to her feet and snatched up her meal tray.

"I need a scrubbing," she said and almost ran from the table.

"Hmm," Ardra thought as she watched the surveyor hurry away. "Is she upset because she lost a friend or because she feels guilty? I've never seen a Jahanite twitch like that. I wonder if she's picked up the Eifen mannerisms of her bond? If not, she's the most nervous of all the suspects."

Twilight colored the sky grey when Ardra walked out of the cafeteria. She considered the direct, civilized route to the barracks up Main Street but a nagging doubt made her need to prove to herself she wasn't a shimpuppy. She opted for the circle route to her room and walked up the alley between the clinic and Administration then pressed on, through a thin line of skeleton trees where she picked up a natural trail that led up the west side of town to the back of the barracks.

A light breeze swirled and switched in direction, now south, now north, now in-between. When it came from the north, the air carried a new human scent cluster to Ardra's nose, so she wasn't surprised to round a clump of hookbush and discover company.

On a wind-worn rock sat an elder Olidan woman dressed in traditional rapcloth, a loose-woven fabric with leather seams. The olive mottlings of the woman's face were much disrupted by creases, and her hair lay down her back in a long, black braid, the customary solution to an Olidan's unruly curls. She looked to the west, away from the town, with an expression that said she was watching a drama unfold. Ardra followed her gaze but saw only emptiness.

"How be the meal?" the woman asked. Obviously, her sense of smell was as keen as any youth if, in swirling winds, she could pick up the faint food odors that clung to the PKF officer.

"Fine if you like Eifen beets," Ardra replied. "Myself, I prefer the heritage beets like Ruby Princess."

"Foods unrelated but for the name. Our name's Elya Udell and we're the team anthropologist." The woman continued to watch the invisible show to the west. "T'were fine news to hear that the powers were sending you here, Ardra. Here we were wondering if anything would ever be done about Cara's death and news came that another collar was on her way. Then someone said it be a Wythian and we relaxed."

The woman's speech, dress and manner all proclaimed her to be Olidan born and raised. The Olidan language had no singular form for the first person pronoun; there was no "I", only "we" and its use spilled over into Standard. However, her use of the familiar name was puzzling, considering they were meeting for the first time.

"We've heard a lot about you," said Udell.

"Yes, I've seen that word spreads fast in Retro," Ardra replied.

"Not from Retro, from family. You're kin. Father was a Wythian before he bonded and took the Udell name. T'was his sister, Kenna, and her bond who emigrated from Olid to avoid the child limit."

"Kenna Wythian is my mimima—my mother's mother's mother." Ardra added the explanation of the title, in case Udell didn't use the Oursonian shorthand for kin.

"Kenna started her own thread of Wythians on Planet Metro."

"Sorry, I didn't realize there were Udells in the family."

"Nor would you. You're three generations removed from Olid and its ways. But you still carry the family name through the matriarchal line. Not all Olidans born on other worlds keep to that tradition. So many of the races carry the name through the father that it seeps in and erodes the lines on other planets."

"Wythian's a proud name," said Ardra, who often needed to reign in her pride when it came to family and family accomplishments.

"And you wear your name well," said Udell.

"As far as Cara Stine's murder is concerned, you know, the PKF never gives up on a murder case," Ardra said.

"So it's told, but those that be near to the victim want it resolved, not kept open. We know Ivy Rosil, how she works."

"Really?"

"T'were like yesterday when we knew her first. Rosil was a chief then and working with a team investigating corporate wrongdoing on mining outposts. They flitted in to outpost Melsa twelve where we were doing hospital time for a wee scrape. Undercover and posing as investors, they were, and not convincingly to our eye. She flashed a lot of money around the bars and shops while she was there and nobody was thinking it was from the PKF expense allowance. Word was, they never did gather evidence enough for a charge. Us, we don't know how she dropped from chief to sergeant, but it's no surprise."

Ardra scraped through her mind for something positive to say about Rosil; even though she chafed and complained about the sergeant, Rosil was in command and a PKF colleague. All Ardra could manage was, "I'm sure she wouldn't let her personal life interfere with the investigation." But Ardra was not sure.

"It's you we're sure of," Udell responded.

"From what you've learned of the Wanderites, do you think either victim could have been killed by one of the locals?" Ardra asked.

Udell shrugged. "It's certain they know more about the deaths than we do. Here we've talked mostly with the Wanderites in

Retro—Kafka, Vincent, and Elmo. There's hint in ancient Dispersal records of races whose language didn't even have words for murder and violence because such matters were alien to their culture and counter to survival. The Wanderites don't use the words either in their own tongue but it's possible that's more a matter of avoidance, ignoring the subject, rather than a lack of its existence. They're often making veiled allusions to it. It's the rare, rare society that doesn't know murder, and we've yet to meet one personally."

"What sorts of things might motivate them to murder?" Ardra asked.

"Protecting their own where they see a threat. That's nearly universal."

"Greed, ambition, jealousy?"

"Can't say. We're all descended from the same ancestors, though."

"Can you tell me anything about these symbols?" Ardra asked. She squatted down and sketched the dotted ellipse, the esses, and the bent triangle in the sand.

"Where have you seen them?"

"I'm not sure I should say . . ."

"Context is important."

Ardra wavered. It was important to hold back at least one detail. "They encircled the area where Surveyor Stine was murdered," she said, careful to make no mention of the pebbles or the total number of symbols or Lesting.

"Well now! Current use!" Udell looked pleased. "We've seen these only carved on rocks near certain oases," she said. "And the carvings are ancient, more than a thousand Standard years old as judged by erosion factors and growth of Wanderer lichens. They're a sign of cleansing, so t'was explained to ourself."

"Cleansing?"

"That can be symbolic, you know, getting rid of the bad."

Ardra cleared her throat to forestall an exclamation. "Peekay," she thought. "That gives more weight to the pebbles. What badness did the Wanderites see in Cara Stine that her co-workers missed? Lesting, on the other hand, was obvious."

Aloud, Ardra asked, "Do you know what Kafka might mean when he speaks of the ground running in rivers? Perhaps it's an expression that doesn't translate well to Standard."

The anthropologist pondered for a while. "We've not heard such a phrase in Standard," she said slowly. "Do you know its sound in the Wanderite tongue?"

Ardra admitted she'd yet to hear the local language. "Do you think Surveyor Stine or Forecaster Lesting were threats to the locals?" she asked.

"As a group it's sure we intruders are all a threat to their way of life," Udell replied. "Our presence has already corrupted three of their people to our drugs of leisure. They've abandoned their clans to smoke root in our tavern and sleep in our alleys. Our version of civilization may be better or worse than theirs, no one can say which, but one thing is for certain, their culture can't stay the same. Even were there not a fleck of useful ore on this entire planet and no place to farm or ranch, the second colonization of Wanderer is inevitable. We, the daughters and sons of the Great Dispersal, are instinct-bound to blanket the Universe."

"Surely, they could refuse us. The Interstellar Council would respect their wishes."

"Their way is to share. They wouldn't know how to refuse."

"I guess there's always been mutual benefit before when the dispersed races found each other. But this is the first group of descendants who have lost their technology and regressed so badly without resurging. How did it happen?" Ardra asked.

Udell shrugged. "Is it such a loss? Ourself, we can't say it is. T'would be nice if we could get the Interstellar Council to outlaw the colonization of Wanderer. These folk would do better and be happier without our intrusion. Sure there's nothing we have that they need."

"How about sanity?"

Udell chuckled. "What's that?"

"Well, it isn't talking to your wrist or seeing things that aren't there," Ardra insisted.

"Have you ever seen a mirage?"

"That's different."

"Hmm, maybe."

Udell and Ardra were silent for a moment and stared out over the plain. The grey light blurred distant patches of scrub brush and cactus and snuffed out all but the brightest stars overhead. "It doesn't seem attractive to me," Ardra said. "At least I'd like to know why I was seeing something that wasn't there."

"It's certain we'll find out all the inner workings of the Wanderites. We've too many probing minds to leave anything alone," Udell muttered.

"Would you like to see this survey mission fail?"

"Who, ourself? Never likely. Well . . . we hadn't been thinking that way. Besides, there's not much ourself could do to make it fail."

"You'd know enough about Wanderite customs to leave incriminating evidence at the scene of a murder. And if random murders became commonplace, the Council would be forced to re-evaluate contact between our two races. They couldn't sanction a war, nor could they afford to lose a steady stream of colonists."

Udell tilted her head up and tested the air. "We smell a dust squall," she announced. She got to her feet, shook the legs of her rapcloth straights into place, and smiled at Ardra. "T'were right what we said before about having a Wythian here to handle the case." Still smiling, she headed out into the plain; she carried nothing and seemed to be headed nowhere in particular.

A soft chuckle made Ardra aware that she was smiling and shaking her head at Udell's retreating back. Surveyors were a curious lot. They were nothing like the tricksters and self-appointed saints she had come to know on her beat back home on Metro. Was Udell a saint, Ardra wondered, perhaps an avenging do-gooder out to protect the bizarre innocence of the Wanderites?

Then there was the new information about Rosil. If she had already been demoted from chief would she worry about losing her sergeant's rank? But why would she shield Kafka? Did he have a means to blackmail her? Once a chief, now a sergeant. No wonder Rosil was in a chronic bad mood.

CHAPTER 11

Direction

Two hours. Eternity. Ardra stood alone in front of the barracks and sighed. The young Olidan had slept, she'd cleansed, she'd composed mailcubes for the next supply ship, she'd stared at the ceiling of her room, at its walls, out its tiny window. Two hours stretched between her and nightwatch. Skrif, still topping up its charge in the room, had urged her to play her anchoran.

"What's the use?" she snapped, then added, "What's the use of anything?" as she stomped out of the room. Even if she did find the right threads in the tangle of the murders, even if she did earn her way off this lonely bouncing ball of a planet, she would still be stuck with colony duty. Two hours before nightwatch, two years of colony duty. Perhaps two was her unlucky number.

A single sun skimmed low across the northern horizon and flooded the town with red light. It caught Ardra from behind and sketched the shadow of a giant down the street. Next door to the barracks, the lights of the tavern were feeble competition for the blushing sun.

A quick indulgence? With two hours before work, Ardra knew she could partake of a high volatile, something with a quick half-life. She could have a ghost blink, perhaps even some tinsel juice, and be straight and legal for shift. Her feet stirred and moved forward.

The pursed lips of the tavern door parted at her approach and, as she stepped into the room, a whiff of dark ale sidled into her nose and cuddled up to her scent receptors. "Not this time," she admonished her suddenly active salivary glands.

"Have . . . have there been any positive developments in the case?" Kip appeared suddenly in front of Ardra, wringing his hands and hotfooting.

"Positive developments? What do you mean by that?" she countered.

"Maybe there's an arrest to be made or maybe you've ruled out certain suspects. My bond, you know, is . . . was . . . she was in the same team with Cara Stine and was sharing a shelter with her and Cliff Sennett the night Cara was killed. I shudder when I think of it. What if Blaze had been the one to get up for a trip to water the sand? It might have been my bond to be strangled, that's if it was a random attack, I suppose. Do you think it was random? No, I suppose you can't answer that. Sergeant Rosil has been asking questions that make Blaze sound like a suspect. And you have too. Surely no one seriously suspects her but just asks the questions to be thorough. Don't you think that's the case?"

Ardra tried to look around Kip, to pick out a table, to signal the hostbot. Unfortunately, Kip's height and nervous side-to-side shuffle blocked her view. Eifens were the only race categorically taller than Olidans.

"I'm sorry, Kip, but we have to consider everyone," she said. "After all, your bond and Sennett were the only two people known to have been in the area when Cara Stine was killed."

"But my bond was sound asleep; she's a profoundly deep sleeper. I can testify to that, you know." Kip's shuffle grew into a dance and he started to crack his knuckles.

"Is she here? Why don't we join her?" Ardra spotted her opening, dodged around Kip, and headed through the outer bar ring toward the tables. Some two dozen people, half the population of Retro, created a hum of noise and generated a mosaic of scents in the room. Wall speakers added an underlayer of music.

"Blaze is out on a spot check," said Kip as he trailed along. "She and Cliff have been stuck on spot checks since . . . it happened. She hates spot work. They haven't been out on a deep foray since . . . before."

Ardra selected a table to one side of the room and placed herself in the chair with the best view. She could see the entrance on her right, the pit area to the left, all the tables in the middle, and the sweep of half the bar circumference. Kip fidgeted into the chair opposite her.

"Let me buy you one." Ardra lifted a finger in the direction of the hostbot and it swooped down from its raised surveillance dais then wove nimbly among the tables and stray patrons. Its mechanical innards sighed musically as it halted before her. When Ardra was standing the hostbot reached no higher than her waist so even when seated she was a head taller than it. The design was intended to intimidate no one yet still be able to reach the tops of the tables.

"How can I serve you, Officer Wythian?" it intoned, now self-programmed to recognize Ardra and use her name and title.

"Ghost blink," she said. "And?"

"Retro ale," said Kip.

The hostbot acknowledged the orders and dodged through the tables toward the dispenser arc.

"Did you know that Cliff was crazy about Cara?" Kip asked. He was now tugging at one cuff of his airy pink shirt, typical Eifen leisurewear. And, she reminded herself, the color was officially called "blush". She had learned that back during her time at the Academy on one evening when a crowd of cadets took time to unwind in the party dome that offered traditional sports. They tried their hands at the Eifen sport of glowslap, a game of concentration and reflex, that required players to block triggered light sensors in an order based on the preceding sequence. Ardra had led the field with a score that broke the 300 mark. Then a pink-shirted Eifen cadet stepped up to the target and racked up more than 700 points in a blur of motion.

"Acute!" she'd said. "You move like a pink shearfunnel."

"Pink?" the Eifen said as a puzzled pinch formed at the bridge of his hooked nose.

"Pink," she said, and pointed at his shirt.

"This isn't pink," he laughed, "It's blush." Then he laughed some more, as if she were colorblind.

Then Ardra tuned back into her present.

"But Cara wouldn't have anything to do with Cliff," Kip continued. "First she was involved with Les and when she dropped him, she started to see Lute. Some men can't stand rejection, maybe Cliff took the attitude that if he couldn't have her, no one could. Do you think?"

"What gave you the idea that Cliff Sennett was pining for Cara?" Ardra decided to play along with Kip. Maybe he'd tell her something she didn't already know. He seemed nervous tonight, even for an Eifen.

"Blaze told me that Cara told her that he was always pestering her. Not when they were working, mind, but here in town. Here in the tavern he would send her drinks and pipes and bowls. She rarely indulged, you know. Of course, it was great to be sharing a table with her, Blaze always said, because she would pick up whatever Cliff was plying Cara with on a particular day."

"Do you know why Cara broke up with Les?"

"I don't know what she ever saw in him in the first place. He was her opposite in all ways. He was moody and argumentative and selfish while she was cheerful and outgoing, friendly to everyone. There's no one in Retro who doesn't miss her. She was beautiful, too. She had the prettiest smile you're ever likely to see, and her skin was smooth as silk . . . at least . . . that is to say . . . I mean, it looked very smooth." Kip started to wring his hands again.

"Were you involved with her, Kip?"

"Me? No. No, of course not. Well, I'm bonded . . . happily bonded, you know." Kip's hazel eyes flashed and darted.

"Hmm," said Ardra.

"Ah," said Kip. "Here are the drinks."

The hostbot re-appeared by the table, its chest tray extended and laden with their order. First, it used one hand array to lift a blue tankard crested with foam from the tray to the table before the Eifen. Not a drop was spilled and the foam rode undisturbed on top. Then, with two arrays the robot scooped up a slipseed coaster and beverage globe and arranged them before the Olidan.

"Ten credits added to seven credits for a total of seventeen credits," said the hostbot. Ardra acknowledged the charge and submitted her identitab for scan.

Kip watched the hostbot as it left and Ardra watched Kip. Idly, she wondered if he'd been involved with Cara Stine. He didn't seem the type but, if he were, that might have given his bond a motive to go with her opportunity in the Stine murder. Jealousy was a classic and more believable than Ardra's previous guess that Stine's cheerfulness had annoyed Blaze. But if Blaze had killed Stine, why would she go on to kill Lesting? It didn't make sense.

Kip turned back to the table and wrapped his bony, twitching fingers around the handle of the tankard; Ardra noted that he was left-handed. The forensic report on Lesting suggested a right-handed attacker.

With her right hand, Ardra scooped the beverage globe off its coaster and cupped it in her palm. Ghost blink was properly served at core body temperature so it gently warmed the skin that cradled it. Ardra looked through the glassite globe into the grey swirls of liquid and recalled Dispersal planet lore of adepts who could divine the future from murky glass balls. All she saw was murk.

"Well," Kip said. "Here's to fire and firewater." He raised his tankard to the Jahanite toast.

"For Eternity," Ardra responded. She lifted the globe's drinking port to her lips and drew a stream of liquid into her mouth as the air intake whistled softly—F sharp, she decided. The ghost blink slithered over her tongue and steamed up toward her palate. Unlike power drinks such as boosters that hammered the senses, the ghost hinted at flavors, high tones, low notes, then silence. Most of its effect was absorbed in the mouth and moments later swirled into the blood stream where it initiated a frisson that cascaded through the body and out the fingers and toes.

"Trudge really has the touch," said Kip as he thumped his tankard back on the table and wiped foam from his upper lip. "Retro ale is the best surveyor post ale I've ever tasted."

"I'll have to give it a try," said Ardra. "Not before my shift, though." The ale smelled interesting, a dark balance of hops and molasses.

"Tell me more about this fellow, Lute Cullen," Ardra continued. "You're not the first to mention his involvement."

"He's a botany specialist with a lab assignment but an inclination for survey work. He likes to get out in the field even though he doesn't look like the type. Blaze shakes her head over him and wonders how he manages to keep his hands so clean; there's never any dirt under his fingernails, and this from someone who's forever grubbing after all sorts of plants in all sorts of places. He's pleasant, he's good company, and he's good in a conversation. I like him fine. It made sense Cara and Lute would get together because they were both so good looking and agreeable, made for each other, you could say."

"Did they get along?"

"They're both get-along types, she was and he was . . . is . . . You know, I believe they were destined for each other. I never saw a cross word between them."

"Do you know if Botanist Cullen and Forecaster Lesting had any arguments?"

"Les? Well, he hated everyone but I don't think he and Lute had much dealings with each other. No, wait! Lute was trying to get a retroactive climate summary for Wanderer. He wanted to find out what the climate had been like over the last few hundreds of millennia so he could make an analysis of the progression of plant life. Lute and Blaze, who also wanted the summary for her own work, were trying to go under him to get it done because Les had decreed that this was a low priority and had the chance of being completed about the time that weird pillar of stones finished tumbling to the ground."

"Go under him? You mean they were trying to get Forecaster Veray Beld to do the work?" Ardra asked.

"Veray and Murl, yeah that's right. Murl dabbles in more than the tech side. You know, they were always doing work behind Les' back. It was the only way anything new got done in the forecasting office and it wasn't too tough because Les spent so much of his time hanging around here in the tavern. He'd order a booster, then sit and stare at the steam coming off the drink until it cooled down, then

152 PARKER & PARKER

he'd send it back to be reheated, and so on. After a couple of months of this, the hostbot started acting weird because its self programming for his preferences started conflicting with its mandate to sell and turn a profit for the tavern. It went twiggy and started bumping into tables and people. One night Trudge lost his temper and threw it out that window next to the dispenser arc." Kip craned around and pointed to a small, boarded circle on the outer wall.

"Good thing it's built tough, the hostbot, I mean," Kip continued. "So now that Les is dead . . . er, gone and not pestering the hostbot any more to reheat and reheat and reheat his drink, the little server is back to avoiding obstacles and peace reigns, as much as it can in a tavern."

"I understand Les hated diggers and was inclined to call Trudge rude names," Ardra said. She drew again from her beverage globe and watched Kip's eyes.

"Yeah, and whenever he spat filth at a person he made sure there was an audience and the insults were loud enough for everyone to hear. I mean, if you want to know who he insulted, who hated him, who are suspects, I'd say that's everybody in Retro. Of course, I didn't kill him and I sure know Blaze didn't kill him. He used to call me Twitcher. "Hey, Twitcher," he used to yell at me across the room or across the street. There wasn't a derogative term for a race that he didn't use and then he was always inventing new ones. Mind you, he was all syrupy sweet and full of fine words whenever he had to deal with anyone of rank or position. That's how he got ahead, we all figure."

"What else can you tell me about the botanist," Ardra asked. The eagerness of every person to trash Les Lesting's memory was wearing thin for her. No matter how foul his mouth had been, he didn't deserve such a violent end.

"Lute? Like to meet him? He came in a couple of minutes ago and he's been sitting at the bar with one eye on our table. You know how it is in a small community like this. Everyone's interested in meeting the new face in town. That's you, by the way. You should meet him; he's right over there. I'll call him." Kip waved an arm and Ardra swung sideways to get a better look.

A man at the outer circle of bar picked up his goblet, stood, and headed for one of the gaps allowing entry to the area of tables. He was just under two meters in height and his movements were smooth and relaxed. As he got closer to the table Ardra noticed softly curled dark hair, caramel-colored skin and features that curved into each other to form a smooth whole rather than a collection of parts. His smile showed even, sparkling teeth and no hint of guile.

"He's a pretty boy," Ardra thought. "Not my type." Then the ghost blink must have caught up with her because her mind turned a giddy pirouette.

Kip introduced the two and Lute pulled a third chair over to the table and joined them. Ardra wiped her palms on the fabric over her knees, under the table, out of sight.

"Isn't Wythian the name of the PKF Academy on Placidon?" Lute asked.

"Named after my mimilo. The badge is in the blood," she replied.

"Let's see," he mused. "That's your mother's mother's brother, which is your mother's uncle, or your great-uncle. Acute! Glad you're here."

They talked briefly about Placidon, the planet of higher learning where Lute had studied botany, Kip had schooled in political science, and Ardra had trained in countering the art of crime.

"So which of the party domes did the PKF cadets shut down?" Lute asked when talk turned to recreation after study hours.

"It varied," Ardra shrugged. "The Super Gee was pretty popular." She smiled at the memory of herself and Dilli making a contest even of their recreation.

Party domes on Placidon were huge bubbles decorated with multicolored lights and standing on stilts over the water in the shallowlands. Each one catered to a particular taste, such as dancing, blasting, giggling, sport, meditation, or spending an evening in quiet conversation. Then there was the Super Gee, a bubble crammed with all the latest twisting, shaking, scream-inducing machinery that the warped minds of the Realm could devise. There were simulators that made you feel like you were being hurled about but you weren't, and then there were the real things bearing names like "The Hammer", "Twist and Shout", and "Eyeball Sucker". The ongoing contest with Dilli was to see who could take the most of the worst rides in succession and still ambulate, feet only, to the next one.

"You'd never get me in there again, not for anything," Kip said. He shook his head and tweaked his ruffled collar. "Blaze dragged me in once when we were courting and she coaxed me onto one of the gentle rides, so she said. Well, my eyes crossed and my lips turned green and I painted the wall with . . . well, then things got even worse. It's a wonder she didn't disown me and leave with someone more bold. Still, I guess it figures you PKF types would be thrill seekers."

"Better to seek thrills in a party dome than on the street, but I suppose the work does draw a certain personality," said Ardra. She eyed Lute and decided he looked like the type to ride all day in the Super Gee and feel nothing but joy. She inclined her head in his direction. "How about the botanist?" she said. "What's a guy like you doing in the raw world of surveying new planets?"

Lute grinned. "It's the best job in the Realm."

"And don't let his baby-soft face and hands fool you," said Kip. "You know, Lute, that drives Blaze crazy. All the anti-ray creams and wind visors in the Realm can't give her the look she wants and there you are doing nothing to protect yourself and looking like you just stepped out of one of Metro's monoliths."

"Good genes," said Lute.

"How many races can you trace in your family?"

"How many races are there? I figure my family has managed them all at one point or other. That is, except for the Wanderites, but that's only because the race was discovered for the first time a year ago. I've a highly cosmopolitan family tree."

"Blaze figures you've got distinct advantages in adaptability," said Kip. "Maybe the Cullens will become known as a long line of surveyors the way the Wythian family is established as PKF material."

"Did you ever think of pursuing any other career, Ardra?" Lute asked. His dark eyes moved to enfold her.

No. Eyes don't enfold. After another long draw on her drink, she answered, "A different career? Never. My earliest memory is of a sparkling mobile that hung over my crib. It was made of the badges of retired greats, and nears, and cousins. Despite its height above the bed I was determined to hold one in my hand and they had to remodel the crib to keep me from killing myself from climbing up the sides."

Lute laughed. "I didn't get started quite that young, but I was a toddling terror around the houseplants. Leaves would mysteriously disappear, leaving only a skeleton of twigs, and my parents could never find out where I stashed them. It's a secret to this very day." He grinned and winked.

"Sounds like a challenge to a detective," Ardra said. Her palms were starting to prick with sweat. Again.

Kip clunked his empty tankard on the tabletop, twitched and peeped where any other race would belch. "That's my limit for now," he announced. "I'm off to a late meeting with the Coordinator and Sociologist of the team. We're trying to devise a plan to reintegrate the townies with their own people. It's a battle from both sides though; the addicted don't want to be saved and the clans won't recognize them as their own. They're outcasts now."

"Good luck to you," said Ardra.

"And good speed in your investigation," Kip replied. He left, casting one last, mournful glance back at Ardra.

Then Ardra and Lute were alone at the table in the quiet half-light of the tavern. The wall speakers throbbed to a Bloohan throat song, one of her favorites.

"I've been brought in because of the murders, you know that of course," she began. Back to business. "Kip mentioned that Cara Stine was starting to be seen with you just before she was killed. Were you involved?"

"I do wish! She was a clever, warm, cheerful soul. But no, she was involved with someone else and I'm not sure who it was. It was someone she didn't want anyone to know about. Maybe bonded. I don't know. We spent time together because we hit it off so well and were great friends for talking about more than health and weather."

"Did she talk to you about Lesting and why they broke up?"

"She claimed that Les was under-appreciated but she didn't talk much about their relationship. I got the impression that he had been the one to break it off."

"Lesting broke it off?"

Lute shrugged. "That was just an impression. I don't know who did what because she didn't like to talk about it. She'd talk about the biology of Wanderer, that was her profession, and she'd talk about the good qualities of each person in Retro. That was her way. She told me I was the most emotionally well-balanced person she'd ever met. I told her she was uncanny." Lute looked into Kip's vacated chair for a moment. Then he tipped his head with a grin and looked over at Ardra. "I wonder what she'd have said about you," he mused.

Ardra noticed that Lute's eyes, though coal-dark, sparkled like a mountain brook in sunshine. They talked further, but she never did get back to asking any probing questions—at least, not any that related to the murders.

All too soon, the clock forced Ardra out of the tavern and back to her room. Skrif was waiting.

"You've left only ten minutes to prepare for shift," Skrif said, its green scan line so intense it outshone the room light. On the bed, her dress uniform and equipment belt were laid out and waiting for her.

"I had a talk with Kip and I met Botanist Lute Cullen," Ardra reported as she stripped off her civilian clothes.

"Did they advance the investigation?"

"Lute claims he wasn't involved with Cara Stine and Kip twitched the dance of guilt." Ardra hopped on one foot then the other and pulled on her straights.

"Perhaps Botanist Cullen was jealous," Skrif suggested. The robot disengaged from the charge pad and moved off the counter with a puff from its minijets.

"Lute's not a suspect. He's guileless." Ardra tugged down her tunic and reached for her belt. "Even better, he's got a plan to ferret out a trail and meet with one of the clans of real Wanderites tomorrow, late morning. He's invited me along. I may be able to split the case wide if I can get the right information from the right people."

"Shall I requisition a vehicle for us?"

"Lute and I will go on foot. Apparently, vehicles send the Wanderites to cover, which explains why I couldn't get near that fellow with my A-pad. You'll stay in town."

"Impossible. I must accompany you."

"If you come with us, it'll look like official business. Rosil will think I'm making a field foray." Ardra pushed her feet into her boots.

"Which you are."

"You stay."

"No."

"Hey, who's in charge here?"

They both knew it was a rhetorical question.

CHAPTER 12

Discovery

"Nothing," Ardra snapped. She was short on sleep, overcooked by the suns, and frustrated. The ghostly voices of Stine and Lesting harassed her mind's ear, telling her she was going nowhere. "Peekay!" she added for emphasis.

"It's only a matter of time," said Lute in a tone altogether too cheerful. "We'll have our luck yet."

Skrif wisely remained silent.

With the robot hovering in close attendance, the botanist and the cop had trudged and trudged east of the town. On foot so they wouldn't alarm the Wanderites of the region, they had searched for trail markers, for footprints, for any trace of the area's clan. In the three hours of their trek they had found sand and rock.

"We haven't even come across any plants that are new for you," Ardra grumbled. She wondered why it felt like she had sand in her boots. They had been walking on firm sand, not the kind to swallow a boot and slither over the top.

"Why don't we take a water break," Lute suggested. "There's a bit of shade under this skeleton tree."

The skeleton tree stood alone in the wasted landscape around them; its nearest kin on any side was twice the distance a stone could be thrown. Normally. In Ardra's current mood she suspected she could hurl a rock at least that far. Not that she would, even though the release might feel good. What if such a missile bestirred a dire lizard, or something even worse?

Ardra carefully checked the ground under the tree for bubble cactus before she joined Lute, already cross-legged on the sand

and smiling. Skrif lifted into a sentinel position and increased its scan rate. There was at least one murderer who might be in the area, there were dire lizards to consider, and there were countless unknowns.

"Fortunately, the desert vegetation is too sparse to hide much," Skrif thought. "Not like Chelidon and its seething masses of trees, vines, and shrubs." Unfortunately, boulders, washes, and gullies, all potential sites of concealment, marred the terrain on Wanderer. Most unsettling.

The two humans drank from water flasks Lute pulled from his pack and they sighed with pleasure at the caress of the liquid in their mouths and throats. Ardra opened her lips to suggest it was time to abandon the project, head back to town, and petition Elya Udell for help. Even though it surely would inspire wrath in Sergeant Rosil, the Wanderites must be questioned.

What was more important, dodging the barbs of a superior or voicing the questions of those forever muted? The indirect approach with the botanist wasn't working; it was time to enlist the anthropologist and be direct with the Wanderites. Just as Ardra drew breath to speak, Lute bounced back to his feet and began to search the area around the rest site.

"Nothing clings to him," Ardra mused. "No drop of sweat, no speck of dust. How does that happen?" Lute was impeccably dressed in dove straights and a purple semisilk shirt. His skin had probably never known the chafe of coveralls. Ardra shrugged and leaned back on her elbows. The skeleton tree that gave her a striped shade was heavy with clusters of grey pods. The occasional gust of hot, dry wind shook the hanging pods and they clattered like dried finger bones. Ardra squinted up as through a giant down-grasping hand.

"Have you found something?" she called over to Lute's hunched back.

His answer was muffled by his turned head; his words were unintelligible, the tone negative. So Ardra put in a system call for her patience program, the one she constructed for herself when her father advised her, "Maybe you aren't patient by nature, but

you can always act as if you are. Kelpans do that all the time, and
if a Kelpan can act patient, so can you."

Ardra sighed, and tugged at the wet black collar that clung to
her neck. She had chosen to wear her black dress uniform hoping
to impress the Wanderites, but now she wondered if there was the
faintest chance they would meet any and justify the amount of
sunlight she had been soaking up with the dark color. Idly she
watched a tiny eddy of wind lift a grain of sand and spill it into
one of the boot prints in front of the tree. Grain by grain, the
desert would erase its memory of her passage here, just as it had
back at the Stine murder scene.

When Ardra had made her timed run with the A-pad out to
the site where Cara Stine was killed, she'd been amazed to discover
that every boot print from her visit the day before had been
obliterated. Small wonder Rosil and the forensibots hadn't recorded
any footprints of note during their investigation. If only there had
been a strange set of prints to alert them to an outsider. If only the
lack of strange prints was reliable evidence that the killer must be
one of Stine's camp mates.

Then Ardra's nose drew her back to the present. Through the
dank smell of her soaked shirt, past the dusty smell of the sand,
and over the tang of the oil on her boots, a whiff of sweet orange
blossom tweaked her nose.

Her eyes scanned from left, a clump of fist cactus, to right, a
few blades of sand grass that formed supple arcs over the ground.
The shape of the sand grass reminded her of the trajectory doodles
she used to draw with her stylus when she was supposed to be
paying attention in history study. They always seemed to be learning
about the Great Dispersal—the Great Bore, she called it. She
couldn't make herself care how many old slower-than-light ships
had left the doomed Planet Earth and scattered through the galaxy
to find new homes.

Back then, her mentor had expected her to memorize ship
numbers and arrival days of all the known races of the Realm, a
task almost as odious as reciting poetry in language study. It was a
pointless exercise. Some of the ships had changed direction more

than once in their search for habitable planets and records were sketchy and had degraded over the millennia. No one had been able to reconstruct the point of origin from the data so what did they matter? It was all ancient, ancient history.

The vision of her old studies receded and Ardra slowly realized that the blade of grass she was staring at was too thick. Then she noticed it was too straight and suddenly she saw its gleaming red eyes. It was a NoName, its long yellow body rigid, unmoving.

"Is that sweet orange blossom smell coming from an ugly thing like you?" she whispered. Something seemed to tickle her brain and she shuddered. What if this reptile really were telepathic, she pondered, what if this creature or one of its buddies had observed the strangling of Surveyor Stine? Was this a witness she could question? Ardra stared at its shining ruby eyes and concentrated "Who killed Stine?" she thought, visualizing the holograph of the victim. "Who killed Stine?"

"It's clear as day!" A voice burst in the air over Ardra's head and she jerked upright while the NoName darted from the sand grass and vanished over a hillock. Lute loomed over her, a smile fading from his face. "I've found a marker but . . . what's wrong?"

"Nothing, it's nothing." Ardra took a deep breath and shook her head; she couldn't believe she had actually tried to mind-talk with a forearm-long, yellow snake with stumpy legs. It probably had a brain the size of a swamp swine louse.

"You had the weirdest look on your face," Lute said as he retrieved his pack and swung it into position. "It was supernatural, almost possessed."

"I was just concentrating."

"So what were you thinking about?"

Ardra briefly considered telling him about her suspicion that there was something psychic about the yellow lizard, but decided against it. If scientists couldn't conclusively demonstrate the talent in people, she'd sound crazy if she pointed a finger at a cactus-munching reptile. Besides, she already tried that gambit with Zoologist Darlis.

"I was wondering," she said, "why this skeleton tree is in pod.

Only two days ago I was sitting under one on the south plain and it was nothing but bare twig. Don't they have a season for seed production? Is everything on this planet a contradiction?"

Lute grinned. "Actually, the explanation is pretty simple. Not all skeleton trees produce pods. There are male trees that produce pollen and female trees that receive it and this tree happens to be a female. The one you remember from the plain was probably a male, but you should have seen others in the area in pod; it is podding season. That is to say, it's a time of widespread podding, even though we don't understand what triggers it. It's not like there can be seasons as we know them here."

"Hmm, did I see one in pod? Maybe. Did I notice? Nope, I had other matters on my mind." And for the moment all Ardra was able to notice was the way Lute's eyes reminded her of the black diamonds in the Coeur Museum's gem collection. She'd worked there as a security guard while taking her preliminary PKF training. That was before the Academy and before she met Haley. Haley and his emerald eyes. Gone.

"Shall we?" Lute asked, breaking her reverie.

"The markers. Right, let's press on. I've got a sudden hunch we're going to get lucky and meet a band of Wanderites just over the next wash." Ardra hopped to her feet, dusted the seat of her trousers, then steadied herself; she had caught a faint whiff of Boolean musk from Lute, dusky, spicy, and so lightly applied he must have used a single microdroplet.

"I hope you're right about our meeting a band," he replied. "People native to an area, especially those who forage, know data racks of information about the local plants. I could learn a year's work in one afternoon of good talk with a herbalist."

"Well, maybe you could, maybe you couldn't," Ardra chuckled. "Have you tried holding a serious conversation with Vincent or Kafka?"

"They can't all be like that," Lute replied.

"I admire your optimism. My first conversation with Kafka was a memorable struggle. He took everything I said painfully literally. I asked if he had a name and he said "yes". Then when he spoke it was all idioms and vague images. He probably gave me valuable information when we talked, but interpretation of poetry was always my weak subject during Basis."

"What sorts of images did he give you?"

"Something about walking between two shadows, which I took to mean that both suns were up when Lesting was killed. Then he talked about a flight of eagles, which turned out to be a formation of hoverjets, I believe. Finally, he said the ground ran in rivers. I have absolutely no idea how ground can run unless there's a landslide but there haven't been any reported. You've been here longer than I have, so what do you think he meant?"

"I can't say I've seen the ground move anywhere around town— not in quakes or landslides. What else might it be? A cave-in, perhaps?" As he spoke, Lute led Ardra to a cluster of fist cactus. The growths were more the size of a head than a fist, but their surfaces were corrugated with ridges and bumps that looked like the fingers and knuckles of a clenched hand. There were four cacti in this group, each jostling a spiny shoulder against its neighbors.

"They're a friendly bunch," Ardra remarked.

"Fists can occur singly or in clusters. Sometimes the seedling cactus buds, or clones, just after it establishes. I'm not sure what triggers them to bud. Not yet, anyway. But look there," Lute pointed to a pink pebble the size of a pea nestled in one of the cactus furrows. "That's a path marker, I bet."

"It must be," said Ardra. The back of her neck prickled with electricity at the familiar sight. "It doesn't look natural. I'd sure like to know where those pink stones come from. All the sand and rock I've seen so far is tan colored."

"Stones plural?" Lute frowned. "You've seen others? Where?"

"Oh . . . ah . . . not along our trail, if that's what you mean," said Ardra and succumbed to an awkward silence.

Lute's puzzled frown relaxed into a smile and he winked happily. "Classified information?" he mused aloud. "Possibly involved in a crime scene? If that's the case, I can understand why it's being kept quiet. The underlying mood of the town still does run to lynching the natives to solve the problem. It may not show on the surface, but people are scared. I think fear is the reason tempers have been so quick to flare lately."

"And here we are trying to get closer to the Wanderites and their pink granite pebbles," Ardra said. "Any second thoughts?"

"Who me? I have a star PKF officer to keep me safe. I fear no evil." He winked again.

Ardra shifted from one foot to the other and swallowed hard. She could feel a foolish giggle rising in her throat.

From its elevated position of surveillance, Skrif observed the two hormone-crippled humans and decided to take the initiative.

"I'll search for adjoining markers," the robot announced. It worked outward from their position in a spiral and examined the terrain for pea-sized granite pebbles in exposed locations. As it looked, Skrif marveled that Lute had spotted the pebble and divined its significance. Despite unreliable memories and instinct-driven behaviors, humans were awesome. Skrif had registered a thousand details where Lute had searched, but the companionbot had failed to recognize the significance of one ordinary pebble on one ordinary cactus.

"From now on," Skrif promised itself, "I'll run a recognition routine to sound an alert anytime I observe pink granite."

After a short time, Skrif located two more trail markers. Added to the one Lute discovered, it was enough to project a direction for the trail. When the companionbot returned with its information, it observed that Lute had found an excuse to take hold of one of Ardra's hands.

"So if we trace back these two branches of evolution," he said as he drew lines down two of Ardra's fingers and into her palm, "we find an intersecting node at the five million year mark."

"Fascinating."

"Should we return on another day to complete our search for a clan?" Skrif asked. It looked like the humans might have developed other priorities.

"Didn't you find anything?" Ardra asked. She reclaimed her hand and rubbed its palm with her other hand.

"Aren't there more markers?" Lute asked. "I was so sure this pebble was no accident."

So Skrif defined the two other markers and the direction they formed.

"That's a line roughly NNE to SSW," Skrif concluded.

"Which way should we follow, Ardra?" Lute asked. "What do you like, north or south?"

"We've got to be able to pick a direction based on more than a guess." Ardra frowned down at the pebble. "Trails usually go from somewhere to somewhere else. Likely it goes from home base to an area for food or water or fuel so the question is whether the stone marks the home side or the objective side."

"I'd put the stone on the home side, myself," Lute suggested.

"Hmm. Hang on for a beat." Ardra dropped to one knee next to the cactus, leaned over and sniffed at the pebble. "It doesn't have any trace of the organic scent," she said in Skrif's direction when she rose again.

"Perhaps it's an old marker and has weathered clean," Skrif suggested.

"In that case, it should be headed to something that hasn't changed in a long while." Ardra drew her locator and took a fix. The instrument took readings from survey satellites and displayed the group's position relative to points already mapped on the surface. "There's an oasis along the direct line of the stone side," she concluded. "Let's try the other way."

"Sounds good to me," said Lute. "It sure is great to have an expert along."

The trio turned to the horizon opposite the pebble side, Ardra took a bearing and they set off. Skrif, elevated and in the lead, focused on its search for tiny bits of granite to fine-tune their route. Directly behind, Ardra felt good as she strode along, weaving around the odd boulder or stubby cactus and holding to a fixed bearing. It helped that the nearskin applied by the doctor kept her boot from chafing the way it had on her first hike. It also helped that they walked in sunlight.

"There really ought to be a sun up during the day," she thought. "It's only natural. Two is overkill, though." Her temperature was already rising from the renewed exercise. She set a stiff pace that Skrif matched from the front. Behind, Lute didn't lag at all, despite his laboratory background and his daypack stuffed with gurgling water flasks.

In time the terrain changed from flat plain dotted with the odd hip-high boulder to flat ground heavily strewn with house-sized boulders, too tall and wide for Skrif to overview from a reasonable height. They worked their way between the rocks, sometimes a tight fit for the robot; it was like threading through a narrow maze. Then the boulders thinned and a weathered gully lay open below them.

A peculiar smell caught at her nose and Ardra stopped abruptly, turning slowly to left and right, trying to fix its direction of origin.

"What is it? Do you hear something?" Lute tilted his head to and fro.

"No, it's a smell I should recognize. Let me see . . ." A breeze tickled its way through the sand grass on the lip of the gully and rose to greet her. The scent deepened. "That's it! It's the smell of deep earth. There must be a cavern or mine around here, and close."

"Fantastic! Success!" Lute cried. "All the evidence we have, all the lack of evidence for active surface settlements, says the Wanderite clans must live underground. The few ruins picked up by aerial surveys have turned out to be ancient and long deserted. So, which way is it?"

Ardra felt her face slide into a wry smile. Once people got used to the idea that an Olidan could pick up scents, they started expecting miracles.

"Down there," she replied, nodding her head down into the gully. It was a safe guess and not inconsistent with the occasional whiffs of deep earth she was picking up.

Lute plunged over the lip and cascaded down the wall of the gully with a skidding of boots and a yelp of enthusiasm. After a pause for one last test of the air from left to right, Ardra followed, boot skiing on the hard sandstone slope. Once at the bottom she walked a tight circle, sniffing.

"Miserable swirling winds," she muttered. "Skrif, why don't

you look for markers that way." She pointed down the gully. "And we'll head the other."

"If we're close to a clan dwelling it might be unwise to separate," said Skrif. "We don't know enough about this new race of humans to anticipate their reaction to our intrusion. You'll note stony bends in this gully. We'd quickly lose sight contact."

"Yeah, I note the bends but there should be a marker somewhere close. Let's be efficient about it. If you don't find something within three minutes, just head back. What can happen in six measly minutes?"

Skrif paused. The companionbot ached to answer the rhetorical question. So much could happen in six minutes, as they both well knew. "I should stay with them," Skrif thought but it turned down the gully and sped off. Perhaps it would find a marker in seconds and they would be on their way as a group.

With Lute on her heels, Ardra turned up the gully. Her nose quested for scent while her eyes raked the ground for pink pebbles. The air fell maddeningly still as they wound around a bend.

That's when the Jex twins jumped them, twisted Lute's arm, and held a lance to his throat. Fortunately, the standoff between the Wanderite's copper lance tip and Ardra's durmet blaster was brief and well-resolved. They managed to communicate, and the Jexes agreed to take Ardra to their chief.

Over Skrif's objections, Lute and Ardra followed the Wanderites and crawled through a small opening in the gully wall. Too wide to follow them, the companionbot remained outside and soon discovered Ardra's audilink had ceased to function. The robot was dismayed.

Ardra was pleased. The small opening in the gully wall opened into a cavern. There, she discovered that an oil used to light the cave had the same scent signature as the oily smudges she had detected at both murder scenes. It was more evidence pointing to a Wanderite suspect.

A third Wanderite, Jexjex, led Ardra and Lute down a disorienting passageway.

"I can't believe we're following this psychotic man to who-knows-where?" Ardra thought.

Then their guide gave a little hop and slowed. "Now look what you've done," he snapped at the thing-that-wasn't-there. He stopped at a fork in the tunnel and waved his lance at the left passage before turning right.

Six paces up the right fork, the ceiling lifted into shadow and they came to a halt in a vaulting room surrounded by a gently curving wall. The surface of the wall was covered with a mosaic of colored pebbles. It seemed to be a pictorial encyclopedia of plant and animal life on Wanderer. Ardra quickly picked out a dire lizard, two skeleton trees, one with and one without pod, a cluster of fist cactus, strands of sand grass, and a hookbush.

"Cool heels!" the sentinel demanded and waved his lance in their faces for emphasis.

"Right," they chorused, frozen in place.

Then the sentinel wafted out of the room and left them to admire the mosaic that encompassed them.

"Every plant species I've logged, and more," Lute whispered, neck craned, mouth agape. "This is magnificent."

"I still can't understand how a Great Dispersal race could have regressed so far," Ardra whispered back. "They carry copper-tipped spears, wear rough-woven clothes, and draw on cave walls. Could the irregular sunlight and darkness really have done this much to them? I wonder if that's why children are never seen on the surface. Probably they keep them below ground to preserve their sanity."

"That herb seems to be important." Lute pointed at a tuft of blue speckled with pink in the mosaic. "Notice how it's surrounded by a larger than usual blank space. I wonder where it grows and why it's special."

"Maybe it's something they eat," Ardra mused. "Some toxin in one of their foods that distorts their thinking process."

"There must be other micro-environments in this region that will support different vegetation because quite a number of the images are plants I don't recognize and they don't look like species adapted to the harsh arid climate so prevalent around here."

"Of course, it could be some genetic deficiency that became dominant in the passing generations. Their medicine has probably regressed with the rest of their technology, leaving them with no solution to their madness."

"I can see two dozen unique herbs just in the first three meters of the mural. There must be lore attached to this work and, hopefully, someone among them will be keen to share their knowledge."

"I say! Those pink dots in the first plant you pointed to are made with the same type of stone that was found . . . that we found marking the trail."

"Do you suppose I'd have time to use my imager to record this?" Lute reached for the straps of his pack.

"I don't think we want to pull out any technology that might make them feel threatened or offended," Ardra cautioned.

"Well, well. Here comes someone different," Lute remarked as a lithe man wearing a dark smock that hung to his ankles flowed in through one of the tunnels that fed into the chamber. He stopped, crossed his arms and lifted his chin.

"Eat my dust!" he demanded.

"Uh, sure," Ardra replied, wondering what he was talking about. The sentinel, who had flowed in after the new man, helped her with this by pushing her down to her hands and knees. Then he put a hand behind her head and shoved until the sand of the cavern floor gritted between her teeth.

Indignation raged against diplomacy as Ardra submitted to the ritual. She counseled herself that, after all, she was the one dressed in black and the locals took that to be a sign of power. So, if this fellow in the long robe were a leader of sorts, he would want a symbolic acquiescence from the presumed leader of the visitors.

As the sentinel released his pressure and she rose spitting dust, Ardra envisioned the lean man before her with his smock caught on the tusk of a stampeding swamp swine. She dusted off the knees of her straights and ignored a muffled snigger from Lute. When she looked up at the revered leader, he was displaying a thin-lipped smile.

"You are called Ardra," he said, "and I am called Jex."

"I'm pleased to meet you Jex." Ardra extended a palm for him to touch with two fingers, as Kafka had in the alley at Retro.

"Ardra and Lute are here to flap gums with me?"

"I am, but Lute is here to flap gums with someone who can name plants."

"One who can name plants," repeated Jex. "Jexjex will take you." He nodded to Lute and then to the sentinel who hopped in the air, yelled "Not now!" over his shoulder, and flowed back out of the chamber. Lute darted after him.

"Lute, it's not a good idea to separate," Ardra called after him, but he either didn't hear or didn't want to hear, and she was forced to swallow a reflexive curse as the sound of retreating footsteps ebbed to silence.

Ardra turned back to regard Jex. He stood with his arms folded and his mouth firmly shut.

"Er, nice cavern you have here," she tried.

With the suddenness of a lightning flash, he beamed. "Our home," he replied. "We live with dancing light under skies carved by our parents and you live with the devils under skies of no substance."

"What devils do you mean?"

"They are everywhere sunlight can fall and they own the planet. It was theirs before we arrived and will be theirs after we are all gone."

"Have you seen them? What do these devils look like?" Ardra slid one hand over her belt and fingered the control panel on its recorder, just to be sure it was on. The conversation sounded promising.

"That is a question with no answer," Jex replied.

"But you're safe from the devils here underground?"

Jex raised his eyebrows at the question. "I am safe everywhere. They have no power over me."

"That must be nice. What gives you that power?"

"Some are born with it and some are not. When children cut their second set of flat teeth they stand before the spirit wall and watch. If a boy sees the spirits dance he knows he is ready to carry a lance to greet the sky flame. If a girl sees the dance she will rise to track the hidden fruits."

"And if no spirits dance?" Ardra asked, trying to keep her brow from furrowing with the concentration required to follow his words as she tried to pull some sense from them.

"Then the child becomes a keeper of home and stays forever in sanctuary."

"I see." But she didn't—at least, not yet. "Have you heard that two of my people have been killed?"

"One called Cara and one called Les. I have heard of this. The devils demanded it and your people had no defense."

"I wonder if you or any of your people saw anything when it happened. Cara was a surveyor and was killed beyond the low hills. It was dark at the time but perhaps one or more of your women were out tracking hidden fruits in the area. Could I speak to a few of your people? I mean, flap gums with some others?"

Jex was silent for a moment or two; he seemed to be practicing wrinkling his nose, and his eyes crossed as he tried to regard its tip. Finally, he said, "There is one." Then he spun and flowed out the entrance he had come in. Ardra hurried to keep up with him.

As she strode along beside him, Ardra eyed the features of Jex and compared the similarities to the other people she had seen in the caverns, then drew a comparison to the three Wanderites who were squatters in Retro. Kafka's round nose was a perfect match for this tribe.

"Do you know Kafka?" she asked.

"I know nothing."

Right. She had forgotten that "know" was too strong a word for these people. "Is there one of your tribe whose name is Kafka now? Probably he used to be called Jex—some sort of pause—jex."

"There is no Kafka."

Ardra had the feeling her question had been inadequate. "There's a man who lives in Retro, the spaceport where the surveyors live, who looks very much like he's your brother. Do you have another brother who doesn't live in the caverns?"

"The unseen are unseen."

"Aha. Ostracized, is he? But he must have existed when he lived here. What was his name then?"

Jex tilted his head and squinted, then patted the backs of his hands together. "There was a brother named JEXjex."

"JEXjex? That's a distinctive name. Is he special?"

"He was our Speaker and now we limp."

"I'm sorry. Maybe we can help him shake his addiction and get you your Speaker back."

"He is where he is."

"But if he came back . . ."

"Never." Jex's eyes widened and darted as he began to make small snorting sounds with his nose. Ardra held her tongue.

Just when the tunnels seemed to stretch to infinity they rounded a corner and turned sharply left through a narrow opening. To pass through it they had to turn sideways, duck, and step over a sill. Jex rippled through but Ardra felt like a rope trying to squeeze through the eye of a needle. When she pulled free of the cleft her ears cringed at the sudden din of several dozen voices talking, laughing, shrieking, and even growling. At the same time a gentle draft brought to her nose the strident mélange of a crowd of bodies.

Ardra now stood in a large chamber with curved walls and a scalloped ceiling. Men, women, and children filled the room. The adults sat on woven wicker benches or large, flat stones; their hands worked at weaving grasses or shelling oddly-shaped beans, and they babbled, to the air or to each other. A group of children played a raucous game of tag. The rules of this game seemed to involve an ebb and flow of the youngsters from one side of the chamber to the other and back again.

Jex led Ardra across the chamber to two women seated on a wicker bench. One gnawed and chewed on a grey stem, and the other turned a round stone in a cupped stone on her lap. Jex pointed to the open end of the bench, growled, "I shall return," and left. Ardra watched as he vanished back out the cleft, then turned to the two upturned faces before her.

"I am called Ardra," she said, trying a smile.

"There are stars on your shoulders," said the woman who chewed and Ardra looked reflexively down at each shoulder. There was nothing but plain tunic to be seen.

"What do you mean?" she asked.

The woman with the stones said, "I am called Keeper Light and she is called Jex-a-jex."

"I'm pleased to meet you." Ardra held out a hand and Jex-a-jex spat on it and giggled. Contemplating the fibrous spittle on her hand, the Olidan wondered briefly if it would be considered rude to wipe it off, then decided that she didn't care. She pulled out her bandanna and carefully dried her palm. "This isn't getting me anywhere," she muttered.

"Is there a place you must go?" asked Keeper Light.

"I'm here to flap gums," Ardra said. "How did you earn a name like Keeper rather than some variation on Jex?"

"The Jex variations are true names, but I did not earn a name when I stood before the spirit wall. All I saw was the rock and flickering light and it is my burden that I did not see the dancing of the spirits. I can never leave the caverns." Keeper's eyes were steady as they examined Ardra, traveling over her face, her uniform, and her equipment belt.

"In other words, you didn't see things that weren't there. Are you telling me that anyone who is half-way sane is held prisoner in this labyrinth?"

"I am telling you that I did not see the dance and I cannot rise above ground."

"But that's incredible. Don't you realize that your clan is run by people who are unbalanced? Why should those who can't see the dance not be allowed out of the caverns?"

"The running shadows would devour their hearts."

"What shadows are those?"

"Your heart knows them." Keeper glanced around to see who was near, then ducked her head and whispered, "The Speaker has told my sister of this and she told me."

"The Speaker? Do you mean JEXjex, the man we call Kafka? I thought he was ostracized." As Ardra stuffed the bandanna back in a pocket she fingered her recorder again. This was getting interesting.

"He is called Kafka now but I still call him father, and even though I shamed him at the spirit wall, he still calls me his daughter."

"Has he told you who killed our people?"

"He has told me that he suffers for it."

"Suffers how?"

"As always he is driven to the smoke you have brought from the stars. He was the only Speaker for our clan and the burden was too great for one man. When I, his daughter, failed to join him in his calling, he started to wander the dry hills. He was trying to run away from himself. Then the star children arrived and he answered the need."

"One of the star children, Cara Stine, was murdered in a plain near our town," said Ardra. "Were any of your people out hunting or gathering in the area near where she was killed?"

"No. No one was there." Keeper's answer came quickly and she started to fuss with the cuffs of her smock.

"Are you sure?"

"Yes."

"You could ask around . . ."

"No one was there." The woman glared up at Ardra and her hands stopped their work and clenched into fists in her lap.

"Maybe someone among your people wants us to leave," Ardra suggested.

"The star children are our true cousins, family beyond clan," Keeper replied. "Our homes are crowded, but soon you will carve your own homes."

"We prefer to live above ground."

"How sad."

Briefly, Ardra considered the woman, Jex-a-jex, who had spit on her hand. Was it worth trying to get a coherent answer out of her when her sister, who was lucid, had yielded only a little that made good sense? She decided to go for broke.

"Jex-a-jex, what happens when the ground runs in rivers?" She hoped the woman would understand the phrase in Standard and had her answer instantly. The spitter leapt to her feet, shrieked and ran to the far corner of the cavern where she huddled in a dark crevice. Even from the distance now between them, Ardra could see the woman's body shaking and hear her low keening.

"Your words have cruel edges," Keeper said. She put down her stones, rose, flicked her smock, and hurried over to soothe her sister.

"There's something you know that you're not telling me," Ardra muttered. She started to look around for another likely subject to question, but the arm-twister of the gully, now carrying a lance, appeared at her side.

"Follow the leader!" he commanded as he tilted the gleaming tip of his weapon at her. She didn't hesitate, but spun and trailed after him as he flowed out of the chamber. For a hundred meters or so she tried to mimic his smooth style of travel, but her boots seemed to get in her way and finally she settled for a high-speed stride.

"Jex . . . jex?" Ardra guessed at the pause.

"My ears flap."

"What's wrong with your brother who was guarding the entrance?"

"Nothing."

"But he was talking to something where there was only empty air. Could you see what he was talking to?"

"There is nothing wrong with him. I see and hear things that do not exist but I choose not to see them or hear them."

"How do you tell what's real from what isn't?"

"When others cannot see it, it does not exist."

"I guess that should be an obvious answer, but how do you know if others aren't seeing it?"

Jex . . . jex came to a sudden stop, pulled his brow down and contemplated the tip of his short nose. The cross-eyed effect made Ardra feel he was making a face at her, but she chose to believe that this was the look of deep thought. After a few moments, he hunched his shoulders and puckered his lips as his eyes crossed even more tightly. She slid her tongue between her molars and bit on it to keep herself from laughing at him.

Finally, the man's eyes uncrossed and he sighed. "When the sight makes me dizzy, it is not real. Usually. If I can touch it, it is real. Usually." He shrugged and continued down the passage until he reached a low horizontal slit in the wall where he flopped to his belly and wriggled through it and out of sight.

Ardra dropped to her hands and knees and peered through the opening to the sight of many feet milling about on the other side. "Backup would be nice," she muttered, thinking about Rosil with her feet up on her desk. Still, she flattened and crawled through after her guide.

"We have heard and we have decided," Jex announced. The leader in his long smock stood before her as she rose to her feet. Several dozen men armed with spears surrounded him, and they all nodded solemnly.

"Decided what?" Ardra asked.

Jex poured a lumpy yellow liquid from a large gourd into two smaller gourds. He picked up the small gourds and handed one to Ardra. She thanked him and watched as he drank from his gourd. Nothing on this planet had been cleared by the toxicologists for consumption yet and drinking this muck would be a bad idea, she knew. On the other hand, there were a lot of easily offended lance tips winking in the trough light in this chamber, and not drinking it might be a worse idea. So she drank.

It was a BAD idea.

CHAPTER 13

The Dire

A swirling, twisting, dizzying blackness tore at Ardra's mind and she tried to force thoughts out at it like hands to fend off a blow.

"Wythian, Ardra, PKF Officer."

But the darkness ripped the words to splinters.

A grey face loomed up before her, flat, square, with vile eyes.

"Rosil," she thought just as an eddy of shadow pulled her focus askew. There were hands clenched around Rosil's throat and they were squeezing and squeezing while the flat face above the hands turned green. Green?

"PKF," she thought. "Intervene." But the strangling hands were familiar and riding high above their wrists were the black cuffs of a uniform.

"This is a dream, a nightmare. Wake up!"

Someone groaned. Then Ardra reached out and started to swim through the waves of blackness, arm over arm, steady, keep the pace steady. She was spinning deeper and she wanted to rise. Even as she could feel her arms stroking through the swirls, the face re-appeared with eyes now bugged out and bloodshot and the skin turning orange. Orange? The hands were clenched tighter and they were red like fresh blood.

"Why did you question the doctor? I didn't give you permission to question the doctor," the orange face shrilled.

"I was just getting my blister fixed."

"Why did you question the forecaster? I didn't give you permission to question the forecaster."

"I was just finding out about the light and dark cycles on Wanderer."

"You must ask my permission. You do not have my permission. You are on report for misconduct. I am in charge. You are not in charge."

"Yes, sergeant. Yes, sergeant. Yes, sergeant."

"Oooo-ugh-ugh-ugh!"

Claws tore at the lining of her stomach and acid burned her throat. "Keep swimming." Her arms felt stronger now.

"Oooo-ugh-ugh-ugh!"

Then the swirling ebbed and a lightning bolt of pain shot through her head. There was a cough. She felt it. Her body had coughed and she felt the air move through her mouth and she felt her chest lurch. Next, she tried a groan. "Rrrrr." It seemed to help reconnect her mind to her body and she assessed her situation.

She was lying face down on something hard and rough. Her arms and legs felt numb and her head was splitting in two with pain.

"Oooo-ugh-ugh-ugh!"

Was that sound real? Hadn't it been part of the nightmare? She sent a command to her eyelids but they were sealed.

"Rrrrr, open!" Then her eyelids slowly pried apart, and she scraped her arms under her body to lever her torso off the ground. She blinked.

"I'm Ardra Wythian, assigned to Planet Wanderer," she reminded herself as she tried to call up her last conscious memory. "Where the Jahan am I?"

She was lying on a flat boulder next to several tall, round boulders. There was a smell of dampness and greenery and another smell, somewhat pungent, that she didn't recognize. It was twilight and the outlines of the rocks were etched in grays. Beyond the boulders she could make out the shadowy fronds of a tree fern, a sure sign of an oasis, according to her orientation lecture. But how did she get here?

"Oooo-ugh-ugh-ugh!" That dream sound again, but fainter now. She tried to stand but found herself back down on her hands and knees, gulping for air and blinking at the darkness that had reclaimed her vision. Then she remembered the cavern and Jex as he smiled and poured out a disgusting liquid. One sip was all she remembered taking, then nothing. Had she offended them with her questions? Had the same treatment been given to the botanist?

"Lute?" Her voice made no more than a croaking sound, and the stillness of the oasis swallowed the name, giving nothing in return. Her throat was parched. So, staying on her hands and knees, Ardra crawled off the flat boulder, toiled around the nearest giant stone, and followed her nose to the water. With each shuffle of hand and knee, she felt an increase in awareness. Finally, she reached an inky pond and lay flat on its shelved bank. She dipped both hands into cool water and washed dust from her face then drank to wash dust and disgust from her throat.

"Rookie choices in the cavern," she chided herself as she dried her face with a sleeve. "I'm smarter than that."

The swallow of water cleared her head a little more, enough that she moved from hands and knees to an upright sitting position. As soon as she completed the motion, she knew something was wrong. Her waist bent freely.

In a panic, Ardra's hands shot down, raked the equipment belt and came up with nothing. Nothing! She clawed at the belt, on the left, on the right; it had been stripped bare and no audilink multiplier, no locator, none of her tools remained.

"Grime!"

Worst loss of all, her blaster was missing. Unwittingly she had armed the Wanderite clan with sophisticated weaponry and there would be reports to file and explanations demanded. Rosil would have her rank for fastbreaker. It didn't bear imagining.

Ardra cleared her throat and filled her lungs with air. "Lute!" she bellowed. "Ahh . . ." she added and grabbed her head to hold its skull together. The oasis was silent around her. Stifling a moan, she considered the situation. If the Wanderites had drugged her to take her equipment, maybe they had done the same to Lute. Even though he didn't have weapons, he had carried more sophisticated items than water flasks in his knapsack. Maybe he was still in the cavern. Maybe her head would stop hurting at the turn of the century.

Then a breeze rustled through the fronds surrounding the pool.

"Ick," she thought as the breeze brought cloying orange blossom scent to her nose. Her stomach convulsed.

A sound that combined a drum roll and a slither came from behind a second cluster of boulders. By reflex, Ardra reached to draw her blaster, but she came away with nothing better than a clenched fist. Her head was clearer now, and she moved to a crouched position and crept up on one of the boulders. The pungent smell she had noticed earlier intensified at her approach. Then she climbed silently up the back of the rock and peeked over the top.

"Dddlllllll," the drum roll sounded again. It was a male dire lizard and a monster, or so he seemed in the twilight. His threat sacs were inflated and every muscle on his burly body stretched at the rough scales that covered it. His in-turned front feet stood just short of a shallow pit in the sand. Ardra could make out a few shadowy ovals in the pit. If that was an egg pit and this was a male, that meant the earlier sound hadn't been part of her dream, it was the female giving the mating croon before she hurried out of harm's way, which was exactly where one PKF officer ought to be going.

The lizard had his head in the air and his tongue flicked out and in as he tasted the breeze. Fortunately, the wind was blowing from him to her and his musky smell filled her nostrils; he was probably unable to pick up her scent. Ardra stayed frozen in position as the dire turned and tilted his blocky head, eyes unblinking, searching for intruders. Then he dropped his head to flick a tongue at the eggs in the pit and she ducked back down behind the boulder. She counted the throbs of her headache as she held still and listened for sounds that said she had alarmed him. There was only a simple scratching.

"Dddlllllll." Ardra's head snapped up. A new drum roll had come from the far side of the pond.

"Huf, huf, huf!" the first male responded.

Now the musky scent of the dire lizard deepened and, surging again with a new breeze, was the scent of orange blossom, thicker and sweeter than she had ever smelled before. There was a frantic scampering of clawed foot on sand followed by raspy snarls and piping squeals. She peeked back over the top of the boulder and saw two shadows become one seething mass as the lizards met head on, reared and slashed. As they fought, their feet trampled the ground around and in the pit and mashed the eggs that lay waiting for spawn in the shallow depression.

"How does the species survive?" Ardra muttered. It was definitely time to leave. She slithered down the back side of the boulder and crept through the rocks, eyes and ears and nose alert for a third or fourth pretender to the egg clutch. Then she stepped free of the stones and fern trees of the oasis and found herself in a hollow at the center of a ring of low hills.

"Lost," she sighed. Nothing looked familiar and, without the locator from her equipment belt, there was no way to get a bearing. How could she hope to backtrack to the caverns and look for Lute when she didn't even know where Retro was?

What to do? She wanted to curse, to strike out at something, at everything, but the throb of her headache was a powerful counter to her anger. There was no sense waiting near the oasis, she decided. If one of the dire lizards survived the duel, he might turn around and decide she was provoking him. There would be little she could do to defend herself against such claws and teeth without her blaster, and the fern trees looked to be flimsy candidates for climbing. The least she could do was climb the nearest hill and hope for a landmark.

Warily, Ardra picked her way up the hill. The grey sky gave her light enough to identify and avoid cacti and shrubs as she climbed, but her skull clanged with pain and her lungs seemed incapable of drawing a decent breath. Even worse were her thoughts.

"Impetuous idiot!" she berated herself. "Marched out in my dress blacks like I was off to save the Realm. Skrif was right, we shouldn't have gone into the cavern."

Speaking of Skrif, where was her companionbot? It figured the robot would be absent now, when she needed its help; normally it was doing all it could to get in her way. And what time was it? Was she late for nightwatch?

When Ardra began the climb, her head throbbed twice for every pace, but by the time she approached the crest of the hill, it had subsided to one pang every three steps. Counting its rate had been her amusement for the journey; it helped keep her mind from wondering what had become of her expedition partner and how much of her nightwatch she had missed.

Then Ardra came to a stop at the top of the hill and suddenly the pulse of her headache seemed trivial. Visible in the distance was the night glow of a town and there was only one surface town on Wanderer—magnificent Retro. Even more magnificent than the night glow was the sight of a green dot off to the right, a green dot that had been traveling at an angle but suddenly veered and grew steadily larger as it hurried toward her. Ardra massaged her temples and waited.

"Skrif, you're the most beautiful bucket of bolts in the Realm," she said when the green dot had grown to a green line in a visor. The robot arrived on an A-pad, tightly grasping the control bar with both hand arrays until it landed. Then the bot let go and delicately lifted away using its own antigravity and minijets.

"Thank-you," said Skrif.

"Am I late for nightwatch?"

"No, it's early yet. I initiated a search for you when Botanist Cullen returned to the town alone. He said you separated voluntarily, but when he arrived and you didn't, I felt I must contact you. I've been running a grid and checking for heat signatures. I lost contact with your com link soon after you entered the cavern and . . . Where is your equipment?"

"Gone."

"Your sidearm?"

"Gone."

"Oh dear."

"Oh dear cubed."

"Repercussions."

"Unthinkable."

"Why are you squinting?"

"I've got a bit of a headache, nothing serious. I probably got too much sun on my walk this afternoon." Ardra put her hand on the A-pad's control bar and paused, reluctant to admit her folly with the drink Jex had pressed on her. "Thanks for bringing the A-pad," she said. "I've walked around more than enough cactus for one day."

"I most certainly agree," said Skrif. "There's no need to worry about spooking the Wanderites on the return trip to the town."

"Exactly."

"Perhaps your headache is serious. Shall I alert the doctor to expect your arrival? Will you go straight to the clinic?"

"Don't fuss. I cooled my brow with some oasis water. The ache's already lifting," Ardra said as she stepped onto the A-pad and powered it up manually. She decided against playing pilot for this ride and simply initiated its homing function.

"Did you acquire any useful information?" Skrif asked.

"Yes. Unfortunately, everything I recorded went with the equipment, but here's what I remember . . ."

Skrif traveled in tight formation next to the A-pad and Ardra recited as much as she could remember from her time with the Wanderite clan; she even admitted to the lumpy yellow liquid. The robot recorded the information in an on-board, personal file.

"So, because the oil they burn in the caverns is the same scent as the smudges on the pebbles used to mark the murder sites, we're definitely looking for a suspect with access to the caverns," Ardra concluded. "That means a Wanderite."

"Or Anthropologist Udell," said Skrif.

"Udell, yes, I suppose. She doesn't seem the zealot type, though. And those Wanderites are unbelievable. It's only the sane ones who stay in the caverns. It's the crazies that run around above ground. Countless suspects."

"It sounds like Kafka is an important man."

"Yeah, important to the clan and important to our investigation. Jex called him Speaker. I wonder what he speaks about. I've got to find the key to make him speak sense to me."

Finally, Ardra and Skrif reached the town. They returned the A-pad to the hangar and headed up Main Street.

"Perhaps you should have Doctor Sethline check your headache," said Skrif as they passed the clinic. "You were drugged and there could be medical consequences."

"It's almost gone," Ardra said. "No need to bother anyone about it. I don't want to create a medical file that Rosil will discover. I'm already in enough trouble with her. Besides, Jex drank the stuff, too, so it must be in some way fit for human consumption."

"I will monitor your health carefully then?"

"Inevitably."

"Does that make equipment replacement your next priority?" Skrif asked.

"I'll have to replace it before the shift," Ardra replied. "I'll need to flex it to make sure it's in top form." She glanced at the timepiece on the administration building to their left as they passed it. "Lots of time, though. I've still got an hour and a half before shift."

"Shall we search for Kafka?"

"Absolutely, right after I debrief Botanist Cullen. Actually, you could look around for Kafka while I do that." Now the pair was abreast of the tavern. "I'll just step in and see if he's here."

By the time Skrif had reversed thrusters and come to a steady stop, Ardra had vanished through the iris door of the tavern.

Skrif contemplated the pulsating bull's-eye of the door and worried. It would be most unfortunate if the investigation became skewed because critical words spoken by the Jexes were now imperfectly on file, reproduced by the memory of a human, a human that might, at this very moment, be most unwell. That nasty substance she consumed might not have been too bad by itself, but she was already sleep deprived and, as always, driving herself too hard.

"No time to fuss about that," Skrif thought. "The sooner I find Kafka, the sooner I can rescue her from the debriefing." The robot re-activated its heat detector and initiated a new search.

"There you are! Wasn't that incredible?" Inside the tavern, Lute sprang from a crowded table and intercepted Ardra on her entrance. Eyes sparkling, mouth laughing, he swept up her left arm and urged her to join the group.

"You've got time before your shift, don't you?" he said. "Let me buy you a round." He wove smoothly among the tables and patrons. The tavern was bustling with most of the town's population, and its hostbot was mobbed.

"You're alright? No adverse effects from anything, I hope," Ardra said as she fell into step with Lute. She swallowed hard as stray curls of rootsmoke and fumes of booster shot straight through her nose and stirred a queasy center in her stomach.

"I'm on top of the universe. Beyond! What'll you have?"

"Spring water."

"You've got time for something more festive than that, don't you? How about some tinsel juice?"

"No, really. The day parched me out and I can't think of anything I'd like more than water." It wasn't the truth. What she really wanted was to lie down in a dark room, close her eyes, and groan herself to sleep. Now that she had confirmed that the botanist was unscathed, the energy that had moved her from the oasis to the tavern drained out through the soles of her boots. She felt like a hollow tree.

Ardra noticed herself wiping her palms on the hem of her tunic and wondered why Lute made her palms damp. He wasn't anything like Haley. Haley would have fussed at her late return, not as much as Skrif, but enough.

"I'm so sorry," said Lute. "I should have left some of the water with you when we split up. I guess I was caught up in the excitement. Spring water it is." He deposited her at a table with Kip and Blaze Myro and Elya Udell. "Same again?" he asked the seated group. The orientation officer, the surveyor, and the anthropologist all nodded with enthusiasm and the botanist departed in search of hostbot or barkeep.

Easing herself into a spare chair Ardra managed a brief smile of greeting to the others. She caught a sniff of nervousness from the table, but it was fleeting. Blaze fidgeted and Kip twitched in

counterpoint and Udell looked like a dictionary definition of
tranquility. Ardra wondered if they were all simply being true to
their heritage or whether preceding rounds of indulgence had
enhanced their behaviors.

"T'were great luck you two had today," Udell said; she leaned
across the table and raised her voice to be heard over the background
babble. "Here we've been tramping the hills for months and only
surface parleys with roving bands to show for it, and there you go
stumbling into the Jex cavern on your first ramble. Don't go
thinking we'll be envious though, any contact and information on
Wanderites be welcome. That boy has filled our ear with his side
of the encounter and we've yet another ear for you to fill."

"I'd like to hear what happened with Lute after we separated
in the cavern. If I can pick up on that before I go on duty it can be
written into my report," Ardra said. She fumbled at her belt where
her recorder should have been then cursed under her breath at the
blank spot; it mocked her. "I'll edit out details of the encounter
pertinent to the investigation and clear a copy of the rest for you
through Rosil."

"We've plenty of time to wait on a copy," Udell said placidly.
"You can't rush Eternity."

"Lute said you were ambushed. What an adventure!" Kip said.

"Just a misunderstanding," said Ardra.

"Got too close to their home, unannounced and all," said Udell.

"Here's Lute, back already," said Blaze.

The botanist appeared next to Ardra, extra chair in tow. He
placed it close to hers and she noted that, as usual, he smelled
clean and looked relaxed. The hostbot, which had tagged along at
his heels, made a circuit of the group, depositing tankard, pipe,
and bowls where appropriate. When the goblet of spring water
thudded to the tabletop in front of Ardra, her stomach sent out a
"No liquids, PLEASE!" message to which she responded with a
tactful "Shut up!"

Blaze and Lute tamped the root in their bowls, sprayed a mist
of highflyer over it, and pressed the igniter switches. A golden
flame arced across the surface of the root, flared, and began to

subside. Lute raised his bowl to the center of the table. "To a day with a great beginning and a better end," he proclaimed. Kip thumped his tankard, Udell raised her pipe, and Blaze spun her bowl. Ardra responded by clearing her throat and calling "Aye, aye!" Then while the other heads bent to slurp, snort, and sniff, she reached out a hand, commanded it to stop shaking, and seized the goblet. The spring water hit her stomach like a rampaging swamp swine.

After a long sighing exhalation of golden smoke, Lute turned to grin at Ardra. "We're a charmed team," he exclaimed. "When I left with that guy who talked to the invisible thing over his shoulder, the best I hoped for was some witch doctor who would give me vague spiritual references to a few herbs. I was led in what seemed like circles forever, then introduced to a withered old woman who acted quite lucid. Apparently, some of the people aren't allowed out of the caverns."

"Yes, I met one myself."

"So this lady, her name or maybe it's her title is Keeper Voice, and she maintains the oral record of all the botanical species in the range of this clan. It was simply a matter of getting her started and then she recited names and uses for two hours straight. She hardly paused to breathe and I thought my hand recorder would overheat."

"Did you speak with anyone else while you were in the cavern?" Ardra pushed the goblet back and forth on the table in front of her, not quite prepared to risk another swallow.

"I didn't even see anyone else—just the twins who jumped us outside, the sentinel, Jex, and Keeper Voice. But I did see countless klics of tunnel . . . I think. It all looked the same to me and the sentinel could have been leading me around in a circle to make it seem like we were traveling a great distance. Not that I care, though, I got such a wad of data from that herbalist." Lute raised his bowl and sucked in a long deep breath; for a moment his eyes spun up until only white showed, but his eyelids soon blinked and the irises snapped back in line.

"How did you get out of the cavern?" Ardra asked.

"The sentinel and his invisible pest bobbed back into the small

chamber he'd left me in with Keeper Voice just as the botanical
recital reached its end. Then he laid some nonsensical clichés on
me, argued with the thing that wasn't there, and marched me out
through a maze of tunnels to a completely different crack from the
one we first crawled into. Once we were outside, he pointed me
toward a landmark and ordered me back to Retro. I thought it
would be rude not to comply." Lute paused to smile and wink at
the assemblage around the table. "Naturally, the sight of the sharp
point of that spear of his had no part in my willingness to cooperate."

"Natch!" Udell chuckled.

"And I wasn't worried about Ardra. I knew she'd have everything
under control."

The people around the table nodded solemnly at these words
while Ardra wondered how much longer she was going to be able
to maintain control of her churning stomach. Despite the best
efforts of the air exchangers in the tavern, wisps of each variety of
smoke and fume were finding their way into her nostrils and
mingling with the odors of at least four unwashed bodies in the
room, the worst of which was her own. The smooth green numbers
of the wall clock seemed frozen in place.

"Didn't your hand recorder bother them?" Ardra asked.

"Not a bit."

"Did they offer you any refreshments? Did they take any of
your equipment?"

"Nope. They just gave me a long talk and a long walk."

"Did you find out what that special plant in the mural was
for?" she asked. "The one set apart from the others and speckled
with pink."

"Apparently they make an extract of it and feed it to toddlers,
so I'm keen to find a sample and investigate its properties. They
say it prepares the stomach for adulthood, whatever that means.
Once the child has cut his or her second molars, the feedings stop."

Kip lifted his face from his tankard and said, "Maybe that's
what makes them crazy."

"Well, really," Blaze nodded.

"Never likely," muttered Udell.

"Hmm," said Ardra. She wondered if the extract helped an adult drink yellow glop unharmed.

"I thought you were parched," Lute remarked. He peered into Ardra's nearly full goblet. "Is it off?"

"No." She shrugged and pushed it around again. From the corner of an eye she saw Kafka's head poke in through the door, turn to the left and the right, and snap back out again.

"Are you all right?" Lute asked.

"Fine." Ardra pushed her chair back and stood. "Excuse me, there's someone I want to have a word with." She spun and headed for the door.

CHAPTER 14

Connections

"Grime! Where did he snake off to?"

Ardra's headache stirred and punctuated her frustration with a single throb. It was still twilight outside and her eyes needed little time to adapt from the gloom of the tavern to the sparse lights of Main Street. With much of the population of the town in the tavern this evening, it was no surprise to find the street deserted. But where was Kafka? A strong breeze had sprung up and his scent had already been lifted away.

Ardra peered up and down the street and into the dark patches that hung about the corners of the buildings; her eyes searched for any sign of movement, especially a gliding movement. Nothing. Kafka had probably gone immobile against a shadowed wall like a lizard on a hot rock. As the image of such a lizard rose in Ardra's mind, a wave of fatigue rose to drown her frustration then retreated, washing away her questions.

Then Skrif emerged from the PKF station and sailed up to Ardra.

"What happened?" Skrif asked. "I found Kafka and told him you wished a word. He said he wanted to flap gums. When we parted he was hurrying to meet with you."

"He just stuck his head in the door of the tavern then retreated," Ardra replied.

"Perhaps something frightened him."

"I'll bet everything frightens him. In fact, didn't he say exactly that the first time I met him?"

"I could search again."

"Maybe I should grab a nap before shift."

"By my calculations, you are sleep deprived."

"I think this planet is getting to me. Look at that. One of the suns is starting to rise."

For a moment, the human and the companionbot contemplated each other. The robot waited for a decision. The Olidan waited for her drive to re-assert itself.

"Avenger!" a voice hissed from the lane between the PKF station and Provisions.

"Kafka?" Ardra's eyes tried to penetrate the gloom between the buildings with no success. "I don't know why I asked," she muttered to Skrif. "Of course, it's Kafka. Let's get to the gum flapping."

"Perhaps you should re-arm yourself before . . ." Skrif hurried to keep up as Ardra stalked over to the lane, then followed her nose to the Wanderite.

In answer to a murky impulse, Ardra grabbed the front of Kafka's oversized work shirt and pinned him against the wall. That's when she realized the Wanderites didn't just look small, they were small. He weighed no more than an average twelve-year-old.

"Don't be shy, little man," she said as she eased her grip. "All I want is a few answers." This close, he reeked of rootsmoke and her stomach seethed.

"You are the answer. You are the Avenger," he proclaimed.

"And you're the Speaker, at least that's what your clan tells me. I visited them today, but I'll bet you already know that."

"You were meant to stay, but you had to go."

Ardra shook her head slowly and glanced toward Skrif, who had parked quietly nearby. "You were worried about me coming here unarmed, but the only danger with this fellow is he'll talk me around in circles until I fall over dizzy."

"Botanist Cullen saw the pebble on the cactus and knew it marked a trail. You'll hear Kafka's words and know their meaning. You're a human among humans," Skrif said.

Despite her frustration, Ardra laughed. "Of course," she agreed. "What was I thinking?" She turned back to Kafka.

"Why did your clan knock me out with that yellow slop?" she asked.

"It was necessary," Kafka replied. "You must fulfill the prophecy."

"And I suppose that's why they took my equipment? To fulfill the prophecy?"

"Yes, yes!" Kafka nodded his head vigorously.

"Well, alright. That melody's over and done. Let's get back to the murder of Forecaster Lesting. I've seen the flight of eagles. Now I want you to show me the ground where it runs in rivers."

"No. No. It's too dangerous for you." Kafka shrank back against the wall.

"I need to see it."

"You mustn't."

"How can I understand, how can I fulfill the prophesy, if you won't show me the rivers?"

The man remained limp and silent.

"No? How about telling me why you were the Jex clan Speaker? What are the powers of a Speaker?"

Kafka pressed his lips together.

Then Ardra remembered the doctor's claim that the addicted Wanderites could be bought. "Tell me about your Speaker powers. I'll get Skrif to post ten credits to the tavern in your name for an answer."

Kafka's head snapped up. "Ten credits?" Ardra reached her free hand into her pocket and felt around until she found her identitab; at least the thieves in the cavern had spared that item. She pulled out the tab and held it in front of his eyes. He stared at it, transfixed, and licked his lips.

"The ghosts of the future speak to me," he said, then looked eagerly at Skrif.

"What ghosts and what do they say?" she demanded.

He scowled. "How many answers for ten credits?" he asked.

"You may be crazy, but you're not stupid," Ardra laughed. "I'll give you the ten credits when you explain to me about your powers. When I understand, you have the credits."

Round nose twitching, the Wanderite was quiet while he considered the arrangement. He squinted with concentration and finally he spoke again. "The ghosts of the future are not ghosts yet and the future is in the echo of their voices, but it cannot be heard. The echoes write faces in the air and I watch the shadows."

"Give me an example," Ardra demanded. "Did you see the dead surveyor's face, Cara Stine? How about Forecaster Lesting?"

"Not those!"

"Who, then?"

"The others . . . yours."

"Mine? That doesn't make any sense."

"These are the answers. I have given you the only words I have." Kafka squirmed and pulled at his shirt, which Ardra released. He gazed mournfully at the identitab.

"One more question, Kafka. What are these shadows that you watch when the echoes write faces in the air?"

Kafka raised his hands in the motion of a plea, then buried his face in them. "They are the sweetness and the pain . . . all my pain. My knees are weak, always they have been weak, and I am too weak to carry the pain. The precious root that your people brought from the skies fills my mouth with bitterness and empties the ache from my mind."

With a sigh, Ardra nodded to Skrif. "Go ahead. Make the transfer," she said. She stuffed her tab back in her pocket and watched as Kafka glided down the alley and turned back up Main Street.

"Con man or tortured soul?" she wondered aloud.

"Perhaps the clan took your equipment because the prophecy doesn't mention such technology," Skrif suggested.

"I'm more than ready to abdicate as Avenger," Ardra said. "In fact, I think it's time I re-armed myself and I don't mean with a lance."

Skrif powered its antigravity and rose to move to the mouth of the alley with Ardra. "I can't imagine how even a human could make sense of Kafka's answers," the robot mused silently. "And yet . . . the words were uttered by a human so they must make sense. Mustn't they?"

Ardra's thoughts had moved on. With any luck, she reasoned, Rosil would be out of the station when she got there and she would be able to file all the necessary lost equipment reports without anyone breathing fire over her shoulder. So far her luck had been lousy, though, and she didn't expect it to change.

At the mouth of the alley, Ardra paused and glanced south toward the clinic. There was a light showing in one front window and she considered stopping in for something to settle her stomach. It would be a good excuse to ask the doctor a few more questions. Unfortunately, she couldn't think of any questions to ask him now, maybe later. Her eyes drifted to the timepiece on the administration building.

"Grime! It's getting close to shift and this uniform feels like I've been wearing it a week," she said.

"I could lay out a fresh uniform in the barracks room and draw a hotvat while you . . ."

"Exactly. Let's fogee."

So Skrif whisked toward the barracks and Ardra hurried into the PKF station, through its main doors, into the glaring light of the entry, the halls.

"Where have you been?" Rosil demanded; her short but powerful frame loomed in the doorway to her office. Looming even larger was the cloud of scent, a perfume with heavy overtones of midapple blossom, that surrounded her.

Instinctively, Ardra drew herself straight. Even though she stood more than a head taller than the sergeant she didn't feel like she looked down at her.

"I went with Botanist Cullen on an exploratory expedition into the desert," she replied. "There was no one else to hike with him."

"Looking for plants?"

"Botanical research."

"Boring stuff."

Ardra shrugged.

"But scenic company," Rosil added.

Ardra's spine tensed.

Then Rosil's eyes narrowed. "You're going on shift pretty soon," she said. "Where's your sidearm?"

"That's why I came in early," Ardra explained. "I need to file a report on what happened to Cullen and myself today. It's a long story."

There was no avoiding the issue now and there would be no holding back information, either. Even though events in the cavern might embarrass her, she knew any detail could be critical to those who came after. That's why she had been honest about the sprites on Planet Brumal after her survival test. No one had believed her back then though, not even Dilli.

"We found a Wanderite trail and followed it to a cavern," she began. Then she summarized their encounter with the Jex clan and finished with a description of the lumpy yellow liquid she had drunk before everything winked out.

"That was stupid," Rosil sneered. "I suppose I shouldn't expect anything better of an officer with so little experience and so much ego. Your Wythian lineage won't deflect lances, you know. The Wanderites don't know to be impressed by the name and you seem determined to do everything you can to offend them."

Ardra slid her tongue between her molars and pinned it firmly.

"First the Lancer, now a sidearm. What next?" Rosil shook her head. "I'll get you a replacement out of the armory before I go off duty. Try to hang onto this one, will you?"

"Yes, sergeant." The back of Ardra's neck prickled and her throat burned.

"Furthermore, I keep telling you not to waste your time on the Wanderites and you keep ignoring me. I don't suppose you learned better while you were out traipsing through the sands, did you?"

"Some of what the Jexes said made Kafka sound like a suspect or a witness."

"Kafka? That's ridiculous, you must be hallucinating from that Spiri . . . that alien drink. Kafka is completely blameless—totally harmless—nothing more than your pet scapegoat." Rosil commanded a time check then said, "You'd better get going on your report. I want to look it over before you file it."

"Right." Ardra walked further down the hall and into the patrol room where she squeezed into the tiny cubicle she had been allotted.

"You're just temporary," had been Rosil's only comment when she made the room assignment.

"No problem," Ardra reminded herself. "It's no more cramped as an office than my barracks rooms are as living quarters."

Ardra voice-activated the workstation and dictated her report from memory. She would cross-check with Skrif's record later to see if her early memory agreed with her later memory. The sequence of events and physical descriptions of places and people were simple matters for her, but the exact wording of the Wanderites' answers to her questions was tricky. Their phrases had made only a little sense when she first heard them, which was why she had been so careful to check that her recorder was running, the recorder that was now missing with her audilink multiplier, locator, restraints, and sidearm.

"Grime," she muttered. The word immediately printed out on the screen below her report. "Dictator," she sighed. "Delete the last word. Turn off the dictation."

Just as Ardra started to review her report, Rosil appeared behind her and leaned a heavy hand on the back of the chair as she peered at the screen. Rosil mumbled as she read, interjecting the occasional "Humph" or tongue click. Finally, she finished reading and said, "This is useless for the investigation. File it under personal journal."

"Useless?" The word blurted out before Ardra could override it.

"That's an order." Rosil thumped the new sidearm down on the desk and added, "I haven't decided yet whether I'm going to file a reprimand for your loss of weapon. That sort of blot would look bad on a Wythian record, don't you think?"

The early tremors of Ardra's personal temper quake vibrated in her toes and she glared at her weapon, almost afraid to touch it before Rosil left the room.

"Stay in town," Rosil demanded as she departed. "And don't be late for your shift."

Ardra was silent as her throat strangled a horde of retorts that crowded for voice. When she heard the outer door hiss and thump shut behind her superior she kicked the metal leg of her desk until it achieved a harmonic whine. Then she took a deep breath, picked up the blaster and snapped it onto her belt.

"That was dumb," she thought. "Why do I let her get under my skin?" Ardra always bragged to her family that she could work with anyone, and she believed it. During her rookie year on Metro she had been mentored by Officer Peri, a Tithenite who took perfectionism to an excruciating height. He had insisted on the exact wording—every word—of each report they filed and was given to protracted periods of contemplation over the simplest evidence. But she had managed to find his mannerisms amusing, not annoying, and certainly not infuriating.

"Blame it on the suns," she thought as she gathered replacements for the rest of her gear from the shelves of the station equipment room. "I've been tired from the moment I landed, even when I just finished a good sleep, and there hasn't been much of that in the last 25 hours."

Even after she tested out the sighting of her sidearm, there was still time for a cleanse and a clean uniform before her nightwatch, so Ardra jogged over to the barracks and into her room. By the time the locking mechanism of the door to room eight had snapped into place behind her, Ardra had shed her equipment and every scrap of clothing into a heap in front of the closet.

She hurried into the bathroom and descended the few steps into the waiting hotvat. Its foamy surface lapped at her chin when she settled; the solution felt like a trillion massaging fingers against her skin.

"Timer. Five minutes," she said. Then she leaned her head back, sighed, and closed her eyes. This was even better than sleeping and eating. Even better than . . . no, let's not get carried away.

Out by the closet, Skrif sorted through the heap of discards. It extracted the equipment belt and the audilink and carried them to the bed. Then the robot placed these items next to the clean uniform.

"That belt needs a good polish," Skrif thought and looked forward to the end of the nightwatch when the human surely must sleep and the belt's gleam could be restored. For now, the companionbot hurried back to the discarded clothing where it picked up each item and inspected seams and wear points for damage.

"Have you any complaints about fit?" Skrif asked as it bobbed into the bathroom and consigned the clothing to the hamper chute. It contacted the barracks cleaner unit and assigned an appropriate level of priority to each item.

"Just the usual gripe about the collar," Ardra murmured over the popping foam of her hotvat.

"I could soften the collar and let it out a few millimeters."

"No, I want it sharp. It's a dress uniform, after all."

"The Wanderites were impressed by it?" Skrif asked.

"Hmm, maybe. It's hard for me to tell what they're thinking or feeling," Ardra said. "I truly don't understand how their minds work, I mean the crazy ones. They don't seem to fit the standard mold of madness."

"There's a fragment of pre-Dispersal writing that speaks of a different madness," Skrif said. "I reviewed it during my time as a molebot in Coeur's Central Library. I never understood it."

"What did it say?"

"'Man cannot be defined as you would define the keys of a piano. And even if you could so define a man and predict everything about him, he would go mad to escape the definition.' What does it mean?"

"It was probably a joke."

Skrif doubted it was a joke. Henta the Hilarious had taught the companionbot a great deal about comedy during their time together and this piece met none of the criteria of humor.

"Five minutes," announced the timer.

With more alacrity than she felt, Ardra scrambled out of the hotvat and into the embrace of a dry-heated towel. Her head still indulged in the odd pang, but at least her stomach had stopped its complaints.

"Actually, I suppose it means we hate to be predictable," she said. "Pre-Dispersal writing can be weird."

"Perhaps the integrity of the piece was corrupted over time. Many such works are suspect in that regard," Skrif said. The robot held out an arm for the used towel, received it, and consigned it to the hamper chute.

"Four-plus millennia of dubious storage can do that alright," Ardra said. "Speaking of data, I've filed a report on the afternoon. When you have a free moment I want you to double check the details against what I told you on our trip back to town."

"Certainly."

"And let me know of any discrepancies after shift. I want to know of anything I might have colored in the recall process."

Once cleaned, dressed, and equipped Ardra headed out into the dawning night. Both light and temperature were on the rise when she and Skrif emerged from the barracks and registered by com for duty. Skrif headed north to patrol the port apron and Ardra turned south.

Voices and laughter trickled through the opening iris of the tavern and soon she intersected with the group that she had left in her pursuit of Kafka.

"Well found, well found!" Blaze called out. She leaned heavily on her bond, who was not much more stable on his feet, and together they wove a new dance step out of the round doorway.

"You'll be starting work? Have you filed a report then? No pressure, mind." Udell was steady on her legs but the pupils of her eyes were less than pinpricks, and Ardra wondered how they drew enough light to see, despite the rising sun.

"The report's done but for a final check through, and I'll set up a file you can access, as promised," Ardra replied. At least someone was interested in the information she had gathered.

While Blaze, Kip and Udell headed to the barracks, Lute lagged back. He was grinning.

"Don't you ever get tired?" Ardra asked.

"Not in certain company," he said. "It won't happen tonight, but sometimes the sky gets dark enough to see stars. "You've never seen so many as you'll see here on Wanderer when the sky is space black."

"I'm glad you made it out of the cavern in good shape, Lute. When I look at the situation in hindsight, I think I should have

stayed with you. They're such an unpredictable lot, these
Wanderites." Ardra backtracked toward the barracks in step with
Lute's idle speed.

"All that plant talk would have put you to sleep in less than a
minute and what good would you have been to me then? Did you
get anything useful to solve the murders?"

"I'm not sure. Maybe. Rosil doesn't think so." As they drew
level with the barracks Ardra caught sight of a shadow oozing along
one wall. It froze for a moment, but she recognized its smooth
manner as Kafka's trademark. She stopped to watch and he moved
further along the wall, then paused and started to work a window
open. Ardra's hand dropped to her blaster.

"What's he up to?" she hissed as she stepped forward to
intercept him.

"That'll be Ivy's room," Lute whispered. He put a hand on
Ardra's shoulder to hold her back.

"Rosil?"

"He's always creeping in there. No one talks about it, of course,
it's all hush-hush."

"Hush? What? Do you mean to tell me that Kafka and Rosil
are . . . are lovers?"

Lute chuckled. "These things happen in a small community.
We surveyor types don't always hold out for the perfect
relationship."

Ardra forced her hand away from her blaster and pulled her
sagging jaw up into line. "That explains a lot," she muttered.

"What did you say?"

"Nothing. I just didn't want to see her being our next victim."

"Meek little Kafka is a suspect?"

"Everyone is a suspect."

"Even me?" Lute's hand, still on her shoulder, slid along to her
neck and gently massaged the tension in its muscles.

"Lute, I'm on duty. Go to bed."

"Stop by any time." He grinned, slowly pulled his hand away,
and strolled to the barracks door. "I'll let you detect the room
number," he added over his shoulder.

Ardra watched him walk through the entrance; she didn't have to detect anything. Seventeen. That was his room—third from the end on the second floor. The light winked on.

"He's not my type. He's just a pretty-boy," Ardra insisted to herself. "Besides, it's too soon since Chelidon. Surely it's too soon."

CHAPTER 15

Battle

"Err . . . oof!" Ardra's ribs chattered from the violence with which she had been thrown to the ground. "Mmm . . . agh!" Her elbow pinged with applied torsion. Sheets of red shot across her vision and obscured her view of the artificial turf crammed into her face. The red she saw was not from the pain, it was raw anger.

A knee descended to press her head further into the fake grass and she felt its rubbery blades tickle her nose as she sucked for a decent breath. The air she drew in smelled like dirty socks. She tried to make her body go limp, to signal acquiescence, but a rage exploded into her muscles and turned them to iron. Finally, she gathered sufficient breath and grunted, "Enough!"

Accompanied by a smug "heh, heh, you're not so tough," the twisting and pressing withdrew. Ardra pried herself to hands and knees and looked up at Sergeant Rosil whose bile-green eyes leered with triumph. The sergeant dusted her uniform knees and indulged in a smirk.

"Some practice . . ." Ardra muttered.

PKF procedure called for weekly sessions during which active officers gathered and practiced blocks, throws, and holds. Half an hour, once a week, whenever the posting situation allowed, was the minimum. First one grappling partner would practice throws and pins with the cooperation of the other, and then they would switch roles. Usually, the combatants changed partners with each new session; everyone had unique moves and a fresh face gave the opportunity for a fresh read. Not so on Wanderer, though. Ardra was stuck with Rosil.

It was early morning, toward the end of Ardra's third nightwatch, and one sun glared redly as the horizon gobbled it down; the forecast called for dark until midday. The two officers had come out to a dusty square of artificial lawn behind the PKF station to take turns working the moves of their trade. However, inflicting pain was not part of the drill.

Pressure relieved, Ardra vacuumed up a full breath, which smelled of synthetic rubber, dust, and orange blossom, a smell whose sweetness was starting to give her a headache. She could also smell Rosil and was struck by the similarity between the woman's characteristic scent cluster and the odor of raw Eifen beets. Ardra hated Eifen beets.

"That's the half mark," said Skrif who kept the official time for the exercise. It was time to reverse the roles; it was Ardra's turn to practice being the controller.

"Let's see what you've got," Rosil sneered. She danced, dodged, and showed no evidence that she planned to cooperate. The long shadows of a nearby skeleton tree drew crooked black lines across her face.

Ardra got to her feet, steadied herself, and took the measure of the woman who was her opponent, not her sparring partner. As a Kelpan, Rosil was short and a step slower but, as she had already demonstrated with Ardra's cooperation, she was powerful. Ardra calculated how much force it would take to break bones once she got the other woman in a wristlock; then she realized it wasn't her wrist she wanted to break.

"I don't know how it happened," she rehearsed silently as she moved in and the two circled and feinted, "We were simply sparring and suddenly there was a snapping sound. Her head sagged on a limp neck. It was a terrible accident."

"There's nothing more loathsome than a person riding the coattails of an ancestor, don't you agree?" Rosil said. Her lips were drawn back so her square teeth glinted like the ice in that miserable gnome cave on Planet Brumal.

"The only thing worse than that is a cop on the take," Ardra muttered. Her field of vision narrowed until there was only the bobbing, grinning ice. "Rrrr . . ." There was a growling sound from deep in a throat, her own throat. The cloying scent of orange blossom grew until her head ached to explode from the intensity.

"You've got a lot to learn, Wythian," Rosil hissed. "You're not anything as good as you think."

Then Ardra saw her opening and moved in like a stream flowing into a newly formed channel. Her timing was perfect.

"Wythian, stand to!" A wall of sound hit her and she froze just as the windpipe under her hand was about to collapse.

"Skrif?" Ardra jerked back, dropped Rosil to the turf and shook her head to bring the world outside their encounter back into a reality. The companionbot had moved toward them but now pulled back.

"No problem," Ardra insisted. "We were just doing some routine sparring."

"Pardon me, I thought . . ." Skrif didn't know how to complete the sentence. Over their time together, Skrif had noted every behavior of the young officer and had concluded that she would never harm another human except to stop a deadly threat. Now that conclusion wavered. How much control had there been in that hand on Rosil's throat? Perhaps the intervention was an overreaction. And yet . . .

Then Rosil coughed and pulled herself off the ground. "Not bad," she conceded. "You've got one good play, I guess."

"Thanks for noticing. Are you ready to go again?" Ardra heard her voice speak the words, but she felt numb. She felt like she had just encountered a stun cluster. Her mind scrambled to understand what had happened, why she had applied so much pressure to Rosil's windpipe, what dark pit had vomited up her impulse to lean on the heel of her hand.

"There's only a few minutes left," Rosil sniffed. "I suppose I can give you and this lump of scrap metal a bit of extra bench time. It's not quite the end of your shift, but I'll start early and sign you off while I confirm our sparring practice."

Rosil tugged her tunic straight then reached out with one foot and gave the companionbot a shove. With no ground contact for leverage, Skrif skittered through the air over the edge of the artificial turf and thudded against the back wall of the station. Although it applied counter thrust instantly, the mechanism was too slow to respond in the space and time available. The companionbot steadied itself and settled to the sand.

"One quarter of the time remains," said Skrif, secure in the knowledge that no reasonable human considered such a sum to be a few minutes.

"You started your timer late," said Rosil. "I figured that out when you called half time. It was more than half."

"But . . ."

"You're not going to argue with me, are you?"

"Of course not," Ardra broke in.

The sergeant glared at the robot then looked over at Ardra. "What's wrong with this robot?" she demanded.

"It's just . . ." Ardra began.

"Probably a glitch from your scrape on Chelidon. Are you sure he's fit for duty?" Rosil asked.

"I'm an it," said Skrif. "Gender is inappropriate when applied to a companionbot."

"He, she, or it, what do you care?" Rosil reached down and rapped on Skrif's side. "You're covered with durmet. That's the toughest skin in the Realm."

"Physically speaking, yes," said Skrif.

"Exactly!" said Rosil. "Wythian? Make sure Daisy here gets checked over by the Zills. I don't want her on duty if she's unfit." Then the sergeant stalked into the PKF station.

"It!" Skrif called at the closing door. "I'm an it!" Its sides vibrated with the resonance of the sound. Then its speaker hissed with manufactured static—Skrif's version of blue language.

"She's even getting to you?" Ardra laughed. "We're in serious trouble now."

"Furthermore, my name isn't Daisy, it's Skrif."

"Are you damaged, Skrif?" Ardra asked. She rubbed the side of her head and flexed her elbow, resolving never again to play sparring dummy with Rosil.

"I'm not at all damaged," said Skrif. "I have the capability to take the force of level nine blaster fire without damage. Such force considerably exceeds my recent impact with the wall."

"But doesn't exceed . . ."

" . . . what happened during that unfortunate incident on Chelidon."

"Right. Why don't you pay a visit to the Zills, just to keep the peace? I'll stop in at the cafeteria for a quick fastbreaker." Ardra was still too flushed with fight hormones to feel hunger, but she knew the sooner she ate, the sooner she could commune with her bed. It was time she caught up on her sleep. Surely she would feel sleepy after a bite of food.

"Are you injured?" Skrif asked as the pair headed around the station. "I observed that Sergeant Rosil sparred with great enthusiasm."

"She'd never have downed me like that if I hadn't been playing by the rules. No one's ever taken me in tournament hand-to-hand."

Just as they reached Main Street, the horizon swallowed the last nibble of sun and an eerie, wheezing chorus erupted from somewhere beyond the administration building. Ardra jerked to a stop.

"What the Jahan is that?" she asked as her right hand sidled up to the butt of her sidearm.

Skrif checked with the Repositor and had the answer in three seconds. "Reed lizards. They're herbivores that respond to temperature changes with song."

"Reed lizards? Like I care," Ardra mused after she and Skrif parted company in front of the cafeteria. "It's not like a reed lizard strangled Stine or clubbed Lesting." Despite herself, she thought back to the lizard that sang like a pan flute from the top of a street lamp. "I guess even Wanderer knows its moments of joy," she concluded.

The instant the cafeteria door opened at her approach, Ardra smelled hot mealymush and grimaced. She'd eaten altogether too much of that during her endurance training. Then she spotted Trudge seated alone at a table near the Dispenser and wondered, as she had wondered during her first review of Lesting's murder, why he hadn't heard or seen anything that night. She hurriedly collected a boat of mealymush and invited herself over to his table. "It must be morning, the sun just set," she said as she sat. Then she shoveled a heaping spoonful into her mouth and chewed. It tasted like puffed rye with a hint of nutmeg. Not as tiresome as she remembered. She swallowed and asked, "What brings you out so early?"

"Some nights are good enough. Other nights I have the phantom aches," said Trudge.

"I'm sorry to hear that. Can't Dr. Sethline give you anything for it?"

"There's some bits of medicine no further ahead than the pre-Dispersal leeches."

"That's too bad."

"Is."

Ardra noted that Trudge's scent cluster was heavily overlaid with spicefern oils; he had probably tried to soak away his pain in a hotvat. She processed another mouthful of mealymush before speaking again. "I spent half my watch breaking up fights again. It still seems odd to me that no one about the tavern saw or heard anything when Lesting was killed. After all, it was broad nightlight, so to speak. Both suns were up, weren't they?"

"Must'a been. They were up when Veray came crashing in, eyes bulging, and throat squealing. Emptied the place on the spot." Trudge gazed down at the wisps of steam that fled the gudday in his mug. He added, "He wasn't long dead."

"You didn't hear anything from where you were inside?"

"Never would. The "No Limits" is built to contain its own noise when things get good. Won't let it out, so won't let it in."

"Pity."

"Better this way. Worse if he yelled and no one came."

"Surely the town didn't hate him that much."

In answer, Trudge confined himself to a simple shrug. Ardra reminded herself that, as a digger, he likely wouldn't have involved himself in another's dispute. People like Trudge didn't believe in rules; they each followed their own laws and respected that other diggers did the same.

"Young Clais figgered Les didn't have time to yell, though," Trudge said. "Maybe he was right about that?"

"Not even the experts on Blooh could be certain what order each of the blows struck his head. Some they could reconstruct, others they left open," said Ardra. "I'd just hoped someone had been entering or leaving the tavern at the right moment. But no one asleep in the rooms on the south side of the barracks heard anything either, according to the report. It was late by the clock."

"Word is you've been to the cavern of Kafka's clan."

"And received precious little enlightenment."

"You saw women there?"

"And kids, too." Ardra took care not to mention a cluster of children in the main chamber who had been playing with green and blue crystals. No need to rouse a gem hunter's instinct.

Suddenly, Ardra noticed her spoon was scraping the last few fragments of mealymush from the boat. She licked the spoon thoroughly and smacked her lips. Her stomach hummed.

"There were a lot of women," she said. Then added on impulse, "If I go back for another visit I could put in a good word for you."

Trudge looked up, met Ardra's eyes, then nodded. "I do believe you would," he said. "Do." His eyes narrowed with thought and his prosthetics sighed as he shifted. "The murdering club . . ." he said.

"Never recovered," Ardra said. "The murderer must have taken it away. A Wanderite could have taken it anywhere and used it for firewood. We know it must have been a bit of construction stud from the fragments in Lesting's wounds. It's too bad it wasn't recovered. There could have been scent or scrape evidence where the killer held it."

"Maybe someone early on the scene thought it needed burning. Saw it lying by the way and . . ." Trudge fell silent.

"And tampered with evidence?" Ardra asked.

"And saw better than to punish the inevitable," Trudge finished. He downed the last of his drink and stood up.

"Did you?" Ardra stared up at the man.

But the barkeep only shrugged and looked away. "Vincent's still in clinic," he said. "Was a nasty cut. Was." He left his mug on the table and click-hissed his way out of the cafeteria.

With a conscious effort, Ardra closed her hanging jaw and watched the man through the window as he angled across the street and entered the clinic. She was more shocked that he had told her about the disposal of the murder weapon than that he had interfered. Not that he had openly admitted it, or ever would.

The cafeteria hostbot, surface-warped but operational again, rolled up to the table and seized the abandoned mug. It paused and its red scanner line glowed in the direction of Ardra's empty boat.

"Take it," she said and the bot emitted a cheery ping as it lunged for the dish and spoon.

"Think about it, Skrif," Ardra whispered to her audilink as she hopped to her feet. "This makes the murders even more connected. At both killings, the murderer used what was at hand and dropped it after the killing. It fits."

Her step was brisk until she reached the door and emerged onto a street meagerly lit by lamps. The dark sky leaned down from above and added weight to her eyelids. Ambushed by a yawn, she turned north and headed toward the barracks. As she passed the lane between Provisions and the PKF station, she looked down its shadows to the place where she and Rosil had sparred. Nothing. It couldn't have been real.

By the time she reached the barracks, Ardra was certain she was being followed. Unaware of her keen sense of smell, her shadow hadn't bothered to stay upwind and she had felt his presence in her nostrils all the way up the street from the cafeteria. She knew the direction of the breeze and knew where he must be.

"Skrif?" she whispered, keenly aware of the prickling hairs on the back of her neck. "If you're available for backup . . ." She gave the robot directions so they could pincer in on the stalker.

For five minutes, she dawdled before the barracks, time enough for Skrif to move into position. Then she spun and sprinted up the barrack's south lane. Her long legs vastly overmatched her quarry, who was forced to backtrack a piece when Skrif appeared. Soon, they had Kafka cornered against the back wall of the barracks.

"Avenger!" he cried and sank to his knees.

"Kafka, what the Jahan are you up to?" she demanded. "You were following me. Why?"

"The ground shall run in rivers."

"And what does that mean? Am I next? Well, I'm ready for it. Just let the killer try to take me down. We'll see who wins that one."

"Avenger!" Kafka rolled into a sobbing ball.

"You just tell whoever it is to come and get me. It's time I lived up to this nickname."

A moan was Kafka's only answer and Ardra stalked back out to the street.

"Oh dear," said Skrif.

"You know, I don't think Kafka has the spine to kill anyone," Ardra said. "But what about his daughter? Maybe that's why Stine was strangled and Lesting was clubbed. No lance. The women don't carry lances."

"Vincent was cut," said Skrif.

"But not killed. What if Vincent knew about Kafka's daughter and threatened to tell? Then Kafka struck to defend his child, didn't have the stomach for more, and ran away."

"And he's following you . . ."

" . . . because he knows I'm next. He knows his daughter." Ardra felt so light on her feet it seemed there must be antigravity units in the soles of her boots. A part of her even sensed Forecaster Lesting and Surveyor Stine smiling over her shoulder.

"Now all we need to do is prove it," she said.

"You mustn't act as bait," Skrif protested.

"It's perfect," Ardra insisted. "I want you to watch Kafka every moment that you aren't charging. He's going to be the key."

"Will you alert Sergeant Rosil to the situation?" Skrif asked.

It was another rhetorical question.

CHAPTER 16

Rage

The silver line of teeth was bared in a grin. Trudge leaned on the circle bar in his tavern and grinned across it at Ardra. He knew. Ardra was sure if she dared look directly at the man's teeth she would see her own reflection, flushed with guilty pleasure.

It shouldn't have happened. She had intended to go straight to her room after she left Skrif to monitor Kafka. Just inside the barracks, though, she encountered Lute on his way out. It didn't happen. Surely the memory was only the creation of her imagination, a fantasy drawn in exquisite detail but possessed of no substance. Surging fire.

The door to the tavern swiveled open and Ardra dropped her eyes to her hands, clenched together on the bar. If the body coming through that door was Lute . . . she knew she couldn't look at him without spelling her emotions on her face. Finally, she raised her eyes, but only to gaze at the teeth. They still grinned. Footsteps whispered behind her, right to left, and she smelled the anxious sweat of Kafka. Not Lute.

"Feel like you're settling in now? Do?" Trudge asked.

Ardra forced a shrug and a casual tone. "I've given up expecting light or dark when I walk out any door. That must mean I'm starting to feel at home."

"We all have our own way of making a new marble a home. Me, I feel right as soon as I've worked some of its dirt under my fingernails. You're looking better relaxed this evening." His grin broadened.

"There's no such thing as a secret in Retro, I suppose," Ardra grumbled.

"Not if you're after using the barracks. Heh, heh. He's a pretty boy that Lute. Is."

"Gimme a spring water," Ardra growled. She wanted something more powerful, like a booster or supernova, but her shift would start in a few hours and the effects of such powerful kicks didn't clear as quickly as high volatiles like the ghost blink.

"I need to keep my hydration level up," she added, knowing she ought to head over to the cafeteria and put food into her stomach. The idea of a sensible meal seemed incongruous though. Sensible wasn't on the menu today.

Trudge waved away the lurking hostbot and fetched the water himself. He placed the goblet before her with a thud. Ardra guzzled half of it and stifled a sigh. Her mind refused to believe she had spent so much time in Lute's room; it was almost midday when she tiptoed through the empty halls of the barracks and slipped into her own room, her own bed. And slept soundly.

"Your platform's still not working?" she asked Trudge with a nod to two coverall-clad technicians crawling over and under the holographic unit.

"Been trying to get Piper or Tate to have a look-see but they've been tied up with wrecked Lancers and such." Trudge winked and Ardra relaxed into a chuckle. Why did she think a digger, even retired, would think censorious thoughts of her? He never would.

"I've been keeping to my feet recently," she said with a wry smile. "So repair needs in the hangar should quiet down."

The outer door swished open again and a gust of air brought Ardra's nose the bouquet of hot sand. She sighed, knowing that the sunlight forecast called for two-shadow sunlight through most of her impending nightwatch. There would be more of those reflexive looks over her shoulder at nothing, more frying in her black uniform, and a few late fights followed by empty street with no one to question.

The bar's hostbot hadn't rushed to greet whoever had entered, so Ardra turned for a look. Skrif hovered smoothly and quietly in the entryway. After she had sucked down the last of her spring water, Ardra nodded to Trudge and went to join her companionbot. Together, they walked and glided out of the tavern.

"Well?" she asked when they were out on the street.

"As per your instructions I have been monitoring the actions of Kafka," Skrif replied. "From 08:27 this morning (after you retired to the barracks) to 10:18 he slept in the lane on the south side of the clinic. Upon rousing, he proceeded to relieve himself behind the building. Most unsanitary. Then he walked a short distance into the plain to the east of Retro and sat under a skeleton tree. I maintained maximum separation from him and used maximum magnification to observe his actions."

"Which were?"

"From inside his shirt he pulled a woven pouch and emptied its contents, a dozen pink granite pebbles, into his hands. For the next two hours he stared out over the plain and fingered the stones. At 12:37 he shrieked, jumped to his feet, returned the pebbles to the pouch, and ran to the barracks. There he lurked outside your room and peered through the window at intervals. When you left the barracks and proceeded to the bar he followed your progress by slinking through the shadows of the buildings on the west side of Main Street."

"He's up to something. Did he spot you?"

"Nothing in his actions indicated that he was aware of my surveillance."

A breeze drifted out of the lane on the north side of the tavern and brought the smell of anxious sweat. Kafka.

"I do believe he's slipped out the back and is hovering on the north side of the pub," Ardra whispered. "Circle around behind to cut him off if he decides to bolt. I want to talk to him again. Maybe I was wrong about his daughter. Maybe it's him after all and he didn't use a lance because he'd sold his off for credit at the tavern."

With the faintest hiss of air blade, Skrif spun and vanished behind the south side of the building while Ardra strolled casually to the mouth of the north lane. From the corner of her eye, she picked out the crouching form of the Wanderite.

"Avenger!" he murmured. Instead of fleeing, he slid forward to meet her halfway down the lane.

"JEXjex," she replied. "Kafka, what do you have to tell me?"

"It's you. The Avenger."

"Here I am, alright."

"The demon spirits of the air must be fed. It's you."

"Why don't you tell me about that pouch you're carrying and the pink granite stones in it? While you're at it, tell me what these symbols mean." Ardra drew the ellipse and the double esses in the sand with the toe of her boot.

Kafka peered down at the scratches, then moved his head closer. He sucked in his breath sharply. "You know? You know the lines to free the dancer? Do you carry the stones?"

"These lines are supposed to free someone? Who?"

"I must follow."

"Follow who? Who's next on your murder list? Me? Is that why you're following me around today?"

"I must, I must . . ."

"Give me just one straight answer, you miserable, cussed, . . ." Ardra reached to grab the front of Kafka's shirt but froze when Skrif called softly from the other end of the lane.

"Rosil!"

Looking around, Ardra spotted the sergeant across the street, just stepping out of the PKF station. While Kafka shrank back into the shadows of the lane, Rosil sauntered over.

"Picking on the locals, are we?" she sneered as she came to a stop next to Ardra.

"Kafka and I were just discussing Wanderite customs, sergeant. I'm positive they hold the key to our murders."

"Our murders, is it? Our? I thought I explained who was doing the solving and who was walking the beat."

"You did, and I'd accept the situation if I saw any progress at all being made in the investigation. However, nothing has been added to the file since I arrived, nothing that I didn't generate, and unless something is added . . ."

"You want action?" Rosil interrupted. "I'll give you action. I'll give you Wanderite customs. Come with me." She spun, marched out of the lane, and turned south.

With a hurried, "Carry on, Skrif" thrown over one shoulder, Ardra matched strides with her commanding officer. "Where are we going?" she asked.

"I need you to come with me to the tower."

"You mean the Wanderite tower of stones? The one that's supposed to signal the end of time when it collapses?"

"It's time you faced up to the reality of this place, these people."

"It's quite a trip out, isn't it? Usually I take time to have a meal before I go on duty. I haven't had fastbreaker yet."

"That can wait."

"The tower will still be around after I eat. It's supposed to stand until the end of time, you know."

"You're coming with me. Now."

Ardra's face began to burn from within and she clawed back that old familiar anger. This time, the anger she felt sprang from her submission to orders. There had been the order to accept colony duty, the order to come to Wanderer, the order not to interfere with the investigation, and now this arbitrary order to travel to a nonsensical stack of rocks.

As they approached the vehicle hangar, Ardra worked through her hatred of Rosil. For starters, today the woman reeked of Brewrose, the cheapest, most cloying cologne in the Realm. No doubt the sergeant had doused herself with malicious intent. Furthermore, any idiot could see she was protecting her native lover from charges of murder, protecting him from a proper investigation, protecting him from due justice. Kafka, witless soul, deserved the chance to confess.

At the hangar Rosil claimed a two-seat Carrier and had to physically restrain Kafka from stowing away in the machine's equipment bin. Ardra's last glimpse of the man came as they glided out of Retro and cleared the first low hill; he was running along after them like an abandoned shimpuppy. Even running, it would take days to reach the tower on foot. By vehicle it took well over an hour and the two suns of Wanderer floated high and hot when they arrived. Even though it was full evening, the ground sizzled.

On a swayback hill, overlooking the plain where Rosil parked the Carrier, stood a twisted cairn of scarlet stones. Countless centuries ago, each rock of the structure had been cut from red granite into a jigsaw shape, every angle different. The pieces fit together to form a spiraling pillar that rose endlessly toward the stars. At its base, a clutter of fallen shapes gave evidence that it had once stood even taller, but had lost height to the relentless drag of gravity.

"Elya says the Wanderites can't explain why or how this tower was built," said Rosil after she and Ardra exited the Carrier.

Ardra shaded her eyes and looked up at the structure. It was more intricate and impressive than she had expected.

"But their ancestors must have carved it and shaped it," Ardra said. "A tower to nowhere. Somehow that fits around here."

"When the first Wanderite came to Retro—that was Elmo—I asked if the tower was in glory of a god but he didn't say a word. He just shrugged and his eyes darted everywhere. Kafka says none of them ever approach the tortured pillar or even set foot on the hill that bears it."

A trickle of sweat slid down the side of Ardra's face, from temple to jaw. When she glanced at Rosil, she observed no such reaction to the heat. Not even one dewdrop of sweat marred the Kelpan's skin. Some Kelpans joked that only solar core heat could thaw them after the thousands of years their race had spent in the chill of their ancestral planet.

What did it all mean? Who did it? Those were the questions on Ardra's mind as she stood silently on the sand next to the Carrier and lifted her eyes again to the tower. She wasn't interested in the pillar; it was ancient history. Instead, she questioned the puzzle of the unsolved murders and their ritualistic markings. The word "aha" seemed to be on the tip of her tongue. The pieces were all there.

"Wythian!" Rosil shouted from a position partway up the hill. "Are you interested in daydreaming or investigating?"

Ardra swallowed a retort and it scorched down her throat to smolder in the pit of her stomach. Her stomach snarled; where was her fastbreaker?

"Coming!" she called and hurried to catch up with the older woman.

In single file, Ardra and Rosil toiled up the hill to the base of the pillar. The poor footing and the scorching heat left them speechless until they reached the summit. There, they halted and craned necks back to peer up at it.

"Unbelievable, isn't it? Yet, here it is," said Rosil. Her voice spoke of awe.

"I wonder if anyone will ever find evidence of the original ship that brought the Wanderites here from the Dispersal planet," Ardra said. She blotted sweat from her brow with a sleeve and struggled to keep her breathing as measured as her superior. It was impossible for any race to match the stamina of Kelpans, so well adapted to the high gravity and low oxygen atmosphere of their home world, but impossibility never deterred this one Olidan officer.

"An engineering marvel, that's what it is," said Rosil.

"It would be easy enough to build such a tower with a hoverjet or even a historic dirigible," said Ardra. "Maybe they had lighter-than-air craft before they lost their technological abilities and the archives that came with them in the Great Dispersal."

"We could learn a lot from these people," Rosil said. "That's what Elya insists and I believe she's right."

"If someone pulled a keystone out of this thing it would collapse and that would be the end of time. Typical legend hyperbole," Ardra said. She fought the urge to kick it over like a kid's sand castle at the beach on Planet Celestia. Maybe doing something like that would get her booted off Wanderer and shipped back to Metro. Not a bad idea.

"So what are we doing here?" Ardra demanded. "And why did you need me to come along?" Her scalp tightened, a forewarning that her headache intended to return.

"The answer's supposed to be here," Rosil replied. "Kafka says it's part of the prophecy, this tower, and you're part of the prophecy too."

"Yeah, right. I'm the Avenger, whatever that means." Ardra glared out at the featureless plains and hills around them. The occasional skeleton tree twisted up from the ground in an agony of thirst. Colorless tufts of cactus or thorny bush huddled in isolation.

Reaching out with a toe, Ardra cornered one of the fallen red stones of the tower and toyed with it. Then she flipped it over the crest of the hill. It skipped and tumbled down the slope, spraying out a burst of sand here, caroming off a cactus there. Halfway down, it rattled the twigs of a hookbush, and flushed out a dozen NoNames. The yellow lizards fled in tight formation, like a flock of birds; their snake-like bodies twisted down the hill. Their pale bodies blurred against the beige sand.

"Ugly little things, with their bloody eyes," Rosil remarked.

"They stink too," Ardra added, just as a breeze carried their scent to her nose and its sweetness made her gag. Orange blossom.

"I've been thinking of asking headquarters to reassign you," Rosil said. "Can't say you've given me any good reason why I shouldn't."

"How about—I'm here to investigate areas you won't touch, like Kafka as a suspect," Ardra retorted.

"Just thought I'd let you know while we were out here in private."

Ardra said nothing but thought, "What a peach!"

"Might as well head back to Retro if the famous Wythian isn't going to be inspired by this work of wonder." Rosil spun and stomped back down the hill toward the Carrier.

A giant steel hand squeezed Ardra's heart and lungs as she followed in Rosil's footsteps.

"Will you try to keep pace?" Rosil snapped over her shoulder.

Surprisingly, Ardra had dropped behind. She searched for the will to catch up and fought to get her mind off her tormentor. Just one simple shot . . . her hand caressed the butt of her blaster.

"A lance-waving Wanderite sprang from nowhere," she rehearsed silently. "How could I have missed? Something jarred my elbow. There was nothing I could do."

Then thoughts began to drop into Ardra's mind. Like stones in the tower above, they nestled against each other, each finding its fit, and together building a shape.

Kip said Blaze was a sound sleeper.

Rosil was only out for herself. Lousy cop. Lousy cop.

Daly knew how all the equipment worked at the forecast office.
Ardra's hand clenched and unclenched on the weapon.
The ground ran in rivers.
An ice pick stabbed in her brain. A hot ice pick.
Sennett said he snored sometimes.
The blaster was light in her hand.
Kafka said the ground ran in rivers.
Lousy cop. Lousy cop.
She knew she had all the pieces. If they would only . . .
Two dozen red eyes stared out from under a bush.
Piano keys.
Click.
Aha!
Ardra raised her weapon and fired.

CHAPTER 17

Onward

"There'll be a citation in this for you, Wythian."

"Maybe a promotion."

"How did you figure it out?"

Words of praise piled around Ardra like the historic gold coins of Jahan, and she mentally let them run through her fingers. Most of the survey team crowded next to her in the tavern, each anxious to be the first to buy her a round.

"Such a relief."

"Now that we know the enemy . . ."

"I kept Kafka under surveillance as you ordered," Skrif reported. "He was desperate to follow when you left for the tower."

"He was the answer," Ardra said. "Kafka and piano keys. There's this pre-Dispersal quote Skrif repeated to me. It popped into my mind just as Sergeant Rosil and I were coming down the hill from that insane pillar of rocks. Something to do with the fact that humankind refuses to be predictable and if anyone could ever explain and predict our every action—describe us like keys on a piano—we'd go mad, just to prove we couldn't be controlled or manipulated. When I first heard it I thought it was the stupidest thing, but suddenly, under the gaze of that pillar, it made sense."

Her audience clucked admiringly and Ardra smiled again at the shiny coins. Then she remembered the expression on Rosil's face out on the hill below the tower and her grin broadened.

"What the Jahan?" Rosil shouted and whirled when Ardra's blaster hissed. The sergeant's grey face purpled with indignation. Under the fingers of a hookbush lay the shattered fragments of a dozen NoNames; Ardra had obliterated the creatures with her weapon, set on broad beam. The breeze freshened and her headache lifted like a hoverjet on a mission.

"I know what tied the murders together," Ardra said. "And you're right, Kafka didn't kill anybody."

"And what does butchering a bunch of lizards have to do with murder?" Rosil demanded.

Ardra felt her face smile, really smile, and the relaxation it brought spread through her body like warm syrup. She could have answered Rosil's question by saying, "Well, killing them stopped me from killing you," but she was too busy marveling at the sensation of liking the woman. Rosil was right; they were on the bleeding edge of the Realm.

An expectant silence brought her back into the No Limits Tavern and her circle of attentive admirers. Zoologist Darlis and Anthropologist Udell, heads together in heated discussion, entered from the street and she waved them over.

"Here's the woman who can give you the right kind of explanation," she said. "Chup, tell them about the NoNames."

"Don't believe those little lizards beat Lesting to death. Don't," grumbled Trudge.

"When I first asked Kafka about Lesting's murder, he told me that the ground ran in rivers," Ardra explained. "And when Rosil and I were out at the tower we saw a cluster of them in tight formation wiggling down the hill—pale bodies on pale sand. They looked like a stream of sand flowing down the slope. Then I remembered how the smell of orange blossom cropped up when I saw them or when a fight was happening. Tell them, Chup."

"It's fascinating!" The zoologist beamed.

"Hah."

"Sure."

"Ugh."

"No truly," Darlis persisted. "The NoNames are the favorite prey of dire lizards, creatures who outweigh and outfang them enormously. How to survive? Apparently, the NoNames developed a pheromone, a potent, airborne chemical that can stimulate dire lizards to rage against each other. The dires are exceedingly sensitive to the stimulus, one tiny whiff and there they go. We've already seen the effect this has had on them—as much as possible, they avoid contact with others of their own kind. When they do meet up, one of them dies."

"So what? Th'are just lizards," Tate interrupted with a scowl.

"Unfortunately for us, we humans have a similar receptor reaction. There are some differences. It takes a baseline of cumulative exposure to prime our system, then we require a high threshold exposure for an outburst."

"That's what Kafka meant by the ground running in rivers. It's when the NoNames school to mate or shift ranges," said Ardra.

"Also, some of us are more susceptible than others, but we've all felt the effect," said Darlis. "I know I have."

"Hmm." A general mutter passed through the surveyors and most of them looked down at the floor, or the bar, or their indulgence of choice.

"Kafka can read susceptibility. He knew I was on the edge," said Ardra. "He just didn't have the words to tell me. Even though he tried, I didn't understand."

"But what's that got to do with piano keys?" Lute asked.

"It's the way the Wanderites survived," Ardra explained as she examined a scratch on one finger rather than look in his eyes. "We, the so-called sane, are predictable as keys on the piano and, therefore, susceptible. The Wanderite's form of madness short-circuited the NoNames' influence on their behavior. They didn't understand why, but they knew that any of their people born without the madness had to remain underground in their caverns so they were isolated from the NoNames. If they didn't see hallucinations on the spirit wall, they couldn't be exposed to the lizards."

"The Council ought to sign the planet over to the diggers. Ought. We're . . . er . . . they're solitary by nature, like the dire lizards, and perfect for Wanderer. Are." Trudge's silver teeth gleamed; so did his eyes.

"You talked about Kafka," said Coordinator Hesty. "Where does he fit in exactly?"

"T'was when the Wanderites realized we didn't have the good sense to build our town underground that each of the neighboring clans sent a representative to be keeping an eye on us," said Udell. "Kafka represented the Jex clan and their tradition demands a symbolic exorcism when someone succumbs to the rage. Among themselves, the Wanderites haven't known murder since they moved underground and adopted the spirit wall test for those who venture out. Before that happened, though, there'd surely been a lot of blood-letting."

"Kafka's special in his clan," said Ardra. "He's able to sense when someone's particularly vulnerable to the effects of the lizards and is on the brink of murder. Then he follows the person like a third shadow until the murder occurs, at which time he places special clan symbols in the area of the crime. These are supposed to release spirits. That's why he never had a good alibi for any of the killings. He was always at the scene or getting to the scene at the time."

"Avenger," sighed Kafka. "You are the prophecy. It is real. The ground ran in rivers but you moved not."

"It only worked out that way because I'm used to temper," said Ardra. "I've been living with the Planet Jahan of tempers for all of my life. It'd take more than a current of NoNames to carry me over the edge." These words sounded good in the air of the tavern but, internally, Ardra shuddered. She had come so close. Too, too close.

"Each attack was by a different person," Journalist Sumner said. She had linked into the PKF booking file and had the names of those charged. Now she was gathering the first-hand details to round out her bulletin to the Realm.

"They were puppets," Ardra insisted. "Trust me."

"They confessed," said Sumner. "That's recorded on the booking file."

"They did," Ardra agreed. She remembered it well.

After their return from the tower, Ardra and Rosil had consulted with Zoologist Darlis and Anthropologist Udell. Then the two PKF officers composed the explanation with which each suspect

would be confronted. By the time they were ready, it was late by
the clock but all the better for their purpose. Freshened with zeal,
Rosil and Wythian wakened and hauled each of the suspects to the
PKF station.

First they dealt with the death of Prospector Stine.

"There's a small yellow lizard with red eyes that releases a
pheromone that drives dire lizards mad with cannibalistic
aggression. It happens that we humans react to this chemical, too,
some more than others. This is what drove you to kill Cara Stine."

When the bait was put to Surveyor Sennett in isolation he
snorted and said, "That's crazy as a swimsuit in a needle storm!"

Surveyor Blaze Myro responded with a look of revelation and
said, "A lizard?"

Changing only the name of the victim, Ardra and Rosil
individually confronted the staff of the sunlight office. Senior
Forecaster Veray Beld burst out laughing. Tech Daly exclaimed, "A
lizard!" then buried his face in his hands and wept.

Once Ardra and Rosil knew where to apply pressure, confessions
soon followed.

"I didn't understand it at all," Blaze explained during her
interview in the PKF station. "Cara was my best friend here on
Wanderer. Sure she talked a lot and was often too good to be true,
but I liked her."

"How did it happen?" Rosil prodded.

It happened much as Ardra had speculated in one of her many
theories. On the night in question, Sennett quickly dozed off and
immediately started to snore. Blaze, not the heavy sleeper Kip had
claimed, was restless, and she and Cara slipped out for one of their
chats. Then the ground must have run in rivers, though all Blaze
remembered was a faint sweet smell and a nightmarish detachment
from reality. After it was over, she convinced herself it was a
nightmare, that she had dreamed the murder and woken to discover
the body.

When Rosil and Ardra talked to Tech Daly, the man tore at his
orange hair and ignored the tears on his cheeks. He explained that it
had been his habit to take a leisurely stroll around the circumference

of the small town via the back lanes before he retired for the night. The walk normally allowed him to clear his mind so the Universal Light could enter his thoughts and make his sleep restful.

On that fateful night, though, when he reached the back of the tavern he encountered Lesting, who was harassing Vincent. At Daly's approach, Vincent pulled free and vanished and Lesting turned his sour tongue on the technician. Daly had expected to ride out the tirade, as usual. But it didn't work out that way.

"All I saw were these shadowy hands clenched around a chunk of wood and swinging it, swinging it," he said.

After the murder, Daly rushed to the forecasting office and rigged the controller so it would break down after a suitable delay. Then he scurried to bed to feign an alibi. He was horrified by what he had done, and it had plagued him ever since.

Buoyed by her success at the PKF station and further inflated by the praise in the tavern, Ardra eventually floated to the barracks and slept. Oblivious to the frenzied meetings underway in the administration building, she dreamed of purple clouds shaped like citation ribbons. When Ardra and Skrif had recharged, each in their own way, they re-emerged into another sunny evening and joined the population, all crowded into the cafeteria for a general discussion over evenmeal.

At first, Ardra ignored the raised voices among the crowd, most of whom had finished their main course and exercised unencumbered tongues. The sweetly sour smell of fermentation casserole drew her to the dispenser where she swallowed back a surge of saliva and ordered a double helping. Only when she had secured the feast and found herself a seat next to the barkeep did her ears begin to process the words in the room.

"W'need to escape," cried Vehicle Tech Piper Zill. "If the lizards control us w'could kill anyone. W'could kill someone special." His brown eye looked mournful and his pink eye looked shocked. He clutched one hand of his bond in both of his own.

"For shelter from the threat, we all be invited by the local clans into their caverns," said Anthropologist Udell, who sounded as calm as ever.

"I'm sure I can isolate the pheromone," said Zoologist Darlis. "Once that's done we're bound to find a way to block it or inhibit it so it's manageable."

"Why not wipe out all the NoNames?" Trudge suggested.

"Impractical, if not impossible," said Darlis. "It would be like trying to eradicate the swamp swine on Tithe. There'll always be at least one mating pair of lizards lurking in some inaccessible corner, ready to breed like swampers. Besides, they're part of the ecosystem and we don't know if the species is a keystone or a satellite. Maybe it wouldn't cause a collapse, maybe it would."

"Maybe we could train them to avoid us like the Olidans trained the empress lizards," said Forecaster Beld.

"That took centuries," said Ardra through a mouthful of casserole. At the sound of her voice, the group fell silent and turned to her. They waited. She swallowed.

"I don't understand why we don't all just move off planet," she said. "It's not like this place is any great prize. The Wanderites could escape with us." She looked around and saw only incredulous faces. Their responses tumbled forth.

"But the planet's fascinating."

"It's a paradigm shift."

"It's rich in minerals and so much more."

"We could learn a lot here."

"All we need to do is make sure we're always together in a pack or totally alone," said Lute. "In a large group there'll be plenty of others to restrain anyone who's overcome. If we're solitary, we can get by like the dire lizards."

"Exactly."

"We can do that."

"Can."

"Fortunately for us, the next supply ship arrives in one day," said Coordinator Hesty. "It sounds like most of you want to continue your work. I suggest we spend all off-duty time in the host caverns and emerge for work only in groups of four or more. I'll send word on the shuttle that we need an emergency construction crew sent to sink the town. And what about breather packs? Would we be protected if we all went on mask?"

"My guess is that it would work, but I'd have to test it," said Darlis.

"Right, so I'll also order a complete set of class one Jahan breather packs," said Hesty. "Now, let's organize ourselves into buddy groups."

Even though the fermentation casserole tweaked Ardra's taste buds delightfully, as that most favored dish always did, she felt a sigh slip from her lips. Around the cafeteria, voices rose in a joyful hubbub and around her table, eyes sparkled with anticipation. Surveyors were a weird lot.

"It's like the good old days. Is," said Trudge, seated to Ardra's left. His silver teeth gleamed in a trademark grin, and Ardra expected his grin would spread even wider when he saw the gems in the cavern.

"There's four of us around this table," said Lute, who sat directly opposite. "We could form a group." His eyes danced across the mirrored surface to join Ardra's. Diamonds and emeralds.

Next to Lute, Elya Udell nodded her agreement.

"What about the Wanderites?" Ardra asked. "Won't they want to leave?"

"A blessing it might be for the Wanderites who don't see the spirit wall move," said Udell. "T'would not be so for the others, they'd be out of place."

"But they wouldn't need to be crazy once they're off planet."

Darlis leaned over from the adjoining table and answered, "It's a genetic trait like your sense of smell, Ardra. Even though your family emigrated from Olid three generations ago you still have that trait. The Wanderites, the normal Wanderites, can't escape their heritage by simply moving away. Like all of the races, their ancestors arrived having been dosed by cosmic radiation despite the generation ship shielding, and that stimulated the mutations. Then the planet and its creatures, especially the NoNames, provided the selective pressures. Here on Wanderer, this special madness is desirable."

Desirable. The word sounded alien to Ardra, almost hostile. When she first came to Wanderer, her biggest desire had been to leave. Now her work was done and she would have to return to Eagle III Station to receive another assignment. She would have to leave Trudge and Elya and Lute. Only one day remained to her before the supply ship arrived.

Down in the crowded Jex cavern while she waited for the supply ship, Ardra spent hours composing a plea for compassion to be submitted with the PKF report to the Superior Judicial Authority. Every time she thought back to the tower and her walk downhill behind Rosil, a queasy dread cramped the muscles of her stomach. There was also the time she and Rosil had been drilling hand-to-hand combat behind the station. She had been lucky.

"Avenger! You broke the chain." Kafka beamed. He was back with his people now, dressed in a smock, and armed with a shiny-tipped lance.

"I'm glad you're happy about it," she said. "Now that the scientists know the cause, they can work on a solution. Soon, perhaps, your daughter will be able to step out of the cavern and see the skies."

"And laugh when the ground runs in rivers."

"Even though Zoologist Darlis is fighting against it, I suspect a lot of NoNames are going to be fried on sight from here on," Ardra said. It was a good thing she wouldn't be staying. She wouldn't have to fight the urge to join the barbecue.

All of the survey team and a mob of Wanderites gathered at the port for the departure of the supply ship. The vessel, shaped like a fat dart, dominated the port apron and awaited its passengers. Message cubes, survey samples, and hopes were already on board.

A few mouths managed awkward words of encouragement to Blaze Myro and Murl Daly and many hands clapped Kip Myro on the back in mute support. Rosil filled Ardra's ears with duty instructions for the journey. Now it was time.

"Send me word if you're sent somewhere that's wilder than Wanderer. Do," said Trudge.

"I will," said Ardra. "But I hope you never hear from me."

"We be glad you were here," said Udell.

"W' fixed the Lancer," said Piper. "If y' go w' might run out of work."

Ardra laughed. She moved through the gathering and made her farewells. When she said goodbye to Lute, his eyes were the flat, unreflective black she had used as a child to paint camouflage on models of smuggler ships. It seemed today he didn't dare let his heart into his eyes.

Finally loaded and locked, the supply ship began its ascent and climbed through the atmosphere until it thinned below any significant friction threshold. The crew initiated the ship's first space tuck and charged the hyperspeed rams.

In her cramped passenger quarters, Ardra ordered the bunk beneath her into recliner position and picked up her anchoran. She thought of the people on Wanderer and how they had been driven to act. Then she thought back to Haley and Planet Chelidon.

"There are certain forces we're powerless to refuse," she concluded. She could forgive him now. Haley had been incapable of any other action. The giant dragonflies, the pseudodonata, had needed him and he'd gone back into the maelstrom one time too many.

In its padded crate in the cargo hold, Skrif sat in a dormancy just shy of hibernation. All mechanisms and all higher functions stood idle; only its audilink to Ardra's room remained open, monitored by a simple watchdog program. The watchdog roused slightly when the first notes of her anchoran pealed through the connection. If there had been any ears in the hold, they would have heard a single ping as the companionbot gave voice to a smile.

GLOSSARY

Excerpted from "The Green Realm Encyclopedia—511 A.R. edition."

anchor music—A style of music currently popular throughout the Realm. Although anchor music can be played solo, its origin and most common usage is in duet. The main feature of this music is the anchor note, which is fixed for each piece and is played on even beats. In duet, the lead player sounds tones above and below the anchor note and the echo player follows with a mirror counter. Although the anchor note is fixed in length for each musical piece, the melody notes are shortened by mutes of various lengths as improvised by the lead player. The challenge for the echo player is not to be caught out by an unanticipated change in mute length.

anchoran—A compact and highly portable synthesizer. A player can place the anchoran on his or her lap while seated, or suspend it from a chest harness while standing. The player controls damper and volume keys with the thumbs, the octave with one forefinger, and individual notes with the other seven fingers. A voice for the anchoran can also be set at the beginning of each piece of music; examples of such voices include: dirge, bounce, lullaby, croon, and flourish.

antigravity—A technology developed by the Bloohans at the same time they developed the artificial gravity they needed to make their spaceworld more habitable. Antigravity is effective only in counterpoint to a large mass such as a planet and only in association with a small mass such as a transportation vehicle.

A-pad—The most basic unit of transportation in the Green Realm. The principal structures of the A-pad are: antigravity base, directional minijet, vertical riser, and control bar. Additional features may include a bracing bracket and a verbal command center. Typically, A-pads have a one meter diameter base and accommodate a single standing rider. Due to the open design of the A-pad, the antigravity ceiling of the unit is fixed at two meters AGL (above ground level) and its max speed is 10 mps (meters per second).

A.R. (After Reunification)—For some 4500 years, the races of the Great Dispersal lived in isolation on their respective home planets. When the Thalians developed space tuck and hyperspeed, they set out to find their kin in the prime range stars surrounding their location. The first race to be discovered was the Lavarites, who had their own calendar, begun when they landed on Planet Lavar. So that confusion would be limited, a Standard time scale and a Standard calendar were created. Year zero was the year Thal and Lavar were reunified. All years before this reunification were numbered B.R. (Before Reunification) and all years after were numbered A.R. (After Reunification).

armlounge—An upholstered chair with arms, a foot rest, and recliner functions.

ayduck—An aquatic fowl native to Planet Tithe. The ayduck has lime-green eyes and ghostly white plumage with grey markings. It is named for its "aye-aye" call. The eggs of the ayduck are prized for their buttery flavor.

Basis—The body of learning that forms the groundwork of education before an individual selects a specialty.

batbird—A flying creature native to Planet Olid. A batbird is a tiny, winged aviate with a melodic whistle but ugly green flight membranes and suction cup feet. Children are told, "It's a portent of good luck if a batbird lands on you."

beverage globe—A hollow glassite sphere tattooed with leather for gripability. It has three ports for loading, venting, and drinking, and it is used to serve high volatile liquids.

blaster—The regulation sidearm carried by all members of the PKF. This device is designed to fire energy pulses ranging from the mild (used for simplistic communication) to the severe (explosive bursts). Its settings run from zero to ten.

blood red—A precious gemstone much sought after by freelance prospectors. Harder than diamond and red as ruby, the blood red is often flawed but, when flawless, it is priceless. Planet Chelidon is noted for its veins of blood reds. (*Warning*— consumers should be wary of "special deals" offered by freelance prospectors in spaceport districts. Their professed blood reds are often simple rubies or garnets.)

Bloohan—A race of the Great Dispersal, native to Spaceworld Blooh. Bloohans generally exhibit the following features: pink eyes, yellow and straw-like hair, pale and blue-veined skin, weak immune system, and a small and delicate build. They are noted for their team spirit in all endeavors and their hatred of solitude. They believe in a Fundamental Force.

bokstem—The edible stalk of an epiphyte native to Planet Olid.

bonding bracelet—A bracelet worn by an individual who has pledged life bond to a partner. A bonding bracelet is only slightly larger than the circumference of the wrist and it is annealed in place during the pledge ceremony. To be removed, the bracelet must be cut into halves.

Carrian—A race of the Great Dispersal, native to Planet Carre. Carrians generally exhibit the following features: blue eyes, carrot orange hair, ebony skin, keen distance vision, and the build of a brick. They are noted for their cheerful, optimistic dispositions. They believe in Universal Light. Keen distance vision was important to early Carrian survival because it enabled them, while at sea, to sight a shearfunnel in time to flee its path.

Coeur—The capitol city of Planet Metro.

companionbot—A general-purpose robot with top-of-the-line linguistic capabilities. Physically, a companionbot is shaped like a blunt, inverted cone. The broad base consists of an antigravity unit and directional minijets for mobility. The blunt tip is a scanning visor with full-circle view. Two multi-jointed arms are affixed near the base and, when not in use, are snapped into a resting groove around the robot's circumference. Companionbots assume varied roles, depending on their currently downloaded specialty—valetbot, for example.

conplast—A moldable building material that cures hard and strong.

coredrill—A sturdy, tower-shaped robot specialized for mining duties. The coredrill has minimal linguistic skills, brace pods near its base, and massive, powerful arms affixed left and right, just below its visual scanner.

crack impacter—A power chisel used by prospectors.

darkmoth—A flying insect native to Planet Wanderer. The darkmoth has large, deep brown wings and sharp mouthparts. It feeds on carrion.

data cube—A standard storage device for digital information, compatible with all forms of archiver and retriever systems. Blank data cubes are transparent yellow and, once data is placed on a cube, it can be assigned any other color for filing reference. The more data on a cube, the less transparent it appears.

digger—The slang term of reference for a freelance prospector. Diggers are the non-conformists of the Realm. These individuals come from every race and every circumstance and are united only in their disdain for the rules of others and their use of the dialect known as Real. Each digger has a unique code of conduct and is beholden to no one. Diggers never use their birth names but choose a name that indicates their mode of going. Examples include Amble, Slither, and Trudge. These chosen names are always unofficial.

dire lizard—A predator of smaller lizards and native to Planet Wanderer. The male has inflatable threat sacs, a burly, muscular body, a blocky head, in-turned front feet with claws, and a hide with rough scales. The dire has a pungent, musky smell.

drillbug—A micropredator and one of the millions of insect species native to Planet Eifeif. Before the arrival of humans, it fed on the blood of the small, rodent-like animals so abundant on the globe, but it was quick to adapt to the new food source that descended from the stars. The drillbug is the fastest flying of all Eifen insects and also one of the most annoying to humans. On rare occasion, the bite of this species transmits the dreaded drillbug fever.

dungsnake—A small serpent native to Planet Ourson. During cold snaps, this snake will burrow into fresh dung to draw on its warmth.

durmet—A metallic composite of exceptional strength and durability.

eagle—A general term applied to several dozen raptor species native to Planet Handeen.

Eifen—A race of the Great Dispersal, native to Planet Eifeif. Eifens generally exhibit the following features: hazel eyes, oakwood hair, oakwood skin, lightning reflexes, and a scrawny build. They are the tallest of all the Green Realm races, their average height being two and a half meters. Eifens are noted for their many nervous tics and mannerisms and are admired for their ability to snatch up a darting insect mid-flight. They believe in Gyah. A prominent, hooked nose is common in the Eifen race and Eifens are extremely proud of their noses. They look with quiet pity upon those races not so well endowed.

Eifen beet—An edible root native to Planet Eifeif and named in honor of the heritage beet due to its bright red color. Gram for gram, the Eifen beet is the most nutritious food item known in the Realm. It is high in protein, vitamins, and minerals, and its low weight-to-nutrition ratio makes this beet especially popular with freelance prospectors. As a result of its sour flavor, the Eifen beet is an acquired, not instinctive, taste favorite.

empress lizard—The most fearful predator of Planet Olid. The mature empress lizard is two meters tall when upright on its hind legs, has serrated fangs, and hunts in packs. The matriarch of a pack is the most strikingly marked of the group and has a dusky mauve body with scarlet feet, nares, throat, and crest. All empress lizards have large, sky-blue eyes.

Eternity—The dogma of the Olidan race. Olidans believe that their every thought and action must acknowledge the long view. They do not make short term plans until they have considered these plans' ramifications for Eternity.

fastbreaker—The first meal of the day. The other meals are known as noonmeal and evenmeal.

Fatalism—The dogma of the Kelpan race, the core of which is expressed as: "The flower is already frozen and so is everything else." Such understanding frees the believer to savor the now.

fogee—A verb used by musicians in reference to times when they compose music as a group. It also is used as slang with the meaning, "to make things happen".

forensibot—Any one of a variety of small robots specialized to gather crime scene data.

formchair—A chair that will conform to the size and shape of the individual seated upon it.

ghost blink—An intoxicant of the swirl class. It stimulates an intensely giddy sensation in the indulger but metabolizes quickly.

giggle bar—A circular establishment that features mirrors, bright lights, floatchairs, and euphoric intoxicants.

glowslap—The most popular sport on Planet Eifeif. A game of concentration and reflex, glowslap requires players to block triggered light sensors in an order based on the preceding sequence. For example, the lights red, red, red, purple, yellow, orange requires the response red, red, orange. In head-to-head bouts, players face identical field displays and each player's score is derived from accuracy and speed. The Realm record score in glowslap of 11,239 was set in 499 A.R. by Kip Myro.

gossamer—An insect native to Planet Simblo. The gossamer is a broad, whisper-thin circle of wing, brightly pink in color. It frequents regions of deep fern forest where it gathers spores of the meg fern. It transforms these spores into swilk, which it uses to form shelters for its egg clusters.

Great Dispersal—A time when a fortunate few populations of humans fled a doomed Planet Earth on generation ships headed in all directions toward promising stars. Of the ships that set out, the lucky ones found habitable planets to settle and survived the settlement process.

Green Realm—An interstellar community of planets in a small section of our Galaxy. The human races who live on these planets are descendants of the Great Dispersal from Planet Earth.

gudday—A popular energizing beverage brewed from roasted coffee and a stiffweed extract. It may be served hot or cold.

halberd—The title given a team captain in the sport of volleywar.

heritage crops—Food, silage, and fiber crops that originated on Planet Earth. Heritage crops are the descendants of seeds and rootstock that were transported to Realm planets by ships of the Great Dispersal.

heritage livestock—A select few breeding animals were included in the original ships of the Great Dispersal: sheep, chickens, pigs, goats, and a small breed of cattle. Genetic diversity was bolstered by the inclusion of frozen sperm and embryos of other breeding lines. These livestock survived only rarely to planetfall and even more rarely to reunification.

hookbush—A shrub native to Planet Wanderer. The most memorable feature of this plant is its protective thorn, shaped like a barbed hook. Every stem and twig of the hookbush is covered with these thorns.

hostbot—A robot with good linguistic skills and a design appropriate for serving food or drink. Commonly, a hostbot will have a snap-down serving tray on its "front" side and at least one hand optic that it will position over tankards and bowls to check for need of refills.

hoverjet—A streamlined (atmosphere only) transport vessel. As the primary transportation tool of survey teams, the hoverjet is indispensable for both reconnaissance and rescue missions. It is fast and fuel sparing, thanks to its efficient design, and highly manoeuverable, thanks to its antigravity lift and fold-up wings. Hoverjets have the best safety record of any multi-passenger transport.

ignite—A powerful explosive developed by the Jahanite race. A few grains of ignite, properly placed, can bring down a building. Ignite is often packed in micro-straws protected by buffer cubes.

insect—Any creature with a chitinous exoskeleton and less than 10 legs.

intoxicants—There are many categories of intoxicant enjoyed by races of the Green Realm. Euphorics include silver screw and tinsel juice (both high volatiles served in glassite spheres). The best example of the swirl category is the ghost blink. Descents include ale and root. Powers include booster and supernova (steaming beverages served in tankards).

Jahanite—A race of the Great Dispersal, native to Planet Jahan. Jahanites generally exhibit the following features: space black eyes, auburn hair, ruddy skin, long limbs, and acuity of hearing, especially in the infrasound range. The ability to hear infrasound has given this race a slight edge, a whisper of forewarning, when a volcanic event is imminent. They are noted for their tremendous courage and their swiftness in short sprints. They believe that Fire is Life.

Kelpan—A race of the Great Dispersal, native to Planet Kelpa. Kelpans generally exhibit the following features: bile green eyes, limp, mousy brown hair, smoky grey skin, pencil-thin lips, and a short and powerful build. They are noted for their strength and stamina, a result of the high gravity of Planet Kelpa and the low oxygen content of its atmosphere. They are notorious for their hair-trigger temper. Generally, Kelpans have extremely poor night vision, a result of having developed on a planet where the only habitable region is constantly sunlit. Kelpans believe in Fatalism.

klic—A kilometer.

Lancer—A powerful, streamlined, antigravity craft designed for a single rider. It is shaped like a missile.

Lavarite—A race of the Great Dispersal, native to Planet Lavar. Lavarites generally exhibit the following features: grey eyes, chestnut brown hair, thick, leathery, lemon-yellow skin, deep bass voice (both males and females), and a medium build. They are noted for their air of measured calm, for which they credit their belief that all spirits are centered with song. Their thick skin developed as a defense against the winter needle storms of Planet Lavar and their skin color derives from a biological antifreeze compound that protects them against frostbite.

life span—The average life span throughout the Green Realm is 160 Standard years. Exceptional individuals may live to 200 Standard years. Typical life span varies according to world of residence and professional occupation.

locator—A device the size of a deck of cards that is used in orienteering. Its functions include: satellite triangulation, map archives, compass, absolute altitude, temperature, air pressure, and route history.

lulltime tea—A beverage made from the sap of the lulltime plant, native to Planet Simblo. This insectivorous plant produces a sweet sap in its bowl-like center. When a Simblese insect imbibes the sap, it loses motor function and tumbles into the bowl to drown. It sinks to the bottom of the bowl where tiny hairs sweep it into a digestion chamber. The effect of the sap on humans is to cause a non-narcotic drowsiness.

mealymush—A hot cereal made from a mixture of edible seeds soaked in fruit juices and simmered for several days.

midapple—A highly prized fruit that grows on shrubs and is native to Planet Thal. Like most plants native to Thal, these shrubs use the purple pigment, ionophyll, for photosynthesis. However, they differ from other Thalian flora by bearing their flowers, and subsequently their fruit, on the midveins of their leaves. All species of midapple have a crisp, juicy center and a chewy, flavor-rich rind. The flavor of the rind varies according to species and is described as being "nutty or spicy, but not really".

nearskin—A synthetic skin substitute, originally developed by the Eifen race.

needle storm—A weather phenomenon on Planet Lavar in which water forms into tiny crystals that are driven through the air horizontally by high speed winds.

novel chirp—A portable audio book the size of a card. The novel chirp features a miniaturized speaker that produces a remarkable quality of sound.

Nutritube—The brand name of a concentrated paste that can serve as a nutritionally complete, if unappetizing, meal. Nutritube is mandatory in all emergency supply kits.

Olidan—A race of the Great Dispersal, native to Planet Olid. Olidans generally exhibit the following features: emerald green eyes, curly black hair, mottled olive skin (in muted patches and swirls), a keen sense of smell, and a lean build. They are second only to Eifens in height and they are noted for their patience. Their keen sense of smell developed in their early struggle to survive in the dense jungles of Planet Olid where their only advance warning of predatory lizards was to detect their scent. They believe in Eternity.

Oursonian—A race of the Great Dispersal, native to Planet Ourson. Oursonians generally exhibit the following features: chocolate eyes, chocolate hair, chocolate skin, a burly build, and great grace of movement. They are noted for being emotionally vulnerable and placing a high value on their extended families. They believe in Reincarnation.

party dome—A type of spherical building that stands on stilts in the shallows of Planet Placidon. The colorful lights that decorate the exteriors of party domes are a visual announcement of the offerings inside. For example: crimson for thrill rides, magenta for dance chambers, gold for indulgence lounges. It should be noted that Placidon law protects party dome owners from any claims for damage filed by adult patrons. UAOR! (Use At Own Risk)

PKF—The Peace Keeping Force, the cops of the Green Realm. PKF rank ascends thus: Patrol, Officer, Sergeant, Chief, Supervisor, Senior, and Director. An individual of any rank is referred to as a member or officer of the PKF.

Planet Brumal—An ice planet. Discovered in 474 A.R., Brumal has been surveyed but not colonized. Temperatures in the equatorial region range from -80 to -10 degrees Celsius.

Extensive ice caves on the planet indicate that temperatures were milder in the past. It should be noted that there is no scientific evidence to support digger rumors of ice gnomes on Planet Brumal.

Planet Carre—A watery planet of the Great Dispersal, Carre joined the Realm in 205 A.R. Landmasses on Planet Carre are limited to thousands of rocky islands. There are no continents. Carre has a single large moon that causes extreme tidal action in certain regions of the planet and facilitates the sport of rip riding.

Planet Cauldron—An outpost planet, Cauldron is volcanic and barren. It was discovered in 421 A.R.

Planet Celestia—A planet of the second dispersal, Celestia was discovered in 450 A.R. Although it is still early in its survey and colonization phase, Planet Celestia is a popular vacation destination in the Realm. Resorts are a growth industry here, and their favorite slogan is: "Celestia—everything that Kelpa is not."

Planet Chelidon—A colony planet discovered in 495 A.R., Chelidon is characterized by thick jungles and forests, and insects of all sizes and shapes. Both company and freelance prospectors believe that Chelidon will prove to be the richest mining resource in the Realm.

Planet Earth—The source planet for all races of the Great Dispersal. No trace of this origin planet has yet been found during reunification efforts.

Planet Eifeif—An arid planet of the Great Dispersal, reunified in 253 A.R. Planet Eifeif is remarkable for its phosphorescing cloud motes and is the ancestral home of the Eifen race.

Planet Gavial—A planet of the second dispersal, Gavial was discovered in 183 A.R. Gavial is renowned in the Realm as the home to many communities of artists. These communities act as magnets and draw the most creative and the most dedicated from every other world and every race. The inhabited regions of this planet are characterized by erosion-sculpted towers of rock and countless canyons; its stark

landscape is often cited as a source of inspiration. *Note*—
researchers disagree on the causes of Gavial melancholia. The
prevailing view, that individuals of susceptible temperament
are prone to immigrate to this planet, is disputed by those
who believe there is a biological or chemical trigger in the
environment, as yet undiscovered.

Planet Handeen—A planet of the second dispersal discovered in 261
A.R., Handeen is best known as the native planet of the
affectionate race of beings called tiffins. Recently, it achieved
extra notice when archeologists discovered evidence of an extinct
Great Dispersal race near the spaceport, Metar. The small area
currently settled features rolling plains of heritage grains and
low hills covered by gyroca forests. *Warning*—the Realm Advisory
Panel (RAP) cautions against immigration to Handeen. Until
archeologists discover why the descendents of Ship 53 perished,
this planet is considered a world of undefined risk.

Planet Jahan—A dangerously volcanic yet fertile planet of the Great
Dispersal. Planet Jahan is known as the cornucopia of the
Green Realm.

Planet Kelpa—A wintry planet of the Great Dispersal. This planet
is habitable only in one region, a region that continuously
faces the sun of its solar system; the rest of the planet is too
frigid. Kelpa's atmosphere is low in oxygen and its gravity is
significantly higher than any other world of the Realm.

Planet Lavar—A Great Dispersal planet of extreme seasons, due to
its eccentric, elliptical orbit. Its thaw season is renowned for
riotous blooming followed by rapid growth and maturation
of every variety of plant. The heat season features high
temperatures, high humidity, and dry hurricanes. The winter
is famous for its severity and its needle storms. Lavar was the
first of the planets to be found by the Thalians.

Planet Metro—The first planet of the second dispersal, Metro became
part of the Realm in 127 A.R. Also known as the test-tube
planet, Metro is a stony globe with no native life and no surface
water. Thalian scientists, eager to create new planets for
expansion, balanced its atmosphere with strategically placed

Aerobic Generators and mined crustal ice for water. The technologies that made Metro habitable were a great success but, with the subsequent discovery of a number of naturally habitable planets, have not been used again.

Planet Olid—A planet of the Great Dispersal, Olid joined the Realm in 31 A.R. There are eight small, habitable continents in the vast seas of Olid. Thick jungles or forests cover each continent, depending on its latitude. Reptiles of all sizes inhabit all continents and seas. Olidans live in symbiosis with their planet, so there are no cities and its spaceports are the minimum size required for safety.

Planet Ourson—A planet of the Great Dispersal and the planet that, from heritage records, seems to be most like Planet Earth. Ourson joined the Realm in 403 A.R.

Planet Placidon—A planet of the second dispersal, discovered in 246 A.R. Rich in fertile land and blessed with abundant fresh water, the settled (polar) regions of Placidon enjoy the second mildest climate of the Green Realm. Renowned throughout the Realm for its party domes, Placidon is also a hub of higher learning and is often referred to as "Planet U". Pet swamp swine gone feral have been reported in the party dome district near Ruther. Patrons are advised to keep to the boardwalks after dusk.

Planet Simblo—A colony world, Simblo is a warm-to-hot planet of fern forests filled with swarms of biting, stinging insects and myriad forms of insectivorous plants. Most celebrated of its native creatures is the gossamer.

Planet Thal—A planet of the Great Dispersal and the origin point of reunification. Thal's continents feature gigantic coastal mountain ranges with peaks rising as high as 25 kilometers. Prairies irrigated by serpentine rivers dominate the interior of the continents. Thal's major cities and spaceports are situated in the prairie regions.

Planet Tithe—A planet of the Great Dispersal, Tithe joined the Realm in 402 A.R. Dominated by fresh water, there are only two small, crescent-shaped landmasses on this planet. Clouds, both high and low, usually wreathe Tithe. Its inhabitants enjoy an average of 11 clear days in a Standard year. Wild swamp swine are a hazard everywhere on Planet Tithe.

Planet Wanderer—A hot planet and the precarious home to a severely regressed race of the Great Dispersal. Planet Wanderer proves the impossible by its very existence. In an orbit that can scarcely be estimated with advanced chaos mathematics, this globe maintains its marginally habitable place in association with the tightest, most stable binary star set in the known Galaxy. Currently in the process of survey, Wanderer has not yet become a full member of the Green Realm.

Prime Range Stars—Stars that are stable and in a temperature range similar to Planet Thal's sun.

Purism—The Thalian belief that one should strive to achieve a perfection of body, mind, thought, and spirit. It is generally misunderstood to be limited to the notion that exquisite hereditary traits are to be treasured and nurtured. Although this notion underlies the physical cornerstone of the belief, it is not a justification for certain extremisms attributed to Purism.

Real—A dialect of Standard, Real is spoken throughout the Realm by diggers.

Reincarnation—The dogma of the Oursonian race. It is believed that reincarnation forms a circle than runs around the triad of (1) organic life (2) the elemental and (3) energies.

reunification—The mutual discovery of races of the Great Dispersal once separated by time and space and now rejoined. In the Green Realm, reunification took place in this order: Thal, Lavar (0 A.R.), Olid (31 A.R.), Carre (205 A.R.), Eifeif (253 A.R.), Jahan (272 A.R.), Kelpa (318 A.R.), Blooh (399 A.R.), Tithe (402 A.R.), Ourson (403 A.R.), Wanderer (511 A.R.).

root—An intoxicant of the descent class. Cured and shredded, root is served in a smoker bowl with an igniter switch. The indulger mists the root with highflyer then presses the igniter switch. Both the ignition flare and the subsequent smoke are golden in color.

second dispersal—The emigration of people of Great Dispersal races from their home worlds to newly discovered, habitable planets.

shearfunnel—A violent weather phenomenon on Planet Carre. The shearfunnel is a column of air that whirls at high speed and travels rapidly, close to the water surface. Historically, many fishers lost their lives when their vessels were unable to outrun these predatory winds.

shimpuppy—A small, nut-eating creature, native to Planet Thal. The shimpuppy is highly predated in the wild and is timid and known for its scream of fear when alarmed. Its pelt is velvety and purple and its head is frilled. Extremely affectionate, the shimpuppy is prized as a pet.

Ship 53—An ill-fated ship of the Great Dispersal. Colonists on Planet Handeen have discovered archeological ruins near the spaceport, Metar. Remnants of stone structures built by humans of Ship 53 are all that remain of that unfortunate race. Scientists hope to uncover the reasons for their demise. The Handeen delegation has proposed Month 5, Day 3 as an annual day of memory when all those who died in the Great Dispersal may be honored.

ship numbers—As ships fled Planet Earth in the Great Dispersal, they were given numbers based on their order of leaving the doomed planet. Almost all of the reunified races of the Green Realm have records of their ship numbers, which are: Blooh (#62), Carre (#18), Eifeif (#28), Handeen (#53, ship of an extinct race), Jahan (#47), Kelpa (#13, known only from oral records), Lavar (#51), Olid (#52), Ourson (#66), Thal (#24), Tithe (#58).

silk—A heritage product. Frozen eggs of the silkworm were transported in ships of the Great Dispersal. They and their food crop were able to thrive on Planet Ourson.

slaptogether—A composite building material that is produced in sheets. It can easily be cut to needed sizes or shapes.

slipseed coaster—A small, rounded fabric bag filled with slipseed and used to hold a beverage globe in place on a flat surface.

space tuck—A space travel technology developed by the Thalians. Space tuck (ST), when combined with ships powered by hyperspeed, allows inhabitants of the Realm to travel interstellar distances in days rather than centuries. In layman's terms, ST enables a ship to locate and transect dynamic folds in space. This benefits the passengers in two ways—it reduces trip duration and collapses time differentials. Although travel on established ST routes is low risk, travel on pioneer routes is extremely hazardous.

Spaceworld Blooh—Home to the only race of the Green Realm unable to find a habitable planet during the Great Dispersal and unwilling to continue the search. The original generation ship of the Bloohans was placed in orbit around a suitable star. Mining forays to the uninhabitable planets and moons of their sun supplied the Bloohans with materials to expand the size and scope of their habitat until it grew into a massive and luxurious spaceworld. Note—on the Bloohan flag, the spaceworld is depicted in its historical, circular form. Since the development of artificial gravity, the overall shape of the world has grown more creative.

Spirit Slake—A ceremonial beverage of Wanderites. This exotic, lumpy beverage is brewed from a combination of herbs and succulent plants native to Planet Wanderer. The final ingredient, fermented pith from skeleton trees, is added the day before consumption is planned. The more pith added, the stronger the effects of the drink, which can range from mild hallucinations, through intense hallucinations, all the way to immediate unconsciousness. Wanderites are not as strongly affected by Spirit Slake as other races of the Realm.

Standard—The common language of the Green Realm. This tongue was derived from ancient records of pre-Dispersal times and supplemented with cognates taken from the native languages of each race. Standard is spoken as a first or second language on all Great Dispersal planets and as the first language on all second dispersal planets.

Standard Time—A system of time measurement used for reference throughout the Realm. Based on the biological clock of humans, one day is 25 Standard hours long. Other quantities of Standard time are: 100 seconds = 1 minute; 100 minutes = 1 hour; 5 days = 1 week; 25 days = 1 month; 10 months = 1 year; 250 days = 1 year. All worlds of the Green Realm use the Standard calendar annotated with specific dates of local significance.

stiffweed—An archaic plant of Planet Eifeif. Stiffweed is a unique plant with no near relatives outside of the fossil record. This plant, like many on Eifeif, grows in rapid spurts after sporadic rains. During dry spells, it falls dormant. Traditionally, stiffweed is harvested after growth spurts, chopped, beaten, and sun-dried. It is then used as an energizing chew. It should be noted that prolonged use of stiffweed without remedial dental resurfacing will lead to tooth erosion.

straights—Trousers, slacks, pants.

Super Gee—The title of a party dome that features thrill rides. Popular rides in such a dome include Death Hammer and Lance Cannon.

supply ship—A craft capable of both planetary landings and interstellar travel. Its capacity is less than a tuck ship because of its versatility.

swamp swine—The wild pig of Planet Tithe. Pigs were the only species of heritage livestock to reach Planet Tithe with the original ship of colonizers. Some of the founding pigs escaped captivity and thrived in the swamps of this planet. Over the millennia, they reverted to wild form and developed slashing tusks. It should be noted that it is never safe to approach wild swamp swine and only diggers are known to keep them as pets.

swilk—Raw swilk, produced by the gossamer, is collected on Planet Simblo and used to make a confection of exquisite flavor and texture. The finest chocolate bar pales in comparison to a swilk bar.

Thalian—A race of the Great Dispersal, native to Planet Thal. Thalians generally exhibit the following features: gold-flecked eyes, spun silver hair, creamy skin, and a proportional build. They are recognized throughout the Green Realm for their leadership skills and their quiet, yet unshakeable, confidence. Thalians believe in Purism.

tiffin—Tiffins are native to Planet Handeen. The tiffin is a small, bipedal being with snap-away gliding membranes and the intelligence of an eight-year-old human. Ever desirous of contact with humans and the benefits that result from their company, tiffins strive to adopt themselves into human families of any race.

tinsel juice—An intoxicant of the euphoric class, popular in giggle bars. Tinsel juice is a high volatile beverage served in a glassite sphere to control its evaporation. Its mouth and throat sensation is of a hundred tiny tickling toes and its mind effect is a sense of expansive well-being.

Tithenite—A race of the Great Dispersal, native to Planet Tithe. Tithenites generally exhibit the following features: pale crystal eyes, golden hair, pink skin, round face, a rounded build, high buoyancy, and outstanding night vision. They are noted for their perfectionism and their air of resignation. They believe they are JOB (the Just Order of Believers). The higher than normal buoyancy of Tithenites was a survival factor in the planet's trembling quags. Their night vision developed due to the normal low light level of their fog-wrapped planet.

Transport—The smallest of the craft capable of space tuck and hyperspeed.

tuck ship—A true space craft, designed solely for interstellar travel on established routes between Realm planets with orbital connector hubs.

turpeens—A classic mixture of five edible roots, usually served steamed and mashed.

twisted—A term used to describe an individual whose physical or mental capabilities are markedly impaired by one or more intoxicants.

volleywar—The most widely played team sport in the Realm. Volleywar is played with a large, heavy, super-bounce ball in a square room. Each team defends one wall of the room and attempts to bounce the ball off the wall opposite to score.

End walls, floor, and ceiling are used to angle-bounce the ball, which can be advanced only by pass. Body blocks, living ramparts, and scissor pins are the three power moves most popular with spectators, who view through transparent walls. Due to their physical advantages, the number of Kelpan players on any team is limited to three.

Wanderite—A race of the Great Dispersal, native to Planet Wanderer. Wanderites generally exhibit the following features: grey eyes, green-tinged hair, beige skin, a button nose, and a short, wiry build. They are noted for their regressed state of culture and their insanity. They believe in spirit lore.

water dipper—An assistant to volleywar teams. The duty of the dipper is to cater to the needs of the players during tournaments.

wavecloth—A special material developed by the Jahanites, wavecloth repels sparks and embers much as a rain slicker repels drops of water. Hooded cloaks made of wavecloth are traditional wear on Planet Jahan, where volcanic spews, major or minor, are common occurrences. Designed for field use, these cloaks are long and commodious, well suited for protection. The function of wavecloth cloaks gave rise to the popular idiom—"he was caught with his cloak back"—used in instances where an individual has been caught unprepared.

well found—An expression of greeting. This greeting originated after Reunification, as a reflection of the joy all humans felt at the rediscovery of their lost cousins.

Wythian Academy—An advanced training academy for the PKF, located on Planet Placidon. It is named in honor of Gil Wythian, a member who forestalled an infiltration of extremists in the PKF.